A Love to Die For
Part 2

Tortured Hearts

Leigh Oakley

"The heart is not always a reliable compass"

Chapter 1

Kelly had received a phone call from Carl on that fateful day. He asked her to call in and check on Sophie after he'd heard from her father that she'd left the hospital in an emotional state. She knew Sophie's mother was critically ill and of course she had every sympathy with that, but it didn't stop her from feeling angry towards Carl.

Here he was again, contacting her when he needed a favour. She was in the middle of a restyle, but that would be of no consequence to Carl. Hairdressers were a long way down his list of worthy careers and naturally he expected her to drop her scissors and rush off to check on his girlfriend.

She returned to Mrs Milnes and smiled.

"I have to nip out on an emergency I'm afraid, but I'll finish the cut first. Your blow dry will need to be done by a junior, but I'll reflect that in the price."

Mrs Milnes seemed happy at the prospect of a bargain and Kelly felt some degree of satisfaction in making Carl wait a while.

After half an hour, she passed her customer to the junior and set off to drive over to Sophie's parents' house.

She pulled up outside and could see Sophies car already parked. She sat for a moment trying to think of something to say. She knew the news on her mother must have been bad, but she wished Carl had told her a bit more. She wasn't particularly good at this sort of thing and wished he had called Niki instead.

Niki always knew what to say but she also knew Niki would find it more difficult to drop everything at work and drive over. Not like Kelly, who was only a hairdresser, (Carl's words not hers) she was starting to feel annoyed again. Carl might not care if Mrs Milnes was dried off by a junior, but she didn't care if Joe Bloggs had to wait an hour for his exhaust pipe either. Who was he to decide his job as a grease monkey was more important, especially when Sophie was his responsibility, not hers!

She sat for a few minutes debating if or not she should spend the rest of her afternoon comforting Sophie but since she had already made the journey, she decided to go in but return to work as soon as she had confirmed Sophie was alright.

As she went around the back to look through the window, she heard a crash in the garden shed and assumed Sophie was having a clear out or looking for the spare key her mum used to hide in the shed years ago. As she approached the shed door, her chest tightened as a pair of twitching legs came into view, two feet sticking out of the shed door onto the soil, disturbing it with each rhythmic twitch. She stopped and stared, fixated by the sight in front of her.

She couldn't move. Her brain was telling her legs to move but they remained rooted to the spot. She couldn't lift her arms. All communication between her brain and body had shut down. She simply stood on the path watching the legs twitch. They twitched in the damp soil, muddying the bottom of Sophie's jeans, twitched over and over until eventually they fell limp.

The conclusion of this spectacle seemed to release her from the force that was immobilising her limbs and she was able to walk the few steps and pull open the door.

Sophies eyes were half open, vomit hung from her mouth in yellow chunks, slowly sliding towards the pile already spewed on the shed floor. The empty Vodka bottle was under her knee and the empty pill jars stood side by side on her dad's bench.

Kelly suddenly panicked. She'd just watched her friend die right before her eyes and done nothing! She fell to her knees and held Sophie's head on her lap listening to her own voice cursing herself for her stupidity, screaming as she rocked the vomit covered head of Sophie's lifeless body back and forth.

It was all surreal for several minutes until she regained some presence of mind, stopped rocking and stroking her hair like an idiot, and checked for a pulse on her neck. She was still alive! She put her hand in front of Sophie's face and could feel the warmth of shallow breaths from her nose.

Quickly she tried to lay her head back down, but her hair stuck to Kelly's hand with warm sticky liquid. Blood was pouring through her dark hair, through Kelly's fingers and pooling on the floor.

She ran back to the house to use the phone, but the door was locked. She ran to her car to use her mobile phone but then remembered she had left it with her junior at the salon so she could cancel the rest of her clients. Frantically she ran into the road and tried to flag down passing cars but three of them drove past without stopping. She tried a neighbour and then another, banging on doors and windows shouting for help but it was the middle of a working day and not one door opened.

She had run so far up the lane that she decided to turn back and try the other way. Desperation was turning to defeat as her pace slowed until she was walking. Walking and wishing that the moment would be over.

In the years to come she would revisit this moment many times as she struggled to justify it to herself. The moments in which she sauntered back passed the house without looking at it. The leisurely pace at which she set off in the other direction to try other houses. The moment she sat on a wall as valuable minutes ticked by. The fifteen minutes she sat back in her car for no reason at all before she finally got out and knocked on the door of the house that was occupied.

Politely she asked to use the phone, her demeanour no longer publicised any hint of urgency, and the elderly couple could only exchange shocked stares as they listened to the content of the call she was making.

Kelly told no-one of the precious time she wasted. She concluded she was in shock, swiftly vindicating herself for her behaviour that day. Partly because it was probably true, but mainly because the alternative was just too awful to consider.

When she knew the ambulance was on its way, she decided she was more use waiting to flag it down than to return to Sophie. For this she could not vindicate herself. She didn't want to return to that dark damp shed or to spend time alone with Sophie as she tried to cling to life. She might already be dead anyway. She convinced herself that there was nothing she could do, that this was for the paramedics to deal with now. She convinced herself she wasn't lying.

She knew she had to call Carl, but she would deal with that when she could. She knew what his reaction would be, and the attention Sophie was about to receive. Attention she didn't deserve from the man she didn't even want.

When the ambulance arrived, she was sitting on the wall quietly but as it approached, she jumped forward and waived her arms frantically. It was expected. It was normal behaviour. She tugged the paramedic lady down the path to the shed but stood back as the other paramedic, a burly man, caught her up. She let them go in alone. She had seen enough and was relieved that everything was now out of her hands.

The man quickly ran back to the ambulance for a trolly while the lady stayed inside, calling back to Kelly through the hinge of the door.

"What's her name?"

"Sophie. Sophie Taylor."

"Sophie? Can you hear me? Do you know where you are?"

Kelly's eyes were still fixed on the lifeless feet as the burly man rushed by again.

"She's barely alive." The lady whispered to him as he erected the trolly and shoved it up against the door.

They lifted together and plonked Sophie on the wobbling vehicle while the lady held a mask over her face and bellowed the urgency to the sweating man.

"Go! Go! Go!"

Kelly hurried behind them and stood on the pavement while they attached a drip to her arm.

"Are you coming with her?"

Kelly shook her head "I need to find her boyfriend."

It was a weak excuse, but the paramedics weren't interested in anything Kelly wanted to do, or not do. They slammed the door shut and with the siren blaring, they were gone.

She drove back to the salon to retrieve her phone. It was all she could do as she didn't know a single number by heart. She knew Carl would fly to the emergency room like a maniac the moment he knew.

She took a deep breath and made the call.

"Carl?"

"Hi Kelly. Did you check on her?"

There was no easy way to say it.

"Carl, she's taken an overdose. She's on her way to Scarborough hospital."

The phone want dead just as she knew it would.

She then rang Niki who, it seemed, was just as dispensable as a hairdresser when it comes to rushing out of work after all.

Niki looked dreadful when she pulled up outside the pub to find Kelly wating at the door. Her eyes wide with terror and hands shaking with shock. Kelly tried to mirror her emotional state.

"Didn't you go in the ambulance with her?"

"They didn't ask me," she lied, "Carl's on his way anyway and so's her dad."

"I don't think this is just about her mum you know."

"What do you mean?"

"I'll get us a strong drink. Go and find a table."

Kelly sat obediently at the table until Niki put down two large glasses of wine and sat beside her.

"If I tell you, you must promise not to tell anyone, anyone at all."

"I promise." It was a promise Kelly would wish she had never made in the years that followed.

Niki then went on to tell her about Sophie's 'mental state' and her loss of grip on reality. The imaginary love she had invented in her dreams and her subsequent obsession with him.

"This was about another man?"

"Well not strictly speaking since he was imaginary."

"I don't believe this. You think she took an overdose because she was in love with some phantom man? It's ridiculous."

"Yes, that's why you must never tell Carl."

"But...."

"You promised Kelly."

"Yes, I did" Kelly confirmed soulfully.

News from the hospital was sparse and not very encouraging. Kelly spoke to Carl a few times but he sounded distant and confused as he relayed some of the depressing news but on the third day he failed to pick up or to return a text and Kelly was worried enough to call round to the flat.

She knocked for several minutes knowing he was inside and eventually sat on the doorstep

"I know you are in there, Carl. Talk to me ... I just need to see you and know you are alright."

The door clicked behind her and her weight against it pushed it open slowly. She stood up and entered tentatively. Carl had returned to the kitchen where he was sat gulping a glass of whisky.

"Are you alright?"

He didn't answer. Kelly wanted to run and put her arms around him. She didn't because it didn't seem right, it felt like taking advantage. It didn't just feel that way, she knew it was exactly like taking advantage because putting her arms around Carl had been something she'd been wanting to do since she first met him almost two years ago.

She loved Carl; she had always loved Carl. She wished she didn't, but love can't be planned or controlled, it's the one wild card and she had hidden her feelings from so many for so long. The kind of love she had denied ever wanting, had already hit her, and hit her hard. Her heart had been breaking each time she saw him with her best friend, but she had kept her silence because she would rather her own heart break than to cause any pain for her friend.

It was unlikely that her love would ever be reciprocated by Carl anyway, he was out of her league intellectually, in fact he hardly noticed her at all. But now, now it was different. Now Sophie didn't want him and if she had only told him that instead of making a big drama of it, she might have had a chance.

Now it all seemed less likely than ever, but right now she had this one opportunity to hold the man whose affection and touch she craved. Of course it would be taking advantage, and the shame of it would be multiplied by the circumstance but he was only a few feet away and the moment was begging for the solace of human contact.

She moved toward him and as he looked up at her for support, she allowed herself to grasp the moment. It was too much, it was too little, it was too late, it was too soon, but still she remained in his arms until he got up and poured another drink.

He looked over at her as if pleading with her to make this go away. He looked her in the eyes. He didn't notice her glossed and curled hair falling beautifully around her shoulders, or the clever contouring make up around her neck and cleavage, or the corset that was nipping her waist into an hourglass figure. He didn't notice the expensively cut pencil skirt or killer heels nor the potency of her perfume. He looked only at the pupils of her eyes as a friend looks at a friend, with the desperate hope that they will hold out a lifeline so that's exactly what Kelly did.

"Talk to me Carl, I'm here for you, just tell me what you need."

He rubbed his eyes like a crying child and through his hands he muttered.

"Sophie is in a coma. They say there is brain activity which is a good sign but there's no way of knowing if or when she will come out of it or even if she will be the same when she does."

He was talking between sobs and trying to wipe his nose at the same time.

"Oh Carl. I'm so sorry."

"There has been no improvement at all in these past days and that is really not good."

"Do you want me to do anything. Do you want anything?"

"I want my girlfriend and my child to be alright."

"Your child? What child?"

"Sophie is pregnant."

Kelly's heart sank. This was the worst news. Now he had a sleeping girlfriend carrying his child like some sick fairy tale. Snow White in her glass coffin or Sleeping Beauty waiting for her prince to kiss her back to life! Except there was nothing white or beautiful about it. It was black and it was ugly. She was a liar and a cheat, and he deserved better. He deserved someone who loved and appreciated him. He deserved Kelly.

"Well she can't keep the baby after an overdose, surely? Who knows what damage will have been done?"

It was anger talking. Anger and frustration at the injustice of it and her own stupidity in making a promise never to tell Carl about Sophie's lust for some other man.

"Not necessarily," Carl went on "she's only a few weeks pregnant and there's no way of knowing if the baby was affected or not."

"How can it not be affected? That's ridiculous!"

Kelly's harsh words caused Carl to break down.

"I don't know. I don't know anything, anymore."

Kelly wanted to scream that he was damn right about that, but she had to play the part. She had to be the patient, concerned friend just as she had for the last two years, patiently waiting for her chance, for Carl to finally see her.

She was tired of waiting and just when everything seemed possible, just when doubts about the wedding and the relationship had placed it within grasp, Sophie had played her trump card without even knowing it. Now it was like competing with a ghost and instead of comforting a jilted lover she felt like she was consoling a tragic widower. Her chance with Carl was slipping further and further away and she wished Sophie would just wake up and dump him or die. This limbo was pure torture.

She knelt and took Carl's shaking hands in hers and pulled them down from his face. He hadn't shaved for days and she could smell stale sweat from his body, his hands were grubby and his tee shirt was covered in stains but still he was the most attractive man she had ever met and it was pure privilege to be physically close to his stinking body. She fought the desire to hold him closer as his tormented eyes once again searched for hers.

"It's ok," Was all she could say "everything will be ok ... I promise."

Chapter 2

As the days turned to weeks, Kelly became a regular visitor at the flat and bit by bit, she took on the role of housekeeper, cook and faithful friend to the man who was trying to fight his way through every day. Steadfastly she rode the waves alongside him.

The highs and lows of hope and despair, as tests and scans delivered glimmers of light and clouds of darkness in equal measure. One thing was certain though, his baby was growing happily in the sleeping body of the woman he loved. The woman who would rather have died than to marry him, but Kelly maintained her silence and hoped for a miracle.

She hoped that Sophie would open her eyes and tell him she didn't love him, that Niki would intervene and reveal her insanity, or at least to tell him she had desires on someone else or that Sophie would take her last breath and leave him free to get over his grief, while she supported him to the point of becoming his wife.

Of course, she could have moved on herself, instead of wasting months hoping for something that may never happen. She knew that if Sophie woke up and decided to throw her arms around Carl, he would cast her aside in a heartbeat. All the months she had put her own life on hold to stand by his side would be forgotten and what was worse was that he would expect her to be equally thrilled.

She knew the dangers, she knew the probabilities, yet for now, she was content to be in his life just a little and to have the chance to show him some love. She made sure of that, endless love in fact, unconditional love, as she put herself at his complete disposal with not a hint of affection in return. It didn't matter, she knew he was vulnerable and weak, and she was taking advantage again, but she was enjoying the role she had in his life and was causing no harm. Surely there was no harm in two people getting exactly what they needed.

Carl however, still had other ideas of what he needed as he continued to worship the lifeless body of his former love. Lifeless except for the visible movement of her dancing belly as the innocent child kicked at his mother's bloated stomach to remind her that he was alive. Kelly's heart went out to the baby as she watched its fruitless efforts and the unresponsive expression on the face of this breathing corpse.

One day she called to see him after work to find him smiling and a little excited. She had hardly seen him smile at all in the past months and as dread gripped her, she found herself jabbering a silent prayer that Sophie had not risen from the dead.

"They are going to do it tomorrow." he was still grinning.

"Do what? "

"Deliver the baby."

He took hold of Kelly's hands "Our baby. Our little son."

Kelly wished with all her heart that those words had been as accurate as they sounded. Of course, he meant their baby, their son. The son of the man she loved and his cheating girlfriend.

Perhaps the child wasn't even Carl's? She hadn't even considered that! The possibility that the new man in Sophie's life was of real flesh and blood. The idea gave her a moment of elation. It made sense of Sophie's desperate actions. The smile that swept over her face on considering it was the reaction Carl was expecting from his news.

He hugged her fiercely, happy that she was sharing the excitement of it. Why wouldn't she after all?

Tommy, weighing 6lbs 8 oz was put gently into Carl's arms the following afternoon and Kelly was the first person he called. She sat on the floor in the hallway of Carl's flat numbly listening to his rapturous account of the birth with the oven glove still on her hand.

She had been making a special meal to celebrate the birth and the roast had just been checked before adding the potatoes. She remained silent as he gushed news of this perfect baby and the wonderful woman who had given him this gift. His heartfelt regret that Sophie couldn't share the moment but how he would remember every detail for her so he could recount every moment when she finally recovered. He didn't seem to notice that Kelly had remained silent, her reaction wasn't even on his radar amid his exhilaration and hopes for his family.

Kelly wished he would just get it off his chest and hurry up. Finish cooing over the baby, hand it back and get home for his tea. Tommy may have been the guest of honour tonight, but she was thankful he was elsewhere for the celebration.

The champagne was chilling, the lights were low, soon she would be wearing the slinky dress she had been saving and had every reason in the world to put her arms around him in rejoice.

As his key clicked in the door she was waiting. She had been waiting in her perfect pose for fifteen minutes. The one that showed off her curves in profile. She had re-applied her lipstick twice, returned the champagne to the cooler twice and fluffed her hair more times than she could count.

He rushed over to her, grabbed her round the waist and spun her around. She was caught off guard by the sudden unexpected contact but quickly reciprocated by hugging his neck and kissing him firmly on the cheek.

"You should see him Kelly. He's the cutest thing ever. He has my nose and Sophie's eyes and….wow! You look nice tonight."

Kelly was taken off guard for the second time in as many minutes.

"Thank you. I wanted to make the evening a bit special."

Carl frowned a little, causing Kelly to clarify her meaning.

"You know, to greet the little stranger. Something to remember the occasion by even though he can't join us yet."

Carl grinned "That's so thoughtful of you. Thank you … on behalf of myself and my son."

Kelly grimaced as she walked away towards the cooler to get the champagne, quickly transforming it to a happy grin as she turned around to walk back.

"You should have seen Christine Kelly," his eyes misted over "I think meeting her grandson has been the only reason she's survived this long. She sat with her arms around Tommy and Sophie and there was something right there in her eyes. I could hear her whispering to them. It was heart-breaking"

Kelly hugged him firmly as though encouraging him to cheer up before she served the meal.

She allowed him to chat through the meal about prams and high-chairs, about formula and gripe water as he stuffed forkfuls of the perfectly cooked beef wellington, dauphinoise potatoes and buttered baby carrots into his mouth without even noticing. He grimaced on taking a mouthful of the champagne that had cost her a day's salary and went to the fridge for a beer.

Kelly felt ready to explode but she quickly dampened the fire inside her with his rejected glass of champagne and stifled the screams with forkfuls of potatoes. She knew this was not the time to explode, this was the time to box clever so she brought over a pad and pen from the kitchen draw and started a list of the things Carl would need, or rather, the things *they* would need for the baby. She was already jostling for the position of co-parent.

She smiled sweetly and touched his hand often. She raised a toast to the 'little stranger' and looked Carl in the eyes sincerely as she gently clinked her glass against his beer bottle.

She wasn't going to push him. She wasn't going to do anything to make him feel like they were betraying his sleeping princess. She was going to wait and let time bring him to her. She was going to be everything he needed and eventually everything he wanted. Slowly slowly catch a monkey.

Tommy was released from hospital a few days later to the waiting coop of mother hens that had become Carl's flat. For over a week Kelly was pushed aside as the hens took turns on the nightshift feeds and their respective cockerels dared to do nothing other than to sleep in lonely beds and eat takeaways. It wasn't sustainable and very soon the call came that Kelly had been hoping for

"Hi Kelly. I know it's a big ask but do you think you could come over at the weekend to give the oldies a break? Sophie's mum has been taken into hospital."

Kelly was happy to give the oldies a break. A permanent break when it came to the nightshift in fact, but they were watching her every move and she knew that moving in was not an option right now. But she didn't have to wait long for an unexpected lucky break a week later. The landlord of Carl's run-down block of flats had sold to a developer for refurbishment and although the rent would almost double the few remaining residents would remain on the old rate. The only condition was that they each moved out for a month in turn while the rewiring, plumbing and stairways were done. Kelly had more than enough room in her flat and it was literally on the doorstep of Carl's workplace. It made perfect sense and even the oldies couldn't find a strong enough argument to block it.

She would have loved to give up her job and stay at home like a wife and mother, but Sophie's mum hinted at every opportunity that she ought to be out finding a boyfriend. Christine was jealously protecting the nest in the absence of her daughter and making sure one side of the marital bed, wherever it was located, would remain empty until her return. Kelly was amazed that she'd been released from hospital again and was sure that the only thing keeping her alive was the dogged determination to keep her away from her daughter's family.

Sophie's inevitable return was something she talked of often. The things Sophie would do with Tommy, Carl and David, and although her own name was cordially excluded from these anticipations, she fought with every bit of life left in her, to keep the dream alive.

Plans for the future were rivalled only by her incessant reminiscing. Tirelessly she reminded Carl of the happy memories with her beloved daughter and how he could have all that again if he was patient, and faithful. Kelly resented the way she painted the perfect picture on the grubby tainted canvas of the past. She resented the lack of gratitude both sets of parents gave her for the effort and time she spent on their grandson and she resented the ever-present inference that she was muscling in on Sophie's family, true though it was.

During the renovation, the inevitable call came. David called to let Carl know that Christine had lost her fight against cancer and passed away at home, but the relief Kelly had anticipated didn't come. Instead she was overwhelmed with guilt and remorse for the woman who had fought for her child through the worst of times. Sick from the effects of chemotherapy and ravaged by cancer she persevered in her quest to keep a place open for Sophie, relentlessly trying to plug the holes Kelly had been making in the walls of her daughter's life. Kelly had been the predator, the enemy and although the opposition had been removed it was a hollow victory adorned in regret and shame.

Kelly attended the funeral and made sure she did not stand beside Carl at any point, nor hold Tommy. She made her respectful goodbye to the woman she had previously resented knowing that her irritation had been caused purely because Christine had seen through her deceitful plan. She also knew that the woman would have been distraught at knowing she was now leaving the path clear for Kelly to muscle in. She had been defeated, and it had been an unfair fight. Kelly acknowledged that with a heavy heart, a solitary tear and the gesture of leaving the family to have their wake in peace. She returned to her flat after the ceremony and waited for Carl to return to her.

After the month of renovation, they all moved back together, and there was no-one to object. David was still consumed with grief at the loss of his wife while Carl's parents seemed to be warming to Kelly and were grateful that they would not be dragged back into fulltime child minding. Kelly had already reduced her working hours but still they were finding it hard enough to cover the few hours Kelly couldn't.

The flat inside hadn't changed much but the common areas and the outside of the building were now clean and attractive, and it wasn't long before the abandoned block started to fill up with new tenants.

As months passed Sophie remained in her coma, Carl remained in his own room and Kelly became the live-in nanny and general dog's body. Carl was the king and Kelly the pawn. The insignificant pawn who could not get close enough to take him but constantly and silently threatened as he waited for his queen to wipe her from the board. It was stalemate.

Chapter 3

The weeks turned to months and the months turned gradually to years as they became a family unit in every way other than the way Kelly craved. She had played the game patiently, given and given until she had nothing left to give but the monkey was not yet captured. There were days when it didn't matter because Tommy loved her as a mother and Carl loved her as his friend and soulmate. She was sharing a life and family with the man she loved, and it was more than most women got. She gradually nudged the grandparents into the background and became the one who arranged Tommy's birthday parties and selected his first school.

Often, she would accompany Carl at social events as his 'plus one' and although most people accepted her, it was always amidst a few whispers and raised eyebrows to remind her she was the cuckoo in the nest. A nest that Sophie's dad checked regularly when he took his time going to the toilet. Kelly knew he was checking the bedrooms to establish exactly where Kelly was sleeping.

He always returned with a warm smile for the girl who had shown continued respect for his sleeping daughter. For the girl who had been trying her hardest for years to wipe that smug smile right off his face the way she had tried to wipe it from the face of his late wife.

As Tommy reached his sixth birthday, he was a very energetic little boy and Carl decided it was time to look for a house with a garden. He would struggle to make the mortgage payments alone, but still he didn't include Kelly in the financial arrangements or any of the viewings.

As he sat reading estate agent's leaflets, Kelly concluded that Carl had everything, and she was the one making it all possible, but she was the one with nothing.

She had given up her own home, she had given up a chunk of her wage to enable her to do the school runs but she was nothing other than an unpaid nanny and housekeeper. Was it possible that Carl actually believed that she was doing all of this for Saint Sophie? That she shared his belief and hope that one day she would return, and Kelly would just disappear back to her non-existent life, leaving the family she had built for the woman who didn't even want it?

Something had to change. It was time for Carl to recognise and appreciate her. She was tired of tending Sophie's little garden of Eden, of watering the flowers and keeping it perfect for her return. It was time for Carl to give something back. It was he who needed to wake up, not Sophie!

Occasionally, Tommy would spend a Saturday night with David, and it was usual that Carl would go to the pub with his friends while Kelly watched TV with a bottle of wine and a face pack.

"How about we go into town on Saturday night?" She suggested casually as she drained the spaghetti.

"Town? It's hardly a town!" Carl laughed

"You know what I mean. There's a music bar near the front with a Karaoke on Saturday nights. It'll be fun and I haven't been out for ages"

"Karaoke? You can't sing!"

"Maybe not but a girl deserves a night out once in a while doesn't she Tommy?" She knew Carl would cave in if she got Tommy on side.

"It's only fair daddy. You always go out and leave her in." Tommy, as predicted, took her side

Carl watched his son as he picked up a strand of spaghetti and tipped back his head to lower it in his mouth from above. He loved Kelly's spaghetti bolognaise with its special secret sauce.

"Ok ok! We will go to the Karaoke, but I bet it's rubbish."

"Whoop whoop. Dad's got a date!"

Kelly grimaced behind Carl's back. It was the last thing she wanted Tommy to say. She held her breath for a moment, but it seemed Carl had considered the inference too ridiculous to warrant a response. He simply smiled as he shook his head at his son's joke and sat down to eat.

Kelly felt both relieved and angered at the same time. So, it was too ridiculous to even bother denying? As she sat down to her meal, she cast a glance at this annoying, inconsiderate, selfish, wonderful man she loved and thought, "we'll see about that!"

As she counted down the days, she made several shopping trips into Scarborough. She bought new skinny low waist jeans and a crop top which would show off her midriff and belly button piercing. She bought new foundation, glitter eye shadow and a twenty-four-hour lipstick. She was intending to style her layered hair in soft curls and wear her high heeled ankle boots. By the time Saturday arrived all her mantraps were laid out on her bed and dresser.

For the first time since Tommy had been placed in her arms, Kelly found herself anticipating the arrival of the car that would take the little boy out of the way so she could concentrate on getting ready for what might be the most important night of her life.

She had packed his pyjamas, his Furby, Buzz Lightyear and the Bearytales Bear he pretended he was too old for, into his overnight bag hours ago. She didn't want to risk being unable to find any of the vital items that might lead to an unnecessary delay in getting him away.

She needed ample time to get herself ready for her date. It was a wet October day and as she looked out at the drizzle, she decided she may have to rethink her hair. She would go for the wanton Britney look.

At 5 pm the car lights lit the front of the house as they pulled into the drive. It was dark and cold outside, and she had Tommy's coat ready at the door in the hope of bundling them off before they had chance to wander by her and sit down.

"Tommy. Grandad is here!" She called, relieved that he was on time and that Carl was engrossed in the TV, giving her a fair chance of getting Tommy packed off without any conversation between the two of them about why they were going out together.

By the time David parked his car and made it up the stairs Tommy was appropriately coated, wellied, hugged and kissed. She bundled him out of the door and sped off to her room to start her transformation.

"Did I just hear David?" Carl called.

She stopped halfway down the hallway.

"Yes. Did you want him for something?"

"No. Not really. Just seemed like a quick visit."

"Yes. Think he must have been in a hurry." She lied.

He didn't reply and she quickly returned to her plan.

An hour later she heard Carl running the shower. Her hair looked perfect and her makeup was finally done after a few issues. The foundation was the same one she used to wear on special occasions years ago, but today it didn't give her the same porcelain finish. Tiny lines around her eyes and lips seemed to be emphasised by the pigment which clung either side of each one exposing the crack in between. As she mixed it desperately with moisturiser, she knew this was a stark reminder that time was moving on and her body clock was ticking loudly.

Next year she would be thirty. Thirty with no home, no children of her own and no man. She sat in her robe on the edge of her single spinster bed, allowing the body lotion to soak in before getting dressed and, as she sipped on the glass of rosé wine, she plotted to fast track her plan. To ruthlessly accelerate her augmentation from dog's body to wife and mother of two.

Kelly covered most of her outfit with an oversized jacket before leaving her room. She didn't want Carl to see it just yet and the inclement weather was the perfect excuse to wear the sensible coat. She had fixed her hair into a side clasp and tousled it. Then sprayed it excessively, to ensure it stayed in place even in the light drizzle.

Together they walked the few hundred yards to the town centre and chatted about the usual subject. Tommy had become their common interest and he seemed to dominate every conversation they had, but Kelly didn't mind because it gave her the chance to engage with him on a level that felt almost private and exclusive. No other woman could share these conversations and she liked that.

He pushed open the door to the warm lively pub where two girls were already jumping up and down on stage to a tuneless version of 'Like a Virgin.' They exchanged an amused smile and Carl went to the bar.

Kelly took the opportunity to find a table and unburden herself of her coat, but she didn't sit down. She ran her fingers through her hair to separate the strands and leant casually against a wall as though unaware of the impact her bare shoulders and midriff were having on the three men behind her.

By the time Carl returned with her glass of rosé she was chatting merrily to them and Carl seemed taken aback. One of the men put up his hand in an apologetic way.

"Sorry mate."

Kelly jumped in quickly "It's fine. This is Carl, my…"

Before she could allocate Carl a label, he cut in quickly,

"her boyfriend." He handed Kelly the glass which she took with a frown. A frown that was disguising the grin inside.

"Shall we sit down babe?" He never called her babe, but she sat and took a sip of the wine while he gulped half of his pint in one go.

She had rattled him, and he was clearly wrestling with some internal conflict. She wished she had done this years ago.

They continued talking but the conversation was not about Tommy.

"You look very sexy tonight. It's a good job you have me for protection." He joked as though trying to justify his actions.

"What makes you think I want protecting?" It was a subtle confrontation, it was a tease, it was a threat.

"Come on let's dance. It's reggae!" He pulled her to her feet and tugged her to the floor.

Kelly knew he liked reggae and she knew why. It was a beat for dancing in couples without smooching. She had watched him dance with Sophie many times to that beat with their hands sexily palmed and hips against hips as they gyrated to the seductive rhythm. She had watched the spectacle many times as the image had burned her eyes and fierce jealousy had crushed her chest.

He pulled Kelly close and started to sway to the music.

"You shouldn't have told them you were my boyfriend. I might have got a date out of it." She was going to keep pushing.

"You already have a date." He whispered as he pushed her away to look her in the eyes and then pull her close again.

"Do I?" She smiled, gently teasing him with the motion of her naked stomach against his.

Two hours later, after several drinks but more dancing than talking, they tripped out of the pub and staggered playfully home.

"You are a great girl you know." Carl slurred as they reached the flat

"Oh, I know I am." She teased.

"I don't think you know just how great you are though," he continued, "if you weren't lumbered with me you could be out with men falling at your feet?"

Kelly put her key in the door and helped him inside.

"Yes, I know I could. The question is, should I be out looking for a man of my own or not?"

"Is that what you want to do then?" He grinned.

"I think you already know the answer to that." She said more seriously, hoping her moment of sobriety would not scare him away.

He squeezed her hand and she returned the squeeze. He repeated it and so did she. Nothing was said and she dared herself to look into his eyes, just for a second, for one fateful second and she was sunk.

A Love to Die For – Tortured Hearts

He was returning her gaze and she was terrified. Her heart pounded with anticipation, with fear, with excitement but mostly at the enormity of the moment. She had spent years waiting for this moment, years imagining it, years praying for it and now it was here, and she had only a few seconds not to blow it.

She looked down bashfully. He put out his hand and turned her face back up to his. It was all the encouragement she needed as they engaged in a gentle kiss. A kiss so tender, so delicate, so debilitating that she could feel the tears forming in her closed eyes the very second their lips touched. The years of hoping and toiling for this man's love were building into an overwhelming mountain of emotion.

This was it. This was the one moment to define her entire life. Her moment, their moment and it felt perfect, so desperately perfect. He took her hand and led her to the bedroom and no words were spoken, none were needed. The love was tangible. It was thick and heavy, light and airy, dark and perfect, undisputable.

His hands stroked her body as she trembled uncontrollably. Each stroke, each gentle touch of his fingers pulled her soul right out of her body and into the aura that bound them. She had never felt anything like this before. This was not sex, it was something with an identity of its own, almost a third being devouring them, holding them, and binding them together in these moments of inexplicable pleasure.

He held her so gently, so tightly, so completely and as his penis penetrated her, the honour of it consumed her. Just to hold him inside her, to be the subject of his physical pleasure and the object of his need was the most wonderful moment of her existence. This was it. This was the feeling she had craved and dreaded, coveted and feared, longed for and avoided. At last she had found love.

She held his hands in hers as the rhythm of his thrusting started to build pace. She put her arms around his back and pulled him close as he slowed and rocked gently to and fro, kissing her neck, she held his face in her hands and watched his contorted expression of orgasm. She didn't reach orgasm; she hadn't even tried to, because she had been somewhere beyond physical pleasure. Elated that she had felt the love and desire of the man she loved, she had experienced something more spectacular and fulfilling than sex could ever be.

She lay blissfully in the moments of his recovery feeling his heartbeat gradually return to normal pace. Gently he slid out of her and she felt the rush of fluid trickle down onto the sheets. They had not taken precautions and she didn't care. On the contrary she hoped their recklessness would result in a balancing of the scales. She hoped the seed had been sown and it would grow inside her until her importance to him matched that of his sleeping beauty. Surely then she would hold all the aces.

Carl slept soundly with his arms around her, but she couldn't sleep. How could she possibly sleep when something so colossal had just happened? Her mind was racing, her heart was still in the grip of those moments and she was replaying them in her mind so she would remember every single detail of the moments that had changed her world forever.

As daylight broke, she was still listening to his breathing, stoking his skin and trying to contain her excitement, as she waited and waited for him to wake.

Eventually he stirred

"Good morning gorgeous."

"Good morning yourself." She breathed a sigh of relief and smiled. He smiled back warmly.

"Tea and toast?"

She nodded enthusiastically. "A gentleman too eh?"

"Did you ever doubt it?"

"Not for a minute."

She pulled the sheets around her and buried her huge grin in his pillow.

After a few minutes he returned with a tray and an equally large grin.

"I can't believe we did that last night."

"Me neither!" She echoed tearing off a huge piece of buttered toast with her teeth.

"Does this make us ......what do they call it? Fuck buddies?"

Kelly sat bolt upright.

"What do you mean?"

"I don't know," he laughed, "I think I heard it somewhere. When friends sleep together."

"Friends?"

Carl's smile melted away.

"We are friends, aren't we?"

Kelly couldn't swallow the mouthful of toast on the back of her tongue

"I hope we are a bit more than that." She tried to sound light-hearted.

"Well of course," Carl agreed unconvincingly, "more than that, yes we are"

"But?"

"But what?"

"It sounded like a 'but' was coming." She frowned

"No. I just mean that we are more than friends, but I *am* engaged to someone else"

"Which means?"

"I don't know"

"That you love her?"

"I guess so."

"And not me?"

"Of course, I love you too. You are lovely but it's not the same, is it?"

Kelly felt like her chest was about to explode.

"Not the same? The same as what? Not as good as with her?"

"I didn't mean that."

Kelly's hands were shaking as she fumbled for her clothes to cover her naked body which suddenly felt inferior and pathetic.

He put out a hand to try to stop her from leaving.

"Please let me go Carl."

"Don't be like that. You mean the world to me."

"No. No, I don't. Don't say that. If I meant the world to you, I would be your world!"

"Look. I'm sorry. So sorry. I really am."

"Please let go."

"Do you want me to stay away from you?"

Kelly wanted to take the moral high ground so damn much, to stand by her principles, to keep her self-respect. She wanted to tell him to go to hell. To grab everything she owned, and drive away never to return but with each laboured breath she took the hurt and anger was turning swiftly to fear and panic.

She had made a huge step forward and it just needed a bit more work. To scare him off now would be a mistake.

"No. My fault. I will pick Tommy up from David's later. You go."

She always took care of Tommy on her own most Sundays while Carl played football for his Sunday league team.

He kissed her on the forehead and winked.

"That's my girl."

She felt the anger rising again but fought the urge to slap his face.

After he had left, self-hatred burned inside her. There seemed to be no limit to the humiliation she would tolerate. No depth to which she was not prepared to sink. This was wrong, so wrong. It was obvious she didn't have his love or his respect and the more she allowed him to abuse her the more unlikely it was that she would ever earn either of those things.

She slammed both fists into the mattress over and over as though trying to thrust the stupidity from her body. She hated feeling like this, and she hated the life she had created for herself but mostly she hated that she was already planning what to wear and how to style her hair. Pondering over which perfume it was he said he liked, knowing she was about to totter around in high heels all day when she wanted to slob out in her combat trousers, tee shirt and trainers Here she was, trying again to gain the admiration of the asshole who didn't deserve her.

She wasn't going to put up with this much longer she vowed as she got dressed and styled her hair. Something had to change but as she carefully drew the lipliner around the outline of her lips she was shining a different light on the situation. This was no ordinary relationship and Carl had never pretended or lied about how he felt for Sophie. She had been the one to take advantage and muscle her way into his life. She was the one who had seduced him and deceived him with her false friendship, so surely the crimes were all hers, not his?

It suited her perfectly to acquit him and declare her pride and self-esteem intact. It suited her perfectly to grant herself permission to continue to pursue him.

With a final flick of her hair and dab of lip gloss she was on her way to collect Tommy with a gentle smile and understanding heart.

Chapter 4

As usual, Tommy ran into her arms while David greeted her with the usual lukewarm smile of resentful acceptance.

"Can we go and watch daddy play Kelly?"

Kelly looked at her watch and then at the drizzle outside.

"I've got a better idea." She whispered.

"What is it?" Tommy frowned.

"We can go and look through the house brochures daddy picked up. You can tell him which one you want him to choose."

It was David's turn to frown.

Kelly knew she was being insensitive, but she didn't care today. She was fed-up of tiptoeing around him, as though his were the only feelings that mattered. Well, she had feelings too and she had earned her place and the right to be recognised in it.

"That will be nice Tommy," David smiled as he held out Tommy's coat for him, "you can choose somewhere nice for when mummy wakes up."

Kelly smiled as sweetly as she could, but both knew what this was. The gauntlet had been thrown and David had picked up the challenge but, for the first time, Kelly didn't feel threatened. In the absence of the mother hen, David had taken over the task of jealously guarding her solitary egg, the sleeping egg that would never hatch and if he knew what his precious, devoted, future son-in-law had been up to last night he wouldn't be looking so smug.

She took Tommy's hand and left with an enthusiastic wave as she closed the gate, but in the pit of her stomach was a tremor of panic. She hoped he wouldn't mention this to Carl. If he did, she knew he would be angry with her and that would be a disaster. She helped Tommy with his seatbelt and decided that if it was mentioned, she would say it was Tommy who brought it up.

Back at the flat she had a quick tidy up while Tommy watched TV for a while. The usual sting of dusting the photographs of Carl and Sophie was immediately soothed as she entered the bedroom where the event of the previous night was evident.

The sheets were tangled in a single heap, both pillows flattened, one of which bore the bronze haze of her foundation, and her underwear was still on the floor where it had landed. She was about to strip the bed having noticed the stain but then she merely straightened the sheets, deciding that if she were back in her own room tonight, at least he would be reminded of her by her perfume and also by the crusty little patch as he tried to sleep.

As she finished off with the vacuum cleaner, her inner voice was starting to dampen her mood. The previous night had felt like a huge step forward, but it could prove to be the opposite and Carl may return full of regret. She was probably heading straight into a broken heart while she played out her fantasy role, foolishly believing that she could cook, clean and polish her way into his heart.

She returned to the living room and sat beside Tommy, pulling him close as she stroked his white-blonde hair, smiled into his huge blue adoring eyes. She was the only mother he had ever known and the sooner she cemented her position the better. She smiled and placed the leaflets on the coffee table, as she decided that she wasn't going to let any inner voices spoil the day.

She had finally made love to the only man she had ever wanted, and she was still playing mother to the child they had raised together since the day he was born. This was her family now and she was the happiest she had ever been.

She poured herself a cup of coffee and sat down with Tommy to look at the brochures. They all had their individual qualities, but one was a clear winner for them both. A three bedroomed semi-detached house just three streets back from the seafront. It was a corner plot down a quiet cul-de-sac with a huge garden and both she and Tommy fell immediately in love with it.

When Carl finally arrived home and dropped his sports bag in the hall for Kelly to retrieve his washing, she gave the brochure to Tommy and nodded.

"Daddy. We have picked out a house!" He shouted as he ran out of the lounge waiving the brightly coloured paper.

Kelly stayed in the living room and held her breath.

"Oh, you have, have you?"

"Yes. Look at the garden daddy and it has a swing and everything!"

Kelly waited again.

"So, this is the one you want is it?" he teased, "who picked it then?"

"Both of us, of course. Kelly loves it too."

"Oh, she does, does she?" He entered the room with Tommy, who was far too big to be carried, in his arms that way.

"Well we better go take a look at it then I suppose." As he hugged the little boy, he flashed a smile at Kelly and winked.

She was back in the game.

Chapter 5

In the spring of 2007, full of excitement, they moved into the house in the cul-de-sac. They took a room each. Kelly imagined how it would feel to be moving in as a real family with a real marital bedroom and the poke in the eye it would be for David.

The truth was, that taking her own room was not a façade to appease Sophie's dad, the truth was that it had been several months since the night they had made love and there had been no serious attempt to tread that path again, by either of them.

Kelly was afraid of pushing Carl. She needed him to make the first move, knowing that if he did, it would lay the responsibility firmly at his door and put some solid ground under her feet.

Carl wanted her madly, but he was well-aware of the consequences of initiating anything. He wished she would make the first move which he would interpret as her acceptance of his terms. They were back in stalemate.

But later that year on the evening of Tommy's seventh birthday party, she was sitting with Carl feeling totally exhausted after having occupied twenty children for two hours.

"You are, in effect, Tommy's mother you know?"

She smiled in acknowledgement and sipped the wine they were sharing.

"Don't think I'm not grateful for the love and stability you give him. I really am. More than you know."

She put her hand on his affectionately. This was no time to bask in the glory of his words.

"I'm not his mother," she whispered, "I know I never will be but that doesn't mean I don't love him or appreciate what he gives me in return."

Carl stroked her hand thoughtfully for a few moments.

"Sometimes I think I should give up hope on Sophie ever coming back to us."

Kelly's heart missed a beat. The monkey had stepped into the cage and she had to be incredibly careful at how slowly and gently she lowered the door behind him.

"You have done more than anyone could ever have expected." She said as she gently removed her hand from his, turning away to hide the hope and anticipation on her face.

She could hear him breathing gently behind her as she waited for his next sentence.

"I know," he said at last, "I think it's time for me to move on."

"What does that mean?" She asked softly.

"I have no idea."

"You are giving up on Sophie?" She asked, hardly daring to suggest it.

"I can't live my entire life like a monk, in some vain hope that she will miraculously wake up, can I?"

"No. I suppose you can't." Kelly could feel the excitement rising from deep within and lighting up her face.

"I mean. We both love Sophie don't we, and we would never hurt her, either of us would we?"

"Of course not." Kelly concurred still trying to prevent the huge smile inside, from betraying her.

Carl stroked her neck as he stared at the wall. Slowly she turned her face to his and kissed him gently on the mouth. For a second nothing happened, it felt like he hadn't even felt her kiss on his lips as his eyes remained fixed on the wall in front of him.

She kissed him again and slowly he brushed her lips with his and her heart was pounding. She daren't allow herself to believe he would finally be hers but still her heart pounded, and tears of joy welled behind her closed eyelids at the mere chance that he might be.

She trembled uncontrollably as he unbuttoned her dress and for a moment he hesitated as though tempered by the magnitude of his impact on her. Quickly she pulled him close reassuringly and he was back in the moment.

There on the sofa amid the popped balloon skins, streamers and crumbs, they made love for the second time and this time she allowed herself to be lost in it. The emotion of so many shared years and so many half-hopes and half dreams exploded between them in these few minutes of intimacy.

Each thrust drew her deeper and deeper into him, bonding him to her with every sensation that ripped through her body like an earth tremor. She didn't want this moment to end. She was home and nothing was going to take him away from her again. This was the man she had loved for as long as she could remember, and she felt without a doubt, that deep down he loved her too.

"God, I love you. I fucking love you!!"

The words were barely out of his mouth when he collapsed on top of her, but she didn't care. He had said it!

She spent the night in his bed, getting up twice to settle Tommy back down while Carl slept. She didn't mind at all, as she loved taking care of things for him. On the second visit to the over excited boy she had held him close just as she had many times but tonight it felt different. Tonight, she dared to believe he would be hers and that one day he would call her his mummy.

She lay awake in the early hours and waited for day to break. She was swinging back and forth between optimism and dread as she waited for Carl's first words. She knew that she would know immediately if he had regretted the previous night and the anticipation was tortuous.

Eventually she felt him stirring and as his arm snaked around her, she started to feel a little more at ease.

"Carl?" she whispered.

"Don't worry," he said, "I am not going to freak out on you."

"Good." She tried to sound amused whilst she inwardly breathed her relief sigh.

"And I won't call you my fuck buddy."

"You had better not!" She hit him full in the face with a pillow.

"We are ok though aren't we Kel?"

She didn't know what the question meant.

"How do you mean?"

"I mean, we are on the same page here aren't we?"

Her heart was sinking fast.

"Yes. You said you were moving on."

No-one spoke for a second and then Kelly took a deep breath.

"I know you also said that you didn't know what that meant but I think last night gave us both a hint?"

He laughed a little awkwardly.

"Yes, last night was amazing and we could easily build a life together but what would happen if Sophie did wake up? What then? I'm just supposed to tell her she's on her own now? That we have her son and we are playing happy families because I replaced her?"

Kelly wanted to scream the truth. The truth about how she felt. The truth about why she was doing any of this but mostly the truth about Sophie's phantom lover! But she knew he wouldn't believe her, and she also knew Niki would deny it. She wanted to scream "What about me and all I've done for you?" She wanted to scream that she had loved him way before he started dating Sophie. Mostly she just wanted to scream.

"Kelly, I know you love Sophie too and could you really do that to her?"

It was her cue to concur but all she wanted to do was to shout "Yes,Yes,Yes! I would do it to her in a heartbeat." But, as ever, she had to temper her behaviour, play the part and mask the brutal truth with something more palatable.

"Carl! This shrine to Sophie is crazy. I love you and we deserve to be happy. We deserve a chance at a real family. I know you love me too, you said so last night"

Carl dropped back heavily on the bed in a way that seemed to say everything. All the words she didn't want to hear were in that one slump.

"I love Sophie, Kelly. You know that. What you heard last night was just, just......"

"Hormones?"

"Yes, if you like. I care for you very very much, but I can't desert her, I just can't!"

"So why did you make love to me last night?"

It was Carl's turn to feel angry.

"Because I'm a man and you offered it on a plate again. I'm trying to be so bloody faithful, but I have needs and sometimes it's just too hard not to give in to it. I gave in because I do love you in many ways. I gave in because it felt right and mostly because I trusted you not to expect a wedding ring from it"

"What? You talk to me about a wedding ring when your precious Sophie didn't even want one from you?!" The words were out before she could stop them.

"What do you mean?"

"Nothing."

"You know something. Are you saying she didn't want me?"

Kelly could see he was close to tears and her anger and sympathy collided, rendering her silent.

"What did you mean Kelly, are you actually trying to poison me against Sophie? Making things up to get your way?"

"Forget it, you're unbelievable!" She snatched up her clothes to head back to her own room.

"I'm sor..."

She held up her hand "Don't say it. Don't you dare say that!"

He jumped up and caught her by the wrist.

"Maybe it's time for you to find someone else Kell. Someone who can love you in the way you should be loved."

"You know what? Maybe you're right because you are a fucking liability!"

He kept hold of her wrist as she writhed to break free.

"I do need someone Kelly. I know that, but I also know that if Sophie came round, I would drop that *someone* and go running back. So that *someone* can't be you."

"So, what are you going to do when you need a quick roll in the hay or a cleaner, a cook or a babysitter? Find some other sad cow who you don't like enough to even care?"

"Maybe. I don't know."

"Well good luck with that Carl."

"Kelly?"

"What?"

"You are my best friend."

"Whoopie doo!" She escaped his grip, his home and his life. She was gone.

The next few days passed with no contact and Tommy was distraught. He asked constantly for the only woman who had been a daily presence in his life. Carl picked his phone up several times a day, typing and then deleting hundreds of unsent messages. Kelly had done the same.

Tommy was late for school several times just as Carl was late for work. They quickly ran out of clean clothes and ate pizza on three of the four days that passed before Kelly could stand it no longer and rang to ask how Tommy was.

"Missing his auntie" Was Carl's tentative reply.

"Do you want me to call and see him?"

"If you could."

It was the only encouragement Kelly needed to place her head back in the lion's mouth, and after work she rushed home to her mother's house where she had taken up refuge in her old room. She showered quickly and snipped the store tags from the chiffon blouse she had bought in her lunch break. She spent more time than was necessary on re applying her make up but within the hour she was on her way to Carl's.

They greeted each other with a friendly kiss and Kelly knew the gentle essence of her perfume would have filled his nostrils in that short moment of closeness. He lingered for a second which confirmed it.

"Listen Kelly. I really do need you to move on with your life, get a boyfriend, a husband and stop wasting your life on me"

"And what about you? What are you wasting your life on? Something that will never happen?"

Carl didn't answer for a moment or two.

"That's my choice but I can't drag you along with it. How could I even enjoy a life we might build together knowing that at any moment it could be shattered and the guilt I would have to face for your wasted time or for Sophie's stolen family?"

She was beginning to appreciate the moral impact of the position she had put him in, when Tommy entered the hallway.

"Kelly Kelly!! Tommy ran into her arms and she kissed him several times, although the joy was giving away her sinking heart yet again.

They spent an hour playing with Tommy and he showed her the new toys his daddy had bought him, presumably to console him for Kelly's absence.

"I want you stay in Tommy's life as much as you can Kelly but please, please find yourself a man who deserves you, someone who is free to give you his heart.

Kelly sighed and took Carl's hand "You *are* free Carl; you just don't realise it."

"What is that supposed to mean?" He frowned, abruptly withdrawing his hand from hers.

Kelly's patience reached its limit. This yoyo life was killing her. Smiles and frowns, advances and withdrawals, warmth and anger but mostly, his misplaced loyalty and blind stupidity. She finally snapped.

"Fine. Fine. I will get myself a man so fast it will make your head spin. Bye-bye Tommy." She kissed him gently, gave him a hug and left leaving Carl stunned in the hallway with the door wide open where she had stormed out.

Later she sat in her mum's kitchen and poured herself a gin as she tried to take stock of the situation. She knew Carl was trying to protect her and she knew he had feelings for her. Deep down she also knew how awful it would be if she wasted any more time only to be cast aside if Sophie suddenly started to recover. The truth was that she was living another woman's life, nurturing another woman's child and the mess was all of her own making. Yet still it had felt so good.

They had been playing at normal family life, and consequently neither of them had dated anyone. Sleeping with anyone else would have felt like betrayal in this half-marriage they had silently consented to. Maybe Carl would find himself simply satisfying his urges with prostitutes or one-night stands, but Kelly couldn't bear the thought of him touching any other woman, paid or not.

She poured herself another large gin. It was more likely that he was looking for a succession of goodtime girlfriends who wanted no commitment. Girlfriends who would not be interested in playing the role of mother or housekeeper, but happy to welcome him into their bed when it suited them. Women who would not be irreparably scarred if they were dumped unceremoniously on their ass if, and when Sophie, the virtuous Goddess chose to return.

It all made sense she concluded, as she poured again and started to untangle her mother's Christmas decorations. She should have been doing as he asked to show she understood. They could still be friends and she could still be a big part of

Tommy's life. She could still be there at Christmas to open presents and cook dinner.

She could have the bits that his goodtime girls didn't want. She smiled at the thought of taking a new boyfriend but it wasn't a smile of optimism for a new love, it was a smile of anticipation of how jealous Carl would feel when she remained in his life with a new man at her side. Someone who Carl believed had replaced him in every way and more, a man who also shared her bed.

She was playing with fire, but she knew that if she could make him believe it, he wouldn't be able to bear it. They were both embarking on the pretence of finding replacements, but she would never actually share another man's bed as part of the game. She knew that if either of them ever crossed that line, all would be lost. She remembered very well the words her mother had told her repeatedly after her father crossed that line and broke her heart.

"If its real love and you want to keep it, don't ever do anything that can't be undone."

It was a powerful, true and undeniable message. No. She would not cross that line but there was no harm in giving him something to think about.

Hmmm. She smiled confidently as she picked up the phone to arrange a night out with the girls from the salon.

Chapter 6

Christmas came and went, and Kelly split the day between her mother's house and Carl's. The three grandparents had already taken over the cooking and she felt like an outsider. The exchanges between her and Carl were polite and friendly, and she hated it. As she left in the early evening with her collection of cheap, thoughtless, token gesture gifts, she realised she needed to get on with her plan before it was too late. She needed Carl to feel the pinch and that meant making her absence felt.

She stopped divulging every detail of her own life and started to be mysterious about times and dates when she was not available. She had increased her hours back to full time as she explained she needed the extra money to find a place of her own and Carl was in no position to complain.

She knew though, that he resented the constant stream of alternating grandparents in and out of the house for school runs and babysitting. Kelly knew her absence had made his life difficult and that he struggled to fit in the housework and shopping. She also knew he could no longer play his beloved football, or go out on Saturday nights.

It was on one such Saturday night a few months later, that she turned up unexpectedly to see Tommy while Carl was in the middle of getting him ready for bed. The little boy was half in and half out of his pyjamas and Carl was in his sweats which were wet with bath water and stained by ketchup from Tommy's supper.

He opened the door and turned instantly pale. Kelly looked stunning but it was the presence of her companion who was responsible for the long silence in which Carl seemed unable to take a breath. His arm draped casually around her waist and his hand resting on her thigh was a tall, muscular black man with a stunning smile.

"Hi. I'm Jake," he said with an extended hand that turned into a firm handshake, "I've heard so much about you."

Carl was still pre-occupied with the other hand which was stroking Kelly's leg affectionately.

"Please. Come in." He gestured trying to resist the urge to slam the door in the face of this over-confidant predator.

"I can't stay long. I'm on my way to the gym so I just walked Kelly here on my way. I just wanted to say hello. I'll pick you up later doll." He grinned, leaning in for a kiss.

Kelly put her hands either side of his face and kissed him slowly on the lips.

As the Adonis headed towards the door, he patted Kelly on the bottom and winked cheekily. She smiled back.

Jake had seen the jealousy in Carl's face, and he loved it. He had been waiting to do this to Carl since late the previous year when he had taken his car to Carl's garage for new wheel bearings.

He had arrived early to collect the car, but Carl had been having a few difficulties with it, so he decided to wait while they finished the job. As the three mechanics hammered and cursed, a blonde woman arrived with a flask and a huge chunk of homemade apple pie for Carl. She was dressed in pale jeans and an oversized pink fluffy jumper. He couldn't take his eyes off her. There was something alluring about the combination of cream skin, pink jumper and flaxen hair. She reminded him of peaches and cream.

He watched the affectionate way she acted around the dirty grease monkey with her flawless beige complexion and pristine outfit. It was a stark contrast to the grime covered floor and the black oil clogged heaps of metal around her. It seemed like sending a white dove into a coal mine and it seemed unlikely she would get out untarnished. But she kissed him gently without touching anything, smiled and sashayed sexily back out of the coal pit unscathed.

As she left, one of the mechanics nudged Carl as he took a huge bite of the sugar-coated pie.

"Not just a pretty face either eh? Lucky bastard."

Carl laughed out loud, blowing chunks of pastry into the air.

"Yeah, she'll do for now I suppose." He grinned.

Jake knew who she was, most of the town knew who she was and of her involvement with the partner of the 'coma girl' and her son.

"You're plain greedy you are," the man went on, carelessly tossing a spanner at Carl's feet, "I can't get one bloody woman and here you are hogging two!"

"Well you've either got it or you aint." Carl boasted cockily.

Jake was seething. He had seen Kelly several times at the gym, and although he was practically the only black man under forty in the whole town, she hadn't seemed to notice him at all. That's the problem when a girl is in love with someone else, he told himself. She's totally blind because her dating shutter is firmly down.

He didn't know Kelly, but he had seen her upset many times. She was often texting and checking her phone, and on more than one occasion she had left abruptly as though too distressed to finish her workout.

He listened to Carl disrespecting her in front of his workmates and instinctively clenched his fists. If it wasn't for the fact that his car was still in bits he might have knocked the smirk of his grubby face there and then, but he had no wish to be handed his car back with a bunch of dissembled parts in a bag. One thing was certain though, Carl was not a lucky bastard, he was just a bastard, full stop!

A few weeks later he had witnessed another of Kelly's emotional episodes at the gym, which wasn't surprising since he watched her intently at every visit. As she pressed her lips together to prevent her face from crumpling, and snatched her towel to leave, he left his weight machine, grabbed his sweatpants and hoody from his locker and rushed to the foyer before she had time to get changed. By the time she came out he had pulled them on over his shorts and vest and was standing in the doorway with two cups of coffee.

"Magic coffee?" He smiled.

"What?" She wasn't in the mood to be hit on.

"It's magic coffee. Flushes arse hole boyfriends right out of you." He grinned as he pushed it into her hand.

"In that case I'll take them both." She smiled.

They moved to a table and sat down. She hadn't wanted to spill her guts to a random stranger, but it felt good to be able to tell someone what a total arse her boyfriend actually was.

Earlier Carl had told her to get someone else and she'd told him she'd do it so fast it would make his head spin. Now he was texting but still not apologising or offering anything different. He was just texting to continue kicking her.

"So, are you going to spin his head?" Jake laughed.

Kelly looked up into his brown eyes which were dancing with mischief, and felt strangely refreshed at being able to smile instead of cry for once.

"I just might" She smiled.

It was the start of something, but she wasn't sure what, and neither was he. It didn't matter. She didn't know if there was even a place for him in her life right now and he didn't know if he was prepared to play second fiddle to the grease monkey. But there was one thing they both did know. Whether this was a friendship, a romance, or a conspiracy, it would piss Carl off and that was enough incentive for both of them.

Jake had been planning the big introduction to Carl, with Kelly firmly on his arm, for a long time and the satisfaction of that smirk as he walked away had been well worth the wait.

After he left, Kelly started to engage with Tommy, but Carl was too preoccupied to allow her to move on from this without a conversation. Of all the things Carl was planning to say, of all the casual conversations he wanted to have, the speeches he had practised for the unlikely possibility of facing this situation, nothing could prevent him from asking the only question on his jealous, testosterone fuelled mind.

"So. Have you slept with him?"

Kelly kept her head turned away, not out of shame or embarrassment but because she didn't want him to see the wry smile on her face. He was jealous and she loved that he was.

"Why do you ask?"

"I just wondered."

She continued to play with Tommy without answering.

"So?" He probed again.

"Carl I am not going to answer that. It's a personal question and you wanted me to find a man remember?"

She had been right about sex being the deal breaker. She knew he was trying to find out if he still had time to step in or if he would never want her again. She was going to torture him a while longer.

"Yes, I know. Sorry."

Kelly smiled inwardly. It was working like a dream.

"What does he do for a living anyway? Nightclub DJ?" Carl snapped condescendingly.

"He's a junior doctor." Kelly knew she had put one right in the back of the net

The next hour passed with Kelly acting happy and relaxed and Carl unable to disguise the insane jealousy burning in the pit of his stomach. He was subdued and downbeat and although Kelly was feeling sorry for him, she continued as though oblivious until a knock on the door announced the arrival of her new lover.

As she walked away from the house hand in hand with Jake, she glanced back to the hurt and bewildered expression on the face of the man she genuinely loved. She wanted to run back and relieve his agony, but she knew she must not. This game had to be played and played ruthlessly if she was going to finally win.

Later that evening after a meal out with Jake and a few awkward comments over the nature of her relationship with Carl, she was back at the flat of this muscular, charming prospective lover. She was debating the idea of allowing herself to explore his body a little as an experiment. To determine if she could be aroused by someone who wasn't Carl, and if she was therefore, capable of moving on one day if she had to.

They kissed gently and she deliberately turned the kiss into something more passionate as though trying to force the mood to develop. As his tongue found her mouth she listened to her body, waited for the beat of her heart to quicken, for her hands to tremble with anticipation and passion and to feel the urge to touch him. The kiss continued, the mood remained the same, the feelings didn't come.

Half an hour later she was saying an uncomfortable goodbye to Jake at his front door with many reassurances they both knew to be false. She got into her car and picked up her phone to see numerous missed calls from Carl. She listened to his voice messages among which he pleaded for her not to sleep with this man unless she already had. Of wanting to know the extent of her involvement with him and finally his parting message

"I'll tell you one thing.... he's got a fight on his hands!"

She held the phone close to her heart before sending him a message.

"Not slept with him. Don't intend to. Night night x"

The huge smile on her face as she got into bed spelt victory. Carl had finally had the jolt he needed and the jealousy and pain he had felt had made him realise that his love was for her, not Sophie. That this was real and not some fantasy based on a woman he hasn't even spoken to for almost eight years.

This was the start of the relationship she had longed for and the matter of removing Jake from her life was barely a consideration. How easy it was to be callous when you have no interest in someone, she smiled without recognising the irony of her thought and its resemblance to Carl's behaviour towards her. If she had, she might have smiled less broadly, slept less soundly and she might have anticipated the severity of Jakes reaction when she casually turned up at his door to tell him it was over.

"You *are* joking?" He said after an uncomfortably long silence.

"No," she said more gently, "you knew how I feel about Carl. I was honest about it."

"Yes, I knew but I also know how he feels about you Kelly, and you deserve better. Well I thought you did until now."

"Better? Like you, you mean?"

"Yes, like me… or like anyone else who actually gives a shit about you!"

"Carl cares about me, he cares very much."

Jake laughed, a sarcastic, angry, humiliating false laugh.

"Carl cares about Carl."

"That's not fair."

"No! What's not fair is you using me to get your man back, that's what's not fair!"

"I wasn't," she lied, "and it's not like we were lovers or anything."

Jake shook his head and closed his eyes as though trying to recover from the blow.

"Not lovers." He whispered to himself.

"You know what I mean."

"No. Actually I don't. We may not have had sex, but we have made love here where it matters." he thumped his chest with his fist, "or at least I did."

Kelly stared at his face and started to recognise the emotions he was fighting to hide. She knew that pain only too well because she had felt it a hundred times. She had treated this lovely man in the same way she had been treated, yet still she was struggling to find any empathy for him. She was being Carl, she was being the ass hole who talked about 'fuck buddies' and he was the devastated, pathetic, gullible idiot she used to be.

She started to feel smaller and smaller beside this moral giant. She couldn't think of anything to say to him and eventually he was the one to speak.

"Carl wants you now because of me, no other reason. He doesn't love you."

Kelly watched his huge heart breaking in front of her. His full black lip was shaking with emotion as he contorted his face to disguise it. He ran his hand over the stubble of his shaven head and then fixed his big brown eyes directly on hers. She had to break the moment that was too intense to bear.

"Then why is it he can't live without me?"

"Because he loves the things you give him, and he loves being loved and adored. More importantly he is a man, he is territorial, and he thinks of you as his property. In short….ego. But you won't believe it because you don't want to, but remember this Kelly when he breaks your heart again."

He took her hands in his, looked into her eyes and gently pulled her hands to his lips to kiss them. Without another word he closed the door in her face. Yes, he had become her, but the only difference was that he had the resolve to walk away.

She swept Jake to the back of her mind as she embarked on her new relationship with the love of her life. It was a relationship which, although exclusive and a little more regular in love making than before, was still somewhat of a roller coaster as Carl bounced back and forth between guilt and affection, cold and warmth, head and heart. Each day was different and every act between them was only consistent in its inconsistency.

Kelly became a substitute mother, substitute wife and an occasional lover but the situation was far from perfect. At times she felt real love from Carl, but it was temporary, as though his loyalty to Sophie was still preventing him from allowing it to blossom into the kind of love she was sure it could be. It was a love harnessed, constrained and controlled by the beating heart of a woman a few miles away as she slept.

Sometimes her salon time was a welcome escape from the reality of her relationship and sometimes she would find herself carelessly confiding in clients about her personal life. Her personal life was, after all, quite dramatic and compelling so it was sometimes difficult to resist milking the attention.

"It's a terrible situation for a young woman to be in," Mrs Moore concluded as she gave the back of her hair an approving nod from the reflection Kelly was showing in the hand mirror, "bet you'd like to just nip in and pull the plug." She grinned wickedly as she pushed an extra pound coin into Kelly's hand for the tip jar.

Kelly laughed as she got the old lady's coat and as she held it out for her, she was wondering about the legality of withdrawing Sophies life support, and who would need to consent to it. It was not something she could ever approach with Carl, but she knew that if Sophie no longer existed, her life would be so much better. Carl would finally be free from the guilt and loyalty that prevented him from loving her unconditionally. She just wanted to know if it was a likely outcome, that was all, but who could she talk to in the medical profession without raising a red flag?

Later that day Jake received an unexpected text from Kelly.

He agreed to meet her just as she knew he would.

The following lunchtime they were sitting in a café as Kelly tried to test the water on their friendship.

"You got me here for a reason and I'm guessing it's not to tell me I was right?"

Kelly hung her head in shame and said nothing.

"So, come on. What is it? Am I here to pick up the pieces or have you found some other unexpected use for me?"

"I'm sorry. This was a mistake. I shouldn't have asked." She was already on her feet with her jacket in her hand.

"Wait! Wait," he said more softly, "let's start again. So? How can I help?" He was smiling.

Kelly heaved a sigh of relief and sat back down.

He listened to her question intently and when she finished, he exploded with uncontrolled laughter.

"Shush!" she snapped.

"You're trying to eliminate the competition!" he blurted with tears of laughter running down his face "this is priceless!"

Kelly glowered at him, but his laughter was not subsiding. She opened her mouth to speak but another burst of laughter drowned her out.

She tried to glower again but as she watched him rock back and forth, hardly able to draw breath, she could no longer hold back her own laughter and the two of them laughed uncontrollably until their sides ached and they were finally silenced by sheer exhaustion.

"So?" he said as he wiped his eyes once again, "I take it that she's not on a ventilator?"

"No. She isn't" Kelly confirmed as she took out a compact mirror to check the impact of the outburst.

"That means she had brain activity," he went on, "she's breathing on her own so the support she will be getting will be nutrition and fluids."

Kelly nodded.

"It's possible that with the consent of her next of kin, which will be her dad, not Carl, they might withdraw support after this many years, but it won't be a quick demise."

"What do you mean?" Kelly was already feeling like a plotting assassin.

"Well if it were a ventilator and they turned it off she would slip away in minutes but withdrawing nutrition means she would survive for several days, maybe weeks. Her dad would never agree to that. Watching her starve to death when there's still a chance of getting her back?"

Kelly snapped her mirror shut and put it back in her bag. She knew what she needed to know, and it had been a dead end. She looked back at Jake soulfully for a moment, but as she did so she could see the lines starting to reappear on his face as he tried to supress laughter once again.

"Don't start me off again." She said as her voice was already breaking.

They left to take their thunderous laughter out of the tiny café and as they jostled and giggled themselves back to work she realised that in her desperation to rid herself of Sophie she had allowed something else to threaten her relationship. She had re-connected with Jake and she had enjoyed his company more than she should have.

In the weeks that followed she continued to lean on Jake from time to time and a strong friendship was established as the months ticked by, but she drew the line very clearly and displayed no signs of jealousy over his many casual girlfriends.

Even if she had been interested, which she wasn't, she knew that his feelings for her were still strong and was in no doubt that he was waiting for Carl to let her down the way he has prophesised.

He listened to her, dried her occasional tears and held her hand. He was patiently waiting in the wings for the leading man to mess up his lines. He could have pushed harder, but he knew Carl was already hedging his bets again and all he needed to do was to sow the seeds of doubt in Kelly's mind.

Jake had become her lifeline, and she knew it was neither appropriate nor fair to nurture the friendship behind Carl's back. She wished she still had Niki to confide in, but it was no longer an option. Niki was married to Pete and they now had two children but that wasn't the only reason they had drifted apart. The unspoken thoughts Niki harboured about Kelly's intentions towards Carl had dissolved their friendship long ago. Neither of them wanted to embark on a conversation about matters of the heart for fear of opening pandora's box and to do so would undoubtedly result in a bloody war from which there would be no truce.

Kelly's feelings always rose to the surface when she thought of Niki at home with her husband and her children playing happily in the yard, images eating away at her on the way home, reminding her that that time was moving on and her eggs were depleting with each passing month. If she ever wanted a child of her own, she was going to have to force the situation with Carl one way or another. The limbo which had become their life was everything she had asked for but less than she needed and much more than she could bear.

So, one evening, when the mood felt warm and his defences were weakened by alcohol, she started the conversation she had practised in her head a hundred times.

"It must feel wonderful to see your own traits in Tommy. To see the bits of you he's inherited, play out day after day?" She mused as she played with a lock of his hair, her legs flopping over his on the couch.

She thought the subtlety might be lost on him, but it gave her an opening to what she wanted to discuss.

He continued to watch the TV as though she hadn't spoken, and she felt irritated that he hadn't even paid attention to something she had planned so delicately.

"Did you hear me?" She nudged his arm as she spoke.

"Yes, I heard you."

"You didn't answer?"

"No, I didn't," he snapped, "I didn't answer because I know where this is going. Here we go again about marriage and more children and pretending Sophie doesn't exist at all."

Kelly withdrew her hand sharply from his hair and rose to her feet.

"I just want to be a normal family, that's all. Is that too much to ask?"

"Of course, it's too much to ask. We are not a normal family, are we? so we can't pretend to be. No-one else I know has ever had to deal with this… this.."

"This what?"

"Ok. This feeling I have that my girlfriend is wonderful and deserves a real family, but my 'wife to be' is still hanging onto life, hoping to return."

"And are you hoping for that too? That she will come back and replace me so you can throw me on the rubbish heap?"

"I didn't mean that Kelly. You know I didn't mean that."

"I don't know what you meant Carl, but I need to get out of here."

The inevitable departure of Kelly had become more frequent than was healthy, as her virtual husband repeatedly reiterated his lack of commitment. It was another fruitless outburst, but she was unable to calm the dreadful panic she felt when, in her mind's eye she could see the sands of time quietly running out.

She flounced out of his house once again, this time she was determined not to look back. This time would be different because he had blown too many chances, invoked too many tears, squandered too much of her life and left her with the huge burden of regret. Her mum had been right, her friends had been right, and she knew Jake was right. Carl didn't love her, and no amount of her devotion was going to make him.

As she put the key in her car she glanced back to see if he had followed her to the door she had left open. The street was empty, and the door was closed.

"Damn him!"

Chapter 7

She was welcomed back at her mother's terraced house, just as she had been many times before, and her mum made no attempt to persuade her to give him up. Experience had taught her that it was a futile mission and would only result in conflict between her and her already heart-broken daughter.

"You haven't asked me anything?" She said as her mum poured her a glass of wine from the bottle she had already started.

"Why? Has something different happened this time?" She smiled as she folded her housecoat around her and sat back on the couch where she had been when Kelly burst in.

"Yes, I've finally made the break."

There was no reaction as her mum who continued to watch the TV, so she continued.

"I finally gave him an ultimatum. I decided I have pandered to his indecision far too long and I need some control over my future. This time my head has outvoted my heart! Are you even listening?"

"Yes, I'm listening love. Head has outvoted heart." She repeated between yawns.

"Well aren't you pleased? Isn't this what you've been telling me for years? That if I make the break, I will eventually get over him, forget him and find a happier life?"

"Yes love, that's what I've been telling you but only time will tell if or not you have the strength to do it."

"Well this time I have," she retorted, "in fact, I already have a new boyfriend."

Her mother turned away from the TV and frowned in disbelief.

"A new boyfriend? Who?"

"You don't know him, but I've known him a while. He's a junior doctor, now in his final year."

In reality, Jake had a steady girlfriend now, and Kelly had been finding it more and more difficult to secure time with him. Often, this new woman stayed over at his flat and, as she was a nurse at Scarborough hospital, they seemed to have a lot in common. Kelly wasn't intending to muscle in and she was pretty sure his new relationship had no bearing on her dramatic exit from Carl's life, but she did find herself making more of an effort on her appearance than was usual when they met up for coffee.

"Are you flirting with me?" He frowned over the table after she had run a finger over his upper arm and asked if he'd been lifting weights.

"Flirting? Me? Never!" She smiled widely.

He knew she was teaching Carl a lesson. She knew he still had feelings for her. He knew he was in with a chance anyway. She knew he would drop the nurse like a stone. They both knew she was flirting.

She could see that he thought this was a game, but to her it was the chance to move on and to show her mum she had the strength to do it. As they made arrangements to meet for a meal, she had no conscience regarding his girlfriend or any other commitments he was pushing aside, this was Jake and she expected nothing other than his full attention.

The nameless nurse became instantaneous history as Jake and Kelly started dating. Kelly had no intention of rushing into a sexual relationship as she wanted to allow love to grow. She wanted to make love with Jake at a time when he was the only man in her thoughts and in her heart. They spoke daily but the dates were not frequent, partly due to Jake's gruelling shift patterns but also because Kelly was intentionally slowing things down.

She needed to be sure he was the one, before she gave her heart. This was definitely the reason, and nothing to do with the words of her mother persistently resounding when she tried to sleep. "If you really love someone. Never do anything you can't undo".

Three weeks later on a tedious Thursday afternoon her phone announced a text message as she was securing the last roller in Mrs Coopers thinning hair. From a distance she could see the author was Carl and her heart missed a beat. She felt her whole-body flush as she stared at it whilst trying to focus on the question she had been asked.

"Yes, I'll put a bottle of it on your bill." She assured whilst still staring at the message as though it was poisonous to touch. She didn't want to know what he had to say, he was not going to jerk her around again or get her sympathy.

She put Mrs Cooper under the dryer and picked up her phone. Perhaps it was about Tommy and she would never forgive herself if something had happened to him and she'd ignored the message. Her finger hovered over the button. If something had happened, he would call not text. There was no reason to open the message, none at all, she should delete it. Her finger hovered over the delete button and then pressed open.

"I don't blame you if you don't reply but I really miss you Kelly. Please call me."

Who the hell did he think he was? She slammed the phone back down. She was not going to reply. Even if she did, she was not going to reply straight away, she would show him she was no longer sitting by the phone waiting for him. She would give it a few days but already she was mentally composing her reply. She couldn't come up with a message that would deliver the result she wanted, mainly because she wasn't sure what response she was trying to provoke.

As she reached for her coat at the end of the day, she took out her phone and stepped out onto the pavement. She decided to do exactly what he had asked her to do and to take it from there. Her heart was pounding as she listened to the ringtone, but she knew that was a combination of anger and determination to show him she was no longer his emotional slave.

"Hi. You got my message then?" The impact of his voice took her by surprise. The familiarity of it. The magnetism of it.

"It would seem so. How have you been?"

"Getting by I guess."

"How's Tommy?"

"Missing you madly."

"Is that why you called? For Tommy?"

"Yes, well mainly. Not really. For both of us."

"So, what is it you want now Carl?" She needed to keep her voice strong and aloof.

"I don't know."

"Well maybe you shouldn't have got in touch then!"

"We both miss you and would love to see you."

There was a long silence and Kelly was determined not to be the one to break it.

"Kelly. We both want you back in our lives."

"As what?"

"Well....."

"Well what...?"

"Well the thing is…"

He sounded strange and Kelly started to get a bad feeling in the pit of her stomach.

"Carl?"

"Yes."

"What is it?"

"Just that things are not exactly the same as they were. For me I mean. Things changed a bit."

Her heartbeat quickened and a feeling of dread descended as she hoped this wasn't heading where she felt it was. She hoped with all her heart that he hadn't done the thing that couldn't be undone.

"Did you meet someone else?"

"What do you mean?"

It felt like he was buying time.

"You told me you needed to find another woman. Someone who didn't want any long-term commitment, so I wondered if you had someone in mind?"

There was a short silence, but it was a silence that was tearing through the fabric of Kelly's heart with each empty second of uncertainty.

"Carl?"

"I have met someone, yes."

Kelly's felt the blood drain from her face. Another sentence could bring her world crashing down. She left the silence hanging while she tried to prepare herself for what might come next.

"So, who is she?" she said at last.

"No-one you know" he laughed nervously "I went out on a breakdown and gave her a lift back to the garage, we just got chatting, you know how it goes."

"Not really. So it's someone you fancy or something?"

"A little bit I guess"

"Are you still in contact with her?"

"Yes"

Kelly's whole body was shaking.

"You mean you chat or text or what?"

"Both."

"So, is it just a friendship or a romance or what?"

"Oh, it's definitely a romance." He said almost triumphantly.

Kelly couldn't breathe. She felt the blood drain from her face as her legs gave way beneath her. Slowly she slid down the carpark wall onto the pavement where she sat with the phone to her ear, unable to speak. The man she loved had betrayed her and her life was changed forever. His single bullet had shattered her heart into a thousand pieces and the shattered fragments were showering her with tiny cuts throughout her body.

Surely, he knew the separation was only to allow him time to miss her. To make him realise how much he loved her.

She hadn't known it herself until this moment and now everything became clear. The conviction to move on, the promises to herself, to her mother, to Jake. They were all fake. Nothing in her life mattered without Carl. She wanted him. She would always want him.

"She had better be an old hunchback then!" It was a futile attempt at humour, but she hoped he could see through it. She hoped he would hear the tremble in her voice. She hoped he would feel her pain, but it seemed he had no concept of the wounds his careless words were inflicting. Instead he spoke to her exactly as he would to one of his male friends, oblivious to anything other than sharing his news.

"No. She is gorgeous. Kelly, you will love this person."

Was there no limit to this man's stupidity?

"Why would I?"

Carl had not picked up on the true meaning of the question.

"Because she is lovely, and she definitely knows how to enjoy herself."

She held her phone away from her as though preventing it from further attack. She looked at it blankly, this weapon of mass destruction, as she tucked her legs in close to her body like a wounded child. Slowly she returned the phone back to her ear but was unable to say anything at all.

"Kelly?"

She swallowed hard. She held her chest as though trying to steady her palpitating heart and somehow offer it comfort.

"Kelly?"

"Yes?" It was hardly a word, hardly a voice. Anyone with a heart of their own, would surely hear her soul screaming silently, in that single syllable. Carl did not, or so it seemed.

"Did you hear me? She is just lovely"

Kelly was no longer listening to his pathetic insensitivity. She dropped the phone onto the concrete as her mind went back to a Friday night years ago in the lively bar along the seafront when three friends sat drinking wine and talked of love. Oh yes, she could remember her own words "Why would anyone want something that could make them feel so wretched?" For even then, even in those early days of denial she had already felt the pain of loving Carl, and the agony of being relentlessly tortured

Leigh Oakley

by it. The kind of torture felt by a heart that refuses to stop loving
that one person despite rejection, humiliation and the wretched
images of imagination. Oh God! The pain of the images of him
in the arms of someone else.

"Yes. I heard."

"Are you alright luv?" A woman's voice interrupted her
thoughts.

"Yes. Thank you." She replied trying to think of an excuse for
being sat on the damp concrete of the carpark. As the lady looked
down on her expectantly, Kelly just sighed and looked away and
after a few awkward moments the woman hurried off tugging a
small boy away with her.

Kelly looked at the little boy as he grinned back at her. The
woman was lucky, the child was probably her own and nothing
could take him from her. She missed Tommy and, in a few weeks,
she would have been making his Halloween outfit.

"Kelly? Are you still there?"

Carl's tiny voice was just audible from the phone under her leg.
She slid it back into her hand. She needed to know more.

"So, how serious is it?" she held her breath as she waited for
his reply.

"Well, let me put it this way" he laughed "it's sort of early
days if you know what I mean, and I have nothing major to
confess."

At last there was an injection of pain relief. Quickly she was
processing the information with renewed optimism. He used the
word 'confess' so he saw what he was doing as a crime. A crime
against her and against what they had together. He hadn't
betrayed her at all, he was giving her the chance to step in before
he crossed that line. The point of no return. The deal breaker.

She no longer needed a ring on her finger or a promise of commitment. She would settle for being his casual girlfriend, his temporary stopgap, his nanny, his unpaid whore, anything that would stop this bitch from stealing her man and her child.

"Why don't you bring Tommy to see me later?" She suggested in the friendliest voice she could muster.

"I can't tonight. I am seeing her but maybe sometime next week."

Kelly wasn't going to settle for next week. Anything could happen between now and next week. She needed to see him now so she could reclaim him before this woman could get her claws into him. Before she could beguile him further, before she could touch him or kiss him again or make him laugh or exchange a smile.

"Look. I've got to go Kel. Do you want to meet next week or are you not bothered? It's fine either way."

She could tell from the harshness of his voice that she was not in the driving seat here. She could do nothing other than to take whatever he was offering.

"Ok. What about Tuesday? I'll cook us something." She said cheerily

"Yeah I think I can do Tuesday I'll let you know if I can't though as my life is a bit hectic. It's been great talking to you again, but I have to go as I've got another call to make."

"Who to? Do you have to call her?"

"Yes," he laughed again, "I have to call her."

Kelly ended the call and started to pull herself to her feet. The latter part of the conversation hadn't sounded like he had called for a reconciliation but more like a curtesy call to put her in the picture. He said he wanted her back in their lives but did he really expect her to be able to stand by as a friend and witness his new romance at close quarters?

"Your tea's in the oven." Her mother called as Kelly clicked the door shut and hung up her coat.

As she slipped off her shoes, her phone rang again and frantically she wrestled it from her coat pocket to check the caller. She left it ringing as she climbed the stairs leaving her tea drying in the oven. It was Jake and she couldn't talk to him right now. She didn't want to talk to him, not now and not any time.

She was consumed by the conversation Carl might be having on his second call. The call where he would be flirting and making sexy innuendos to his new girlfriend. Totally oblivious to Kelly's heartbreak, he might be making sexy plans with her for tomorrow or the next day or any of the other damn days between today and Tuesday.

For the next few days Kelly did everything humanly possible to keep a foothold in Carl's life. To remind him she was still a stakeholder in whatever he was planning to do. She messaged several times a day and called him whenever she could, reminding him of every good memory she could think of, making flirtatious references to some of their closer moments and generally trying to interrupt any notion he may have of romance with her rival.

Encouragingly, he engaged playfully, giving her hope that she could win him away from this gorgeous fun-loving woman he had described so cruelly. By Sunday evening she was desperate. With no work to occupy his time she had been imagining how those days had been spent. Perhaps he had taken her shopping on the Saturday morning the way he used to with her and Tommy. Had they stopped at the same coffee shop and eaten teacakes with their bags under the table? If he had got a babysitter, they might have gone for a meal on Saturday night or even worse they may have stayed home with a take-out and cuddled up on the couch. Her weekend had been a torturous sequence of imagined scenarios which she was powerless to prevent.

She picked up her phone and rang his number hoping that he might just be alone, that he might just want to talk and that he might just agree to meet her for a quick coffee the next day.

He answered cheerily and from the conversation she could tell that Tommy was in the background but no-one else. She flirted a little and to her delight he engaged and flirted back. Inside she was smiling with relief that he was not closing her out, perhaps he was just playing the game after all. Trying to shake her into coming home with his imaginary romance. She became warm and entertaining and when she suggested meeting for coffee the next day, she was pleasantly surprised when he agreed without hesitation.

As she pulled into the clearing of the small country park next to the tea van she was about to park alongside when she spotted Carl's car further down the track. He had found somewhere more private to talk but it barely seemed necessary on this miserable winter day. They were the only customers. She pulled alongside him and walked over noticing that he had already bought two cups of coffee so she slipped in beside him and smiled warmly as she took one and sipped.

"I love you Carl," her voice was barely audible, "I've tried not to, but I just do."

He took her hands in hers and spoke with equal gentleness.

"I can't be with you Kelly. There would be no future for us, and you deserve a life of your own."

"But you are my life Carl. You and Tommy. You know that."

"And I want you in my life Kelly, more than anything but not as my lover. It crushes me to see you try so hard to win the heart I can't give to you. You deserve someone who can devote their whole heart to you."

"I would rather have just half of your heart than all of someone else's Carl. I want to live for today, I don't care what lies ahead as long as I have you right now."

As she leant towards him for a kiss, he pulled away.

"This is wrong Kelly. I have a new girlfriend."

"A girlfriend? Your real girlfriend is in a coma remember? How did this stranger win the title that I was always denied? Has she met Tommy?"

Carl didn't answer.

"She has, hasn't she?"

Carl didn't answer.

"So, what do you intend to do with this girlfriend if Sophie wakes up then?"

"I will end it with her."

"Does she know that?"

"I think so, but we haven't really spoken about it. She's not like you."

"Not like me? What does that mean?"

"She's just extremely low maintenance, if you know what I mean? She doesn't expect much or want much from this. She's married to her career, wants to study to become a surgeon one day. She has no desire for a family, she just wants someone to have fun with. She's an easy option for me – it's simple with no heartache."

She didn't speak and nor did he. They sat in silence as his words hung in the air. Words about fun and shallowness, loveless words that were a million miles away from the silent moment they were sharing.

He took her coffee and placed it on the floor with his as he leant towards her until his face was only an inch from hers. She took his hand in hers and kissed him so gently that their lips were barely touching. He slid his arm around her waist and pulled her closer kissing her more deeply as he closed his eyes.

It was in that first second of that kiss that her life changed. She could feel it. She could feel that everything had changed. In that tiny fragment of time and those tiny fragments of delicate emotion his betrayal screamed. The intimacy he had shared with this new woman emanated from him, filling the air like a thick, sickening fog. He had crossed the line. The dealbreaker and nothing would ever be the same again.

She fought the urge to push him away. She wanted to slap his stupid face and tell him he had ruined everything, but she also knew that life without him was unbearable. She pulled away slowly as she tried to ignore the monster that was trying to force its way between them. She knew exactly what he had done, but she dare not speak of it. If she did then she knew that everything would be lost.

She looked down to avoid eye contact when she felt his breath on her cheek, and as she turned towards him his lips were again on hers. She responded so gently, so tentatively and this time the kiss was not interrupted or challenged or spoiled. They kissed deeply and her hopeful soul reached out for him as his hand gently caressed her neck and traced tiny patterns down her heaving chest.

She daren't move for fear of breaking this spell, and as his fingers gently stoked her inner thighs, she found herself shaking with anticipation and desire for every tiny touch he made on her body. Slowly he stoked her until she was conscious of the dampness and the aching and the immanent orgasm that approached so quietly and so lovingly that is was no more than a series of tiny shudders but so intense that on feeling it, his groans were more audible than any sound from her.

He kissed away her tears and she could no longer separate hope from fear or dread from desire. She looked into his eyes and knew that no answers dwelled there, she could do nothing other than to kiss him gently and hope. Hope he would love her enough to give her what she wanted most, but not to love her enough to do what he thought to be the right thing for her.

She kissed him goodbye and smiled sweetly.

"Don't worry." Was the only appropriate thing she could think of to say, but as she walked away leaving him with the remainder of his takeaway coffee she was already planning her next move in getting her man back from the gorgeous, lovely, undemanding, fun-loving bitch that had taken him away from her.

Things would never be the same again. Her love for him was damaged forever. Their happy ending, now an empty dream but in this moment when there was nothing more to lose. When love and hatred had collided so perfectly, she was going to fight for whatever was left. This was definitely 'game on!"

Chapter 8

Kelly worked day and night to secure an affair with Carl. She continued to ignore Jake's calls and messages until they dried up. Jake had his pride and he was not going to beg for her attention. She admired him for that but not enough to adopt the same attitude. In contrary, she bombarded Carl with uninvited visits to his workplace bearing coffee and flirting shamelessly. In keeping with his gender, he flirted back. He did more than flirt, he made love to her any chance he got, in the car, in the garage at work or anywhere she managed to manipulate.

She was doing everything in her power to hold his attention, but she knew this 'other woman' was still there somewhere. Lurking in the shadows of his life, seeping through the cracks she failed to fill, trampling on her family and dancing on her memories.

Although he seemed to be keeping her away from his house, he didn't offer to end it with his goodtime girl, and she knew why. If she wanted this woman gone then she had to become his goodtime girl. His disposable playmate who makes no demands on his future, and that was a decision she wasn't sure she could make. The alternative was to put up with being the other woman to the other woman.

Both of her options were bleak, and although being back in his life with no stability at all seemed unthinkable, it didn't feel quite as bad as the nights she lay alone in her single bed imagining where he might be, what he might be saying to her or doing with her and the fist that gripped and twisted her heart showed no mercy.

Beads of sweat covered her body and her heart pounded wildly on the evenings she knew he was out with her. Only when the clock clicked to 11 pm and she knew his mum would be greeting him at the door to be relieved of her babysitting duties, could she finally dry the salty tears and hope to sleep.

At least she got back her contact with Tommy and thankfully, it seemed he had very little knowledge of the devil woman. Despite Kelly's attempts to draw him into a conversation, his take on the new situation seemed to be that Kelly had moved out to look after her mum now and his dad went out more with a friend.

One evening when she had returned Tommy, she put him to bed, read him a story and embarked on the compulsory seduction of Carl which had become as predictable as Tommy's Storytime. She hated that she had become so desperate to compete with this new ghost, marking her territory like a Tom cat in an effort to keep her away.

At least Sophie was the ghost who slept, who stayed put and who's hands were not reaching into their life like the tentacles of a hungry triffid. The status of stalemate had been re-established but this time, the effort required to maintain it, the strain of keeping her head above the surface in this perpetual treading of water was exhausting. Once again, she had showered him in affection, adorned him in unearned compliments and made love to him like a porn star. It was unsustainable. She needed to assess the situation and make a decision.

As they lay together in what she once called the afterglow. Those post lovemaking moments which used to be the quiet reflection of their love, she was now reliving the previous hour as she evaluated her performance, alternately congratulating and reprimanding herself as she re visited her timing, technique and response to every moment of the event.

She knew this wasn't normal and as she examined his happy relaxed face with its contended smile and closed eyes she wondered if he even knew what he was doing to her? Did he realise he was causing her to prostitute herself, as he enjoyed the attention of two women while a third slept soundly with his heart safely captured. Did he not see her fighting for the scraps from his table while he feasted on this banquet?

"Carl?"

"Yup." His response was casual but defensive. He was predicting some sort of confrontation.

"Have you ever.... Have you ever spent the night with her?"

"She hasn't been here if that's what you mean."

"I didn't ask that."

There was a long silence then eventually Carl spoke almost patronisingly.

"Yes. I have slept the night."

Kelly froze.

"Oh God!"

"What?" Carl asked as though genuinely shocked at her reaction.

"That's intimate!" She could barely breath. Imagining them having sex had been hard enough but now imagining him sleeping in her bed, sharing her home, waking together, showering and making breakfast was a new level of pain.

Carl didn't speak.

"What are you doing Carl?"

"I don't know."

"You have three women!"

"I know and it's a bloody nightmare." He laughed.

Kelly flung his arm back and jumped up without speaking. She was halfway across the room with her clothes under her arm when he overtook her and blocked her escape.

"Let me go!" She hissed between clenched teeth.

"That was moronic of me," he confessed without moving from her path, "I'm sorry. I was going to ask you if you wanted to stay tonight."

She stared at him in disbelief. She hadn't stayed over since she moved out.

"You've got a damn nerve I'll give you that!" she laughed sarcastically, "you aiming for a hareem?!"

"Please don't." He said as his voice broke down.

"Carl?"

He didn't reply. He just slid his arms around her and buried his face in her, sobbing like a baby.

"What a fucking mess." He stammered between sobs.

Kelly could feel her heart breaking for him as she stroked his hair and led him quietly back to bed where they lay together for the longest time, just holding each other like their lives depended on it.

Eventually it was Kelly who spoke.

"What does she look like?"

"Kelly don't."

"Just tell me. Blonde, red, brunette?"

Carl sighed "Shut up about her," he tried to endure the silence before giving in, "she's strawberry blonde."

A Love to Die For – Tortured Hearts

At least Kelly could eliminate all the brunettes and red heads from her gallery of imaginary women. Part of her wanted to ask about her body, dress size, lovemaking skills but she knew she was not strong enough to bear any more images.

She slept in Carl's arms that night and he held her so gently for the entire night. In the morning she dared to believe that something had genuinely changed. He seemed more open to her, warmer somehow. Perhaps at last he had felt her pain and was about to relieve her of it.

Later in the day she messaged him, in an attempt to test the water.

"Are we ok Carl? It's just so hard when you can't have the person you want."

"You don't know the half of it Kelly, I fucking love you." He replied.

She stared at the message for the longest time with the broadest smile on her face.

Then she found the courage to ask him.

"What about her?"

"I've already started winding it down, it's no big deal, to be honest. There's not much to her."

Kelly caught her breath.

"Really? I think my heart just stopped" She could hardly believe these messages and had to call him.

"You mean?"

"Yes," he said softly, "I am focussing on you now, not her."

Kelly was silent as she attempted to control the emotion in her voice. She knew very well that this could be nothing more than another dashed hope. That tomorrow he might have another change of heart or a pang of guilt.

As for love, she was elated to hear him say it, but she knew love. She knew the width and depth of it, and she knew it was impossible to hurt someone you genuinely love. Impossible to watch that person suffer the pain of watching you start a new relationship. Impossible to make love with someone knowing that every touch or tender word was breaking that heart. Yes, she was elated to hear him say it, but she knew that whatever he felt for her, it wasn't love.

"Did you hear me? I want you Kelly, not her?"

She could hear the conviction in his voice. His determination to win back her trust and for the first time she felt she had a little bit of the power and she was going to use it to obtain some form of guarantee.

"Why now? What's changed? I was ready to give up on us."

"I just couldn't bear to promise you more than I had to give. I was always holding back just in case.... well just in case I had to take it all back because Sophie returned."

"You hurt me Carl, so badly."

"I know."

"Do you?"

"Yes. I was an idiot. I tried to do something for your own good and that was arrogant and condescending."

"Yes, it was. It was also cruel and hurtful."

"I'm sorry Kelly. I know that now and I also know I don't want anyone else."

"Is that the truth? You are not still going to be holding back?"

"I am yours now. I promise."

"What exactly does that mean?"

"Let's get married."

"You don't mean that?" She laughed.

"Oh, I do. Like you wouldn't believe. I 've put you through far too much and I've wasted so much of our lives when you've been my wife already, in every way that really matters."

"Please don't say this if there's any chance you'll go cold on me again," she pleaded, "I couldn't take any more."

"Darling. It's taken me far too long to get here. I know what I want now. I want the woman who has stood by me when I didn't deserve her."

Kelly was crying silently into the phone but for the first time in years her tears were those of joy and relief.

"Shall I come round after work and make tea for you both?"

"You better had," he laughed, "I'm taking Tommy to the hospital, but we'll be back by seven. He's gonna be so excited when we tell him."

"It's a date!" Kelly ended the call and then clenched her fists in elation and thanked God out loud.

After work she called at the supermarket and bought ingredients to make the chicken hot pot, they both loved. She used her own key to get in and set the table for the three of them, having put the wine in the fridge to chill and lay out Tommy's favourite pyjamas.

When everything was under control, she made herself a cup of tea and sat in the lounge with the TV on which she was far too excited to watch. The only thing that had her attention was the clock. It was 6.30 and everything would be ready on time. There was still half an hour to kill so she started to search through the cupboards in the hope of finding something from which she could make a desert. She had just picked up a box of suet when her phone rang. It was Tommy's voice

"Kelly Kelly, guess what .... mummy woke up!!"

Chapter 9

Kelly used the tone she had rehearsed many times for the unlikely possibility of facing this moment. She recited every word to perfection as she tried to give the enthusiastic support to the little boy she genuinely loved. She ended the call without deviating from her script, but with hundreds of thoughts colliding in her brain as acceptable behaviour, and raw emotion wrestling for a time slot. Then, as she dropped the phone back into her handbag, she looked angrily skyward to heaven, and spoke out loud.

"Great timing, thanks a lot!"

She knew that she was about to walk the delicate line between empathy and manipulation. She needed to box clever, to map out every possible scenario in her mind and how she needed to deal with it, regardless of her feelings.

She turned off dinner, calmly collected her coat and headed for the hospital. As she drove, she went through the situation in her mind and each time there was a different outcome. She tried to convince herself not to panic, and that this could be a good thing.

Carl would soon realise Sophie was not the perfect goddess he had created in his tainted imagination, an image fuelled by guilt, shock, despair and above all, by hope. Silently consuming his heart as she slept away the years with her porcelain expressionless face, she had become his ultimate challenge. The problem he needed to solve, the heart he needed to recapture. His endless and untiring bloody hope.

'Yes.' Kelly thought, this might be the hour of reckoning, when the pieces of his shattered dream may drop conveniently into her lap.

Sophie may reject him entirely and as the realisation of his wasted years begin to dawn, anger and resentment will replace empathy and worship. Bitterness will replace devotion and at last he will be free to fall in love completely. With her.

He would realise he already had his family, and he would finally accept Kelly as his rightful wife. No, he would not desert her now.

Even if Sophie has feelings for Carl and, on learning about their son, is overwhelmed with affection and delight, the ace card was still firmly in Kelly's pocket. Tommy loves her and the bond between them is as strong as any mother and son. It may take a little time, but forcing a new mother on him would eventually result in disharmony and resentment.

This would not be a perfect little family unit for any of them. Sleeping Beauty would not get her 'Happy ever after' because her Prince was already taken. She was confident everything would be fine as she clicked on the indicator to take her into the hospital carpark. Yes, she was sure of it.

As she made her way down the familiar corridor Tommy was running towards her looking distraught.

"What's the matter Tommy?"

"Mummy is horrible." He sobbed.

Kelly hugged him closely to hide her wry smile.

"No, she isn't," she soothed unconvincingly, "She will get better, you'll see."

"I don't want her to get better I want you to be my mum," he stammered, "I wish she would go back to sleep."

Leigh Oakley

Her prediction was unfolding much sooner than anticipated and conveniently, she had her arms around Tommy when Carl came around the corner and put his arms around them both. Instantly reassured by the protective gesture towards his real family, Kelly squeezed his hand.

"It's too soon," he whispered, "we can come back tomorrow."

Kelly's family returned home intact but as they shared the meal she had prepared, she felt unsettled at the prospect of any conversations that might take place once Tommy had gone to bed.

She took Tommy gently by the hand and tried to answer the barrage of questions he was babbling at her as honestly, but as carefully as she could.

"Why didn't she hug me?"

"She will darling, when she's had time to get used to us all."

"Will she come here to live with us? Will we all live together? Where will she sleep?"

"My goodness. One question at a time please." Kelly tried to sound in good humour but secretly she was terrified by the very same questions.

She sat on the edge of Tommy's bed, as she had done hundreds of times, and picked up his adventure book.

"Are you too old for this story now?"

Tommy smiled, "Nope."

As she read the familiar tale, she hoped upon hope that Carl was listening and that as he was listening, he was reminded that this was his family unit. That the vision of her nightly ritual would somehow cement a defensive barrier in the path of whatever was to come.

As she returned, she felt relieved when Carl smiled and patted the sofa beside him. She sat down and he put a welcome arm around her, gently kissing her head.

"Tommy is terrified of her."

"I know." Carl sighed.

"We have to tread carefully Carl. To him, it's probably as shocking as one of his toys suddenly springing to life. He's watched her as still and lifeless as a doll for years then suddenly she sits up and starts talking. I'd be terrified too."

Carl laughed, "you do have a way of putting things." He gave her an approving squeeze.

Nothing was said for several minutes and she could hear her heart gently pounding in fear of what may unfold in the next few hours. Eventually Carl spoke in a quiet broken voice.

"What a mess."

Kelly didn't comment.

It was Carl who spoke again.

"Why now? After all this time, all the waiting and hoping. Someone up there has a warped sense of humour."

Still Kelly dare not speak.

"What are we going to do Kell?"

"What do you want to do?" She asked softly, trying desperately not to blow this.

"I have no idea."

"What does that mean?" She asked with equal softness keeping her eyes away from him.

"This is going to be painful for everyone. We have to be careful and take things one day at a time, see how they unfold."

"Do you still love her?"

"Oh Kelly," he sighed, "how can I answer that?" He kissed her head again and pulled her close.

At that moment she felt nothing but compassion for him and as she looked up into his teary eyes, and brushed back his messy hair, she knew that she was going to support him again no matter what, and that her own feelings would take second place, just as they always had.

That night they slept in the same bed, just as before, but they did not make love. They held each other gently and waited for morning to write the next chapter in their fragmented lives.

Kelly went to the hospital alone at the request of Sophie's doctor while Carl stayed with Tommy for the morning, in the hope that it would be less of an emotional ordeal.

She arrived to find Sophie being hugged by her father and as she approached, Sophie recognised her instantly.

"So how is life for you two?" She croaked. It was a generic invitation for them to update her on anything at all.

Neither replied.

She looked to Kelly in particular and made the question more specific.

"Are you settled with anyone? Still avoiding love?"

Kelly was biting her lip extremely hard, hardly able to say anything at all. She then hugged her friend and eventually said "Oh. You know me. Heart of steel."

Sophie smiled as she wiped away one of Kelly's tears.

Yes, I can see that."

Her father pushed Kelly aside a little while he had another hug and brushed Sophie's hair affectionately from her face.

"I love you so much, and I never gave up on you."

"I know" Sophie was looking Kelly up and down, watching as she attempted to wipe away her tears with tissues from the bedside stand.

"Welcome back. You crazy mixed up lady." Kelly finally choked through the sobs.

"Thank you." Sophie put her hands over Kelly's and kissed each of them in turn.

"Do you know what happened?"

Kelly nodded but frowned in the direction of the old man as though suggesting they shouldn't discuss the detail of it in front of him.

Sophie nodded her understanding.

"How did you feel meeting Tommy yesterday? Quite a shock I should imagine?"

"You could say that. Do you see much of him?"

"Yes, quite a bit." Kelly smiled.

"This is crazy. I can't have a son. I didn't feel like he was mine at all," she then leaned forward to whisper, "I have two daughters."

Kelly pulled back in shock, suddenly considering the possibility that Sophie was brain damaged.

"Daughters?"

"Yes. Rebecca and Tori but everyone here says I dreamt them. Dreamt them in a dream that lasted nine years. Can you believe that?"

"Sounds incredible, but I suppose your brain had to be doing something all that time" She smiled in an effort to make light of the revelation, but inwardly she was allowing herself to hope this was brain damage. She was rushing through the inevitable way this would play out and concluded that she was safe.

The old man raised his eyebrows at Kelly in acknowledgment of the situation, and immediately Sophie put her hands to her ears and closed her eyes as though blocking out the world around her.

Gently Kelly put her hands over Sophie's and guided them back down onto her lap.

"You need to try to deal with this one day at a time Soph.'"

Sophie looked pathetic and defeated but after a couple of moments her face lit up as she leaned forward again to whisper.

"I *do* have two daughters and I know they are still somewhere I can't reach them, but one of them has the same ability as I do to flit back and forth. I always suspected it but now I know it for sure."

Kelly didn't say anything at all, but she was aware that her body language and facial expression was giving away. The fact that she was far from comfortable by her friend's ramblings. Sophie seemed to be oblivious as she continued eagerly with her remarkable revelations, wide eyes starring wildly from her gaunt white face.

Kelly shook her head sympathetically, as genuine empathy started to dilute the jealousy and trepidation she had been feeling as the poor woman continued with equal gusto.

"Because Rebecca, that's my eldest, often spoke of a boy she played with, a boy no-one else had any knowledge of and his name was.....," she leaned forward even further, her eyes as wide as saucers, "his name was Tommy!"

Kelly had heard enough. Enough to know that her salvation had arrived, her prayers answered and at last she had the life she had longed for, right there in the palm of her hand.

She smiled, it could have been interpreted as a smile of support or sympathy but in reality it was the smile of victory as she watched this crazy woman sit back with an air of great satisfaction, having proved she was the mother of two daughters in some parallel existence.

"You don't believe me, do you?"

"I believe that you believe it Sophie, but I think it may be just your mind playing tricks on you."

"I'm telling you!" Her voice was back at full volume and her father was now exposed to his daughter's madness.

"Rebecca spoke of Tommy many times and we don't know anyone of that name, so how do you explain that?"

Kelly wanted to be gentle, but a part of her also wanted Sophie to continue with the craziness that would drive Carl away and protect Tommy from any contact with the mindless rantings of his deranged mother. She gently stroked Sophies dark greasy hair from her drawn face.

"Tommy has visited you many, many times over the years as you lay here sleeping and dreaming Sophie. You must have heard his name several times a month, and I am sure that's why the name came into your dreams. That happens sometimes you know, when you are dreaming, and you hear something that's then incorporated into your dream."

It was the same explanation Anne had given, but Sophie was not to be dissuaded. She had seen and heard Rebecca talking to Tommy and it was far too vivid to have been a dream.

"This was real Kelly. It wasn't a dream. I was there with my family, with the man I love and my children, and now I miss them all so much and I am worried that they don't know where I am, or maybe I've had an accident and been knocked unconscious or something. Or maybe I'm just asleep! I might wake up soon and everything will be ok."

Kelly saw the despair and desperation, and felt the fear and frustration, but there was only one phrase of the last rambling filling her whole being – *the man I love*- the final nail in the coffin of Sophie and Carl had been delivered with a magnificent blow. Perfect.

"Everything will be fine" She soothed, kissing Sophie affectionately on the head.

Sophie's father frowned and tilted his head as though he was reading Kelly's mind, but she didn't care what he thought, she had heard enough, and she quietly made her excuse to leave.

Back at home Carl had prepared lunch and the three of them sat together and tried to talk about normal things, like shopping and homework, but there was an obvious tenseness in the air and after a few half-hearted conversations Tommy was the first to show some courage.

"What's going to happen to the mum who woke up?"

Carl tried to sidestep the question.

"What would you like to happen?"

Tommy thought for a moment and then amazed them with his maturity.

"I know she's my real mum and everything, but she doesn't know me, and I don't know her, and it's not like we thought it would be is it?"

Carl shook his head.

"No Tommy. It isn't."

"I know," Kelly soothed, "we should have known it wouldn't be that simple. Sorry Tommy"

"It's ok," he said nonchalantly, "it's not your fault, but I don't like her. She's weird and she's scary and I wish I didn't have to see her again." He started to cry.

Kelly wiped his tears with her finger and gazed lovingly at the crumpled face of the boy who felt like her own.

"Don't worry. We'll work it out – I promise.".

Her promise was to herself, not to Tommy, and while a part of her wanted to tell Carl all about Sophie's ramblings at the hospital and about her life with the only man she had ever loved, she knew it wasn't the right thing to do.

Carl would find out soon enough, and she didn't want to be accused of scheming against Sophie. It was much more important to her that Carl respected and trusted her, because losing his respect and affection would be much worse than losing him. Even if he did choose Sophie, she knew it was unlikely to last.

Sophie was about to orchestrate her own demise, and when she threw herself off the pedestal Carl had been worshipping, Kelly would be in the perfect position to step up.

Innocent Kelly, the woman who had selflessly been at his side all these years, his lover, his past, his most precious memories, and she hoped and hoped, his future.

She would get her way without compromising her integrity. There was no need to try to force matters.

Two days later Tommy agreed to visit again, and as Kelly walked him back down the same corridor, he held her hand willingly which was something he hadn't done for a long time. It wasn't cool at his age, but today he held it so tightly Kelly's ring was digging into her finger. As they reached the private room, she turned him to face her and tidied his hair and jumper the way she had done so many times at the school gate, and then gave him the comforting smile he needed so desperately.

"It's ok" she whispered.

Tommy released his grip a little, and smiled apprehensively, just the way he had on his very first day at school. The day he had felt terrified, yet trusted Kelly so completely that he walked into the unknown on the strength of that smile.

She walked him toward Sophie who still had her dad beside her. It seemed like he never left, but what else did he have to do other than to treasure every moment with his prodigal daughter?

Sophie seemed to be making more of an effort as she greeted Tommy with a warm smile and patted the bed invitingly. Kelly gently pushed Tommy forward and as he turned back to her for reassurance, she nodded her approval. Slowly he walked over and sat down on the bed uncomfortably, he fidgeted without speaking and kept his eyes firmly on Kelly.

"Tommy?" Sophie's voice was still more of a croak.

He turned to look at her in silence. He felt afraid of her.

"I'm sorry we made such a bad start. You must have been waiting for this for so long, and I must have been a big disappointment to you."

Tommy didn't speak. He didn't like her.

She put her arm around his shoulder and rubbed his arm affectionately, but he was rigid and unyielding as he remained transfixed on Kelly – his real mum.

Kelly felt a hand around her waist which was withdrawn hastily, and before Sophie had noticed.

"I see you two are getting along." Stammered Carl still shocked by his own stupidity at greeting Kelly, without filtering his behaviour in front of his fiancé, and mother of his son.

"Yes," confirmed Kelly trying to disguise her amusement at his mistake, "perhaps we should take your dad to find us some refreshments while you two have a few minutes alone."

Tommy's eyes widened pleadingly but Kelly squeezed his hand gently.

"We'll be back before you know it."

"I'll wait by the door if you want?" David offered, and Tommy nodded with obvious relief.

Kelly and Carl walked to the drinks machine together, but they walked separately with arms folded as though over-compensating for Carl's slip-up. But even when they were out of earshot, they did nothing more than to politely discuss the available items in the machine, and Kelly's heart was allowing fear to creep in. That awful fear that her man was pulling away again. She knew the symptoms as distinctly as the first symptoms of Tommy's migraines. Her heart was pounding but she hid her feelings from him once again, just as she always did and just as she always would do. Still protecting him. Trying to ease the guilt he might be feeling if he was about to drop her like a stone again.

Carl picked up his own coffee and Sophie's tea and then slipped Tommy's lemonade in his pocket leaving her to carry her own coffee and her dad's hot chocolate. Kelly interpreted this simple act as a division of families. A choice his subconscious had made.

As they came back into earshot of Sophie's room, they heard Tommy's voice, which sounded more relaxed.

"This is my mobile phone. Do you want to see it?"

Carl smiled at the positive progress, while Kelly's optimism evaporated as he left her side and strode ahead through the open door to his family.

Sophie starred in disbelief as Tommy pulled the tiny phone from his pocket and flipped up the lid.

"My God. How long was I asleep? My phone is ten times that size!!"

It was this moment. From the shock of holding that phone, that Sophie started to change. It was tangible and undeniable evidence that many years had passed, and neither she nor John owned such a phone. Slowly but surely her conviction started to waiver. The voice of reason was starting to drown out the sweet voices of her imagined children and that same logic was eroding the memories of the years of love and happiness in the arms of John.

Could it be that she had really missed so many years of her own life? Her real life? The years with Carl and her son?

These questions introduced her to a new remorse, a new grief. She started her journey towards acceptance and, just as a grieving mother sorrowfully loosens her grip on the hand of her lifeless child, little by little, she started to let go of the daughters she loved and of her beloved John.

Overwhelmed with gratitude that Carl had shown such devotion, and for the support given to him by her old friend, who seemed to have put her own life on hold, she committed to rebuilding her life with Carl and her son.

As she folded her thin saggy arms around herself in a comforting hug, she settled down to sleep knowing that she had to leave behind the fairy-tale she had created in her years of coma. She needed to accept the loss of her husband and children.

The visitors left, but she couldn't sleep. She tried to make plans for her recovery as she lay awake with her arms still folded around her. She needed to rebuild her body, her relationships, her life.

She tried to rekindle the affection she once had for Carl, but the faces of Rebecca and Tori pulled at her heart and any love for

Tommy was as unreachable as the sleep she craved. No amount of wishing was going to make it happen, it was blocked by images and sounds playing in her head. Sounds of her beautiful life with her other family. The family of ghosts and phantoms, but still the family she loved above all else.

She thought again about Tommy's phone and compared it to the one John bought her last Christmas. It didn't have the flip lid and it was much bigger, but technology had also moved on in her world. Hers was slimmer and incorporated a radio and Tommy's didn't have that.! Perhaps technology had just gone in different directions. Her heart rate was rising again as new hope surged through her.

"Oh God John," she whispered gently into the night, "where are you?"

"I'm right here love. What's wrong?"

She opened her eyes wide and kept perfectly still for fear of breaking the spell. That was John's voice, and it was right behind her, she daren't move an inch for fear of disturbing the moment.

"John?" She whispered again.

There was silence.

"Is that really you John?"

Still silence.

She turned over slowly, gripped by fear. Fear that he may be behind her in their old bed and fear that he may not. Gently she moved. Inch by inch she started to roll over, stroking her arms with her hands as she waited for the plumpness of flesh to return.

He wasn't there. She could see the door to the corridor, hear the distant mutterings of the nurses at their station, and feel the bones jutting against the skin of her elbows. She sat up in bed and covered her face with her bony hands. She was still in the same world, but something had changed.

She had heard John's voice and it was enough to rock her resolve.

The logic and common sense dissolved, as she allowed herself to hope that he was still within reach. The plans she had been making only moments ago were abandoned as a new plan took its place. The plan to return to John, Rebecca and Tori.

It was just as likely that this new world with its tiny phones was her own imagination. She lay back down with a sigh of renewed hope.

"Don't worry darling. I'm coming home." She whispered back into the night and, as she made her promise, a tiny smile danced around the corners of her mouth. Her first real smile since she had been in her husband's arms.

Chapter 10

A few miles away Kelly felt like she had little to smile about. She climbed into bed beside Carl, noticing that he made no effort to acknowledge her lotioned and perfumed body sliding towards him. She was back in the limbo land she knew so well.

She wanted desperately to talk to him but was too afraid of triggering the conclusion she had no wish to hear. While ever she remained silent, there was hope. While ever she pretended not to notice the change, he would feel no need to explain himself. Least said, soonest mended, as her mother used to say. She wanted to reach out to him but if he were to reject her the same conversation would have to be had. The conversation where he tells her again that he doesn't know how to feel or what to do.

Love him though she did, she wished that for once, he would be a man and stand up for her, for them, for what's right.

Her anger grew into frustration as she prayed to be delivered from this merry go round of hell. She prayed that her love for Carl would die but even as the words were silently spoken, she knew it was the last thing she wanted. Loving Carl was her life and without that, the empty space that love left would never be filled.

Her gentle sobs were barely audible but gently Carl's hand reached for hers and she turned towards him, her tears dribbling between them in a salty wet kiss. He held her affectionately and her hands stroked his chest a little more desperately. She kissed him again as her need to regain him grew and grew inside.

A need she was fighting to temper for fear of pushing him too hard too soon. This was the same game she had played for many years, a game she knew well, but a game she felt angry and humiliated at having to play. A game of which she had become tired, and now she felt defeated. She stopped for a moment, to Carl it was probably unnoticeable, but for Kelly it was a pivotal moment of torturous decision.

She could slide out of that bed and out of the door and never turn back. She could take control of her own destiny and rid herself of the shackles of this indecisive cruel man who couldn't see the damage he had done, was still doing, and would no doubt continue to do. Or she could make love to him once again. Try to pull him back past the halfway point again. Try harder, and show him even more love and understanding in the hope that he would finally see that his happiness sits with her.

Her hand still rested on him in the silence. She looked down at her fingers nestling in the hair of his chest and wondered if her hand was about to pull away or to caress him lovingly, she waited for her decision to move her hand as though she had no part in it.

This was between her heart and her body and she watched patiently as her hand moved slowly towards her. It moved down his stomach and her fingers were curling gently around his resting shaft, hoping to feel her fist starting to open as he grew under her touch. There was no reaction, and as she gently began to stroke and massage him, her heart was sinking. He remained flaccid and lifeless in her hand.

Gently his hand moved on top of hers to guide her away, and she smiled understandingly, whilst her inner voice screamed its reprimand at her for making the wrong decision so humiliatingly.

This was her moment to exit, enough was enough, this was her cue. She visualised swinging her legs onto the floor and walking step by step towards the open door, through the door with her head held high and into the exciting unknown of her new life. She drew her knees up, turned on her side sliding her arm affectionately around Carl and curled around him to sleep.

A different kind of silence hung over breakfast. The kind of silence that runs in the background of polite conversation, while Tommy got ready for school. When he finished and went to collect his bag Carl spoke in a whisper.

"I've been thinking Kel. Sooner or later Tommy is going to let it slip to Sophie about our living arrangements."

"Yes, I suppose so." Kelly was deliberately neglecting to acknowledge it as a problem.

"Well we can't let her find out. Not like that."

Kelly slammed the cups down on the worktop and took a deep breath.

"Well maybe we should just tell her Carl. Unless of course you have decided to lie to her, or to take up where you left off with her."

"Of course not. Well.."

"Well what? Are you considering it? You are, aren't you?"

"No! I don't know. I don't know anything anymore."

Tommy returned with his bag "Are we visiting new mum tonight?"

Kelly smiled through another heartache. Tommy seemed happy about the prospect.

"I don't know darling. Would you like to?"

"Don't care either way. Just wondered."

Carl picked up his sandwich and headed out without a word. Tommy followed a few minutes later giving Kelly a casual wave and suddenly, she was alone. She found herself making a phone call to someone she hardly heard from anymore.

"Hi Niki. Do you have time to meet me for a drink?"

"Of course," Niki laughed, "what crisis have you got going on now?"

The bar on the seafront had become a trendy cafe bar, and the quaint seating had been replaced by barstools with laptop points, but the two women were still reminded of those nights years ago, and as Kelly stood to greet her old friend, she knew Niki was feeling it too.

"Wow." Niki whispered as she kissed Kelly on the cheek.

"I know. This feels weird doesn't it?"

"You haven't changed at all," Niki said, holding her friend at arm's length to take a good look, "not the same for me though." She patted her size sixteen stomach, "baby fat that never went away."

"You look great Nik."

"So? What's happening with you and Carl and the love triangle?"

Kelly put her head in her hands in desperation.

"I don't know Nik. I feel like I've wasted my life. I think he still wants Sophie."

"Of course he does. She was the woman he was planning to marry and now she's returned from the dead. It doesn't get any more romantic than that!"

"Should I just call it a day?"

"Yes."

"Why don't you say what you really think?" Kelly smiled.

"I mean. Yes, you should but no, you won't"

"What do you mean?"

"I mean that he's still as confused as he's always been. What's worse is that he always will be. He can't let go of her any more than you can let go of him."

"That sounds hopeless."

"Kelly. If you have the strength to walk away, then do it. Find someone who dotes on you the way you dote on him. It's a better position to be in."

"I know you're right, but it's so hard."

Niki took her friend's shaking hands in hers.

"Hun. It's hard to let go of the one you love but you know what? It's a damn sight harder trying to hold onto them!"

Kelly studied Niki's face. She seemed to understand more than she should for a happily married woman. For a moment she wondered what secrets of her own Niki might be harbouring. What demons might haunt her too?

"You think I should go for the 'set him free' thing?"

"Absolutely!"

"But we both know Sophie doesn't love him. She never has, and the only reason she ended up like that was trying to get away from him to some fantasy she'd created in her head."

Niki frowned as she started to realise where this might be heading.

"Are you thinking of telling him? Is that what this meeting is about? You want me to back you up?"

"No" Kelly assured her "I wouldn't want to be that person. I'm just pointing out that his love was never really reciprocated. We both know that."

"Yep. She was crazy back then and she is now. Chances are, it won't last and when he realises well..... who knows? He may realise that what he had all along with you, was worth so much more than anything he imagined with her."

"You think so?"

"It could happen I suppose. Give her a few weeks and she might start the fantasy all over again."

Kelly laughed a little.

"What are you laughing at?"

Kelly rolled her eyes "She already has Nik."

"You're joking?"

"No. She actually believes she's been with that John person all this time."

"My God. If I were you, I would cut my losses and leave them to it. They deserve each other. Does Carl know?"

"No. She told me in confidence."

"And you didn't tell him? I mean, what happened before, well that's one thing, but if she's still saying she's in love with someone else perhaps you should let him know what a crazy disloyal bitch she's been to him?"

"No."

"Why not?"

"Because if there's a chance for me and Carl then I don't want to carry that with us. You know, me being the one to break them up. I'd rather let him find out for himself."

"Carl hasn't known his own heart for years Kelly," Niki sighed "and having the two of you tug him back and forth won't resolve anything. You have to leave him alone with her. Let him find some closure with her. Then if you still want him, when it falls apart, which it will, then at least he will finally be all yours"

"I know Niki. I think I just needed to hear someone else say it"

"Well now you have."

"Yes."

"Will you do it?"

"I will."

"Promise?"

Kelly hesitated for a few moments.

"Promise."

As they drank a large mug of Latte, Kelly felt certain of something for the first time for many years. She was in control of her life and it felt amazingly good.

She went home and packed a case again, called her mum again to tell her she would be moving back home for a while, then set about making herself look wonderful. Not for Carl, not to try to make him ask her to stay, not to show him what he's missing or for any other of the pathetic reasons she'd had for so many years, but for herself.

She was making tea when Tommy arrived home, and the evening went much as any other. No-one other than herself, would notice anything different, but to her, everything was different. She was happy and confident, relaxed and certain. She was at last, in control.

She poured a glass of wine for Carl once Tommy was settled and then brought down her suitcase.

"What's going on?"

"I'm moving back to mum's."

"What?" Carl seemed genuinely shocked and concerned.

"I think it's for the best."

"No. No, it's not. Why would you do that?"

"You need space to deal with this Carl. So does Tommy."

"No! No, we don't!" He sounded scared and desperate.

Kelly could hardly believe his reaction. He seemed shocked that she would consider leaving him. Perhaps he was just shocked that she'd stopped being his doormat. At last she might earn some respect from him, and it felt good.

"Carl. I need to go. For me!" The power she felt was intoxicating.

"Please Kelly., don't leave me. I need you. Tommy needs you."

She sat down beside him for a moment with her suitcase by the door.

"Maybe you do." She held his eyes on hers hoping he would see the honesty in her face. Through her porcelain complexion, her highlighted cheekbones, her thickly fanned lashes and perfectly outlined lips, to the honesty beneath, and for the first time she felt he actually did. For the first time she felt that he saw her soul.

"What have I done to you?"

She smiled and for the first time she felt superior.

"It's not important."

"What have I done? I'm so fucking stupid."

Kelly patted his hand gently and whispered goodbye.

As she closed the door and strode down the path with Carl's pleas ringing in her ears, she felt more important than she had in a decade. This wonderful feeling of empowerment had been hers for the taking all along, but fear had held all her weapons in their holders and all the keys with her jailer.

"What about Tommy?" There it was, the low shot, the curved ball.

"I'll call him tomorrow." She called back, without turning around or breaking stride. She would not be stopped this time. The car door slammed his voice to silence. This time she was looking after herself.

Carl closed the door and slid to the floor. If only Kelly could have witnessed this, but she was already on her way to a new life.

He phoned in sick the next day and decided to visit Sophie in some sort of vain attempt to redeem something positive from the mess he'd created. Maybe if he spent some time with her, he may fall right back in love again. It was a futile wish because those feelings he had dreamt of, had so far, failed to materialise. But it was the only bit of hope he had, and he needed to believe in it.

"Hey, you." Sophie smiled as he entered her room with two coffees.

"Hey, you." He replied waiting for the years of suppressed love to fill his heart and to banish Kelly's memory from it. Neither were forthcoming.

They had a factual conversation about Tommy and the birth, the christening and all the birthdays she had missed but, while Carl was desperately trying to shuffle her into the life they had missed, he was unnerved by something else. By her frequent questions about Tommy's sleeping patterns and if he had any imaginary friends. She kept returning to the topic, despite Carl's attempts to tell her more interesting facts about their son.

Sophie needed to ask him something.

"Did you ever speak to me about the pregnancy Carl? When I was sleeping?"

"Yes. Lots of times."

Sophie was recalling the moment she thought she'd heard Carl's voice.

"I think I heard you."

Carl looked both surprised and excited.

"Really?"

"Yes. You said we are going to have a baby and that it's amazing"

"Yes, I did. I did say that!"

He squeezed her bony hand and passed her the exercise sheet left by her physio, from her bedstead before rising to leave.

"You need to get fit girl. You're all skin and bone."

"I will." She smiled "Oh yes I will."

He kissed her on the cheek, trying not to notice the stink from her stale mouth or to be repulsed by her thin lank wispy hair and scaly complexion. He would fancy her again soon, he had to, but right now he was trying not to recoil from her, trying desperately not to let his distaste for her skeletal grey body show on his face. He was trying even harder to dispel the comparison his head was making to the pink fragrant softness of Kelly's firmly toned body.

As he left, he called at the nurse's station and asked if he would be able to see her therapist, but they seemed reluctant, almost obstructive.

"You know that her therapist is governed by patient confidentiality?"

"Yes, or course."

"So, she won't be able to tell you anything they discuss without Sophie's consent?"

"Yes."

"So why don't you just ask Sophie how it's going?"

Carl felt offended. No-one had spoken to him at all about her mental state and if, to her, it merely felt like she'd woken up after only a night's sleep.

Sophie had purposely not shared with him her 'other life' her 'other love' or the fact that she'd lived every moment, just the way he had. That she'd made love thousands of times while he'd been saving himself, like the mug he was.

She needed to keep one foot in this lifeboat in case she was stuck here in this hell hole with her faithful boring boyfriend and his equally uninteresting son. She was hedging her bets again, but her heart was pounding in anticipation of feeling John's hands on her once again, of the jokes they would share, of the uplifting joy of just being together which, in comparison to this felt like an eternal Christmas morning.

She watched Carl hover around the nurses' station for a while, hoping he would leave and not come back to her room, giving her the space to think.

He eventually turned to wave goodbye and she raised her arm in reply, unconcerned by the wasted muscle which hung in floppy sickly white skin folds, it didn't matter for soon this body would be left behind and she would be reading a bedtime story to Tori while Rebecca pretends to be too old to listen.

Gently she lay down and drew the sheet over her bony shoulders and started her plot to escape back to the love of her life. She decided that there must be something she was missing, some trigger, some set of circumstances that causes her to cross over lives and if she could remember all the facts, she could probably work out the common denominator.

"Nurse?" She sat up full of purpose "Can I have a pen and paper please?"

At home Carl spent the afternoon cleaning and preparing dinner for Tommy. He was doing all the things Kelly would normally do but in half the time and with twice the enthusiasm. As he trod her path and was reminded of her duties, he was deliberately dismissing the gentle waves of affection for her as quickly as they arose, swatting them away like flies at his new picnic. Irritated by their persistence, yet warmed by their company.

He concluded that Kelly had given him what he needed, and any sentiment must now be eradicated. He had been given everything he had been waiting for, and very soon Kelly would be the friend who helped him out, and Sophie will be back to wedding planning and dress fittings. He was sure this temporary sadness would soon be washed away in the tidal wave of resurrected love that was fast approaching his shore.

Later, as he waited at the school gate, he noticed instantly the fear in Tommy's eyes as he glanced right and left for any sign of Kelly.

"Why are you here dad?"

It wasn't the greeting he'd been hoping for.

"I took the day off today to visit your mum"

"Where's Kelly?"

"She will be at work I expect"

His own words gave him quite a pang as he recognised the lengths Kelly had gone to in order to help him as a single father. Every day she picked Tommy up, and stayed with him until Carl got home, then returning to the salon to do late appointments to make up the time.

He found himself wondering what she would do with the spare hours now she no longer had the burdens he'd allowed her to carry. The empty space she had left in his life had resulted in an even bigger one in his heart. He wished she would call. He wasn't used to being the one who had to tread carefully, because he'd been the one who could do whatever he felt like and she would deal with it.

He took Tommy's hand as he experienced a new feeling. It was a mixture of guilt, regret, sadness and loneliness but it was more than that. It was genuine heartache for the loss of Kelly.

"Is she coming tomorrow?"

"I don't think so, Son. The thing is.... your mum is back with us now."

"What about Kelly?"

"What about her?"

Tommy looked up at his father with such shock and disbelief that Carl felt ashamed and belittled by his own child.

He tried to think of something morally redeeming to say but he was not a man who could easily handle complicated emotional situations. It was simple, he had made a plan that seemed to be for the best and this was no time to be wavering back and forth or be wobbled by some emotion that had no place in his project.

"It's bangers and mash for tea." Was his response to his son's question about the fate of the only real mother he'd known and loved.

Tommy's teary blue eyes searched his father's face for some comfort or acknowledgment of the massive hole Kelly had left in his life, but there was none. He merely smiled and shrugged as though their team had lost a match on a Saturday afternoon. He playfully ruffled the little boys blonde mop of hair, further minimising the event, then followed it with a quick rough squeeze of the shoulder. So that was that. A decade of a mother's love to be dismissed with nothing more than a shrug and a squeeze.

The two figures walked along in silence for a while. Then, oblivious to his son's pain and anger, Carl instructed Tommy to keep his secret about Kelly's role in their life. To pretend she was just someone who called in from time to time.

Tommy's dejected loitering began to change, picking up a purposeful angry pace to which his father was still oblivious. His dad had thrown away his mummy like an old toy without even asking him what he thought or how he felt about it.

She had been tossed out to make room for this skinny, smelly, limping, evil woman who didn't even like him. Now he was being asked to lie and pretend she'd been nothing to him. Tommy marched. He was too upset to speak but with each step another brick was cemented in the wall that would separate father and son for the rest of their lives.

Tommy picked and poked at his tea and when he heard of the plan to visit Sophie later that evening, he responded with silent compliance. His personal rebellion was subtle in his transformation from happy child to glum child and the only blatant protest was his insistence in calling her Sophie and referring to Kelly as mum. Carl reprimanded him whenever he did this, but it was obvious he was not going to relent.

"Now be nice." Carl ordered as he tugged his son step by step along the hospital corridor

"She smells funny." Was Tommy's defence for dragging his feet.

"And don't say that." Carl was becoming irritated that his plan was revealing flaws.

"And she's scary." Tommy was milking this.

"She is not! Now shush we're nearly there."

As the pair approached the nurses' station a young nurse blocked their path with a sympathetic smile.

"You might want to give us a few minutes."

"Why?" Carl snapped, still irritated by his son's behaviour.

"Well maybe you should take the little boy for a lemonade or something give us some time to prepare her."

Carl was not taking any of this nonsense as he pushed by her, striding purposefully towards her private room, still dragging the reluctant Tommy behind him.

As he approached the room, the scene before him caused him to falter but the writhing of Tommy's hand in his was even more compelling as the child tried desperately to escape.

"I don't want to go!"

He turned to Tommy to reassure him and asked one of the nurses to take him for a moment before returning to Sophie's door. The bed, the cabinet and the floor were covered with papers, hundreds of slips of paper all connected by arrows and tape.

Sophie's wobbly handwriting decorated each sheet in an alarming array of random words such as suicide and hanging, autopsy, tablets, nightmares, mountain and strangely the word pepper pot. His blood ran cold and for the first time since the news that his long-lost love had returned, he felt afraid, no, more than afraid, he felt terrified that the creature which had awoken was someone else, something else.

"Sophie?" He hoped to learn that there was some sense to this.

"Yes?" She smiled. The smile dissolved and gave way to a frown as she noted his hostility.

Carl raised his eyebrows to invite a reasonable explanation for the collage.

"I am working on something." She snapped defensively.

"And what would that be?" He joked hopefully.

"I'm writing down everything I remember." She tried to make light of it, but her red face and fidgety behaviour was unnerving.

"Hanging?" Carl said sarcastically.

Sophie started to gather the papers together as though clearing a room of clutter for an unexpected visitor.

"You wouldn't understand."

Carl wanted to give her the benefit of the doubt and quickly reverted to his plan to reunite his family.

"Ok darling. Anything that you feel helps you to remember." He walked towards her tentatively and stroked her arm, fixated on the word suicide, as she continued to gather her secrets and push them into a drawer.

"I didn't expect you to come back today." She retorted almost resentfully.

"I brought Tommy to see you."

"Tommy? That's wonderful. Where is he?"

"I'll go find him if you're sure you're up to it?"

"Yes of course." Her eyes were suddenly wide and alive, and he felt more positive, as he rushed off to find their son while she was so welcoming.

"Why don't you leave us two for a while.?" She urged, smiling widely at her fiancé.

"Ok." He nodded as he gently pushed Tommy forward and then headed for the drinks machine.

Tommy starred mistrustfully at the smelly, weird woman who claimed to have given birth to him.

Sophie captured her lank hair in an elastic band and then patted the bed as she had done before, inviting the hostile boy to sit beside her. He shook his head.

"Come and sit with mummy Tommy"

He shook his head again but made no attempt to leave the room.

"I don't bite." She reassured.

"I know" He snapped.

"Don't you want to sit with me?"

He shook his head again.

"You don't like me very much, do you?" She asked submissively.

He shrugged and kept his eyes on his feet.

"I know I don't feel like your mummy, but I am, and I would love for us to be friends."

"I don't want to call you mummy." He retorted "Kelly is my mummy."

"Ok. That's fine." She said sympathetically, but it had hit a nerve and worse than that, she was now wondering exactly what Kelly's role in her son's life had been. Moreover, what had her role in Carl's life been?

Tommy moved towards the bed and sat down, which felt like her reward for allowing Kelly her rightful place, and although her mission was to return to John and her daughters, she found herself feeing territorial about another woman's presence in the lives of her pathetic fiancée and annoying son.

She could feel herself rising to the challenge of dethroning Kelly even if she didn't want this family of hers. She knew that in order to do that she needed to befriend the child, and that meant giving him some affection no matter how false.

"Let me look at you" she smiled "You have my eyes."

"Everybody says that." Tommy said politely.

"This is hard for me too, Tommy. I've missed so many years of my life, of our life"

"I know." He whispered submissively.

"I don't want to cause anyone any sadness, I really don't. I'm glad Kelly has looked after you for me. She was my best friend and she's a wonderful person."

"Yes, she is!" Tommy gushed, suddenly feeling his new mum valued Kelly more than his dad did. "Can I still see her then?"

"Of course. As much as you like."

"But daddy says….."

"You leave your father to me." Sophie smiled as she gently patted the little boy's hand, wishing she had not interrupted him when he was about to tell her what exactly daddy had said about Kelly.

She still had her hand on Tommy's when Carl returned, which gave him much needed hope for their future together. They chatted for a few more minutes but Sophie was obviously distracted, frequently glancing at the drawer in which many edges of her papers were trapped.

"I think we should be making a move Tommy."

"Ok." Tommy jumped up and skipped towards his father "Sophie says I can see Kelly whenever I like."

"Did she?" He tried to hide his discomfort, but Sophie knew that look. He was squirming.

"Bye." Tommy waved.

"Bye." Sophie waved back, until the two were out of sight and then quickly retrieved her precious papers, cursing that they were now out of order, as she urgently re-arranged them from bed to floor.

Carl entered the house and quickly listened to the flashing answer machine

"Hi. It's Kelly. Hope you are both ok. Will call again later." ...... "Hi again, it's me. You must be visiting or something so just calling to check if you guys need anything. Talk soon............Hi. Hope you are alright. Bit worried. Almost bedtime Tommy so night night and big kiss"

Carl didn't let Tommy listen, nor did he mention it. He needed to keep Kelly away and the best way was to make Tommy believe she didn't care anymore.

He had to keep to the plan, and this was his way of swotting Kelly away like a persistent wasp. He hit the delete button swot, swot, swot.

Chapter 11

Despite the small moments of distraction that were creeping into her life, Kelly still spent most of her waking hours analysing Carl's silence. She tried to believe he was keeping his distance because he didn't trust himself around her, or that it was just too painful for him to get into a conversation with her and be reminded of their love.

"This is a good thing Kelly," her mum told her gently while she was watching her daughter push the food around her plate and stare out of the window. Food she desperately needed to replace the weight she'd lost over the last two weeks, "something had to happen to break that awful cycle of hoping, rejoicing and devastation you're been living with for more years than I care to remember."

Kelly nodded and smiled gently. She knew her mum was right. Mum's always are but it didn't stop her from checking her phone every few minutes in case this time, he had responded to one of the text messages she'd sent that morning. She hated that there was no response.

"No response *is* a response!" Niki reminded her when they spoke on the phone later that day.

She knew Niki was right, just as her mum was right and so was everyone else who had tried to talk some sense into her, but she couldn't believe he would cast her aside so brutally and so childishly.

"If he wasn't still strongly affected by me, then he would at least have the manners to reply."

"Of course he's affected by you," Niki replied sympathetically "but that doesn't mean he wants you back in his life. You'll feel so much better once you put all this behind you and stop hovering in the shadows, waiting for Sophie to mess up or drop dead. It's time to move on."

Kelly hated that phrase. She'd heard it hundreds of times over the years. The 'one size fits all' cliché of advice brandished around by those who have never lost their heart to anyone. The smug self-righteous 'know-it-all's who act as though you had never thought of that before. Do they really thing you are going to say "move on? Wow, thank you. Yes, I'll do that then"?

Niki proceeded to offer ways in which 'moving on' would help her friend to embark on the road to happiness, oblivious to the anger that was building as Kelly listened in silence.

"Look I have to go." Kelly interrupted and quickly ended the call.

She despised the ignorance of those who were stupid enough to believe it was even possible to make the decision to leave a love behind and move on. People who spoke of it as though it was in her power to make that happen, or that she might possess one morsel of control over her heart.

Clearly, Niki had never experienced the all-consuming power of love, and over the years she had concluded that not many people do. As she started to recall the many times she'd tried to extricate herself from it she remembered the young heartbroken man from their last night out many years ago, and wondered if, unlike her, he had finally found his peace. Had he found the secret to moving on?

Later that evening, with still no response to her earlier messages, she suspected that Carl might be once again, trying to do this for her own good. Was he still making her damn decisions for her like she was a child? or worse still, like he believed he needed to protect her from her idolisation of him? As though he was some rock star, and she was his pathetic groupie?

If she was going to hold onto this feeling of control which had started to drift, what she needed was a bloody good distraction.

She picked up her phone again and dialled a different number.

"Hey! Long-time no speak!" Jake sounded genuinely pleased to hear from her

"Yes, it's been a while. So, how's life with you? Married yet?"

"Nope."

"Serious girlfriend?"

Jake laughed out loud.

"What's this really about Kelly? We've hardly spoken since the coma girl story hit the news."

"Yes. I know. I'm sorry. It's been a really tough time for Tommy."

"And for you I expect?"

"I guess so."

"So, do you need a friend right now? You do know I hate you right?"

"Right."

"You also know you're a fucking idiot, right?"

"Right."

"I could maybe fit in a coffee next week or something" His tone was a little dismissive, but she knew how all this looked. He probably knew more than he was letting on about her situation and Carl's reconciliation with Sophie.

"That would be great." She daren't push for more because she knew she didn't deserve more.

"Or maybe I could fit you in this afternoon between girlfriends?" She wasn't sure if he was being sarcastic or playful.

"Jake I, well It's just ….."

"Yeah I know, I get it."

"Do you?"

"I'll meet you at one, but Kelly?"

"Yes?"

"Don't jerk me around."

By the time they met for lunch he seemed more relaxed.

"So? Has Saint Carl finally fallen from grace?" He smiled.

"It would seem so," the relief at his friendly demeanour was obvious, "I don't want you to think that I'm only here on the rebound."

"I'm sure you don't, but that doesn't mean it's not true does it?"

It was no use lying. He wasn't as easy as Carl to manipulate, and the resulting honesty was a relief from the life she'd been living. Jake had always been the one she could trust. In the time she had spent with him there had been no ambiguity in his eyes, no indecision in his voice and no hesitation in his touch.

"Do you have a girlfriend?" She asked tentatively.

"Yes."

"Serious?"

"Why do you want to know?"

Kelly shrugged.

Jake placed both hands on the table and leaned forward until his face was only a few inches from hers.

"Let's cut the crap Kelly. Are you here hoping for a reconciliation? On second thoughts, don't even answer that. I know that you are, so what I need to know is what's the deal here?"

"What do you mean?"

"Well how sure are you that this isn't just another attempt to make Carl jealous. Another game to get him back?"

"I'm absolutely sure."

"So, what are you saying? That you suddenly don't love him anymore and you've realised that you love me? That's bollocks!"

"Yes, it is." She wasn't going to lie to the one man who incredibly, still seemed to have some respect for her. She swallowed hard and looked him in the eyes.

"My love for Carl is toxic. Worse than that, it's pathetic and it's never been returned. I know now that it never will be."

"So what? I'm second prize or something?"

"No! No Jake you're not. I don't deserve your love, but I know it's the kind of love I want. I know the love I feel for you is there, but this juvenile obsession caused me to defile it. I'm sorry and all I want is a chance to earn it back and to show you that I'm free of it now."

"You put up a good case, I'll give you that," he grinned, "you know that I've got you sussed but I like you anyway, right?"

"Right."

"So?" he asked expectantly.

"So, you said you had a girlfriend?"

"Yep, but it's nothing I can't deal with."

Kelly smiled. His delight in getting a second chance with her was obvious and it felt so good to be genuinely wanted.

He smiled back. He had finally won her back from the ass hole who had tortured her for so long, who had tortured him for so long, and now he had the chance to show her what a committed relationship looked like. Better than that, he had the chance to rub the grease-monkey's nose in it all over again!

"I'll be free by the next time we meet." He assured.

She smiled again but this time she felt a chill run down her spine. She recognised this behaviour. It was exactly the breakneck speed at which she would drop him for another chance with Carl and some poor girl was on the other end of her quest to get him back.

The romance between her and Jake was very different to how it had been previously, or so it seemed to Kelly. Perhaps it was that she was paying more attention to him, allowing herself to enjoy his company more openly, or maybe she was genuinely falling for him.

As they embarked on a real courtship, she committed each act of kindness and consideration to memory, as she built a defence against his potential eviction from her life. She was determined to make this work, determined to conquer the art of 'moving on' and this time, in order to prove it to herself, she was prepared to cross the line, to do the thing that can't be undone.

She turned up at Jake's three bedroomed modern 'new build' with a bottle of expensive red, on the day she hoped would change her forever. He'd asked her over for a meal, which she knew to be a euphemism for sex, but she was ready.

As the meal ended and they took the remainder of the wine up to his bedroom she felt warm and excited as he removed the bottle from her hand, placed it on the bedside table and kissed her deeply.

She wanted to take the lead, to be the one in control, but as he unbuttoned her blouse and guided her towards his huge satin covered bed, it was all she could do to breathe in and out. He unwrapped her like she was a precious gift, gently stroking away her clothes with his soft hands as she simply allowed herself to be absorbed in his exploration of her body.

She had hardly touched him at all when he eased himself on top of her, but it didn't matter. She was no longer craving control or domination. She was selfishly allowing him to pleasure her and enjoying every moment of it.

Eventually she slid her hands over his chest, comparing his dark, athletic body to Carl's boyish frame. From his huge chest, taut stomach and the curve of his solid round buttocks. She stroked the solid tense mass of muscle in the arms which were effortlessly supporting his weight as he thrust slowly and deliberately into her. The value of the words he whispered compared to the grunts and huffs of nothingness she was used to. In comparison, Carl was emotionally retarded. Carl, with his childish behaviour and careless insults, his average body and unkept hair. The man who had no concept of the damage he caused with his selfish stupidity.

He was no match for the man in who's arms she was now laying after the orgasm that had almost rendered her unconscious. This was too good to be true, too wonderful for words and oh god, too soon to enter her heart, which was still so full of Carl.

His black fingers stroked her hair as she lay on his chest with tears of frustration welling in her eyes. Why could she not love this man, the man she felt so safe with? Was she simply yearning for Carl just because she couldn't have him? Was pure pride standing in the way of her own happiness? She held Jake tightly as she tried to force her heart to love him, tried to will her soul to need him and to order her head to forget Carl the way he seemed to have forgotten her.

She imagined Carl watching them as she turned her face towards Jake's and gave him a tender kiss, as she stroked his chest just the way Carl loved her to, as she pulled him down on top of her to make love again. Yes, this would hurt Carl, this would really hurt, and the thought of his pain urged her on. In her passion for Jake she was reeking the revenge Carl deserved. He couldn't feel it because he couldn't see it, but she was doing it just the same and one day he would know of it, and that made it all the sweeter.

Within a few days she moved in with Jake and filling her days with work and her nights with Jake did help to distract her from imagining Carl's every moment. But, as August slipped into September Tommy's birthday approached, handing her the excuse she longed for. She was excited to buy him the iPhone he had coveted for so long. The one Carl couldn't afford for him. She charged it up and added her own number on speed dial before lovingly wrapping it.

Jake made no secret of the fact that he wasn't happy about it. He tried to convince her that she was undermining Carl, but she stood her ground, knowing that Jake was smart enough not to try to dissuade her. He was learning his place admirably, just as she had learned her place with Carl.

Chapter 12

On the day of his party, she turned up at the house half expecting to see Sophie at the door. She had prepared herself for the worst by allowing herself to picture Sophie in her old kitchen, using her pans and mothering her son. Over and over she played the images in her mind as she tried to desensitise herself. She wanted to see Tommy so much that she forced herself to deal with it, and consequently stood boldly at the front door of her own house, as she rang the bell with Jake's hand reassuringly in hers.

Carl opened the door and shuffled uncomfortably for a second before glancing at the joined hands and hardening his expression.

"Kelly!"

"Hi. I brought Tommy a gift. Hope you don't mind?"

Carl minded. He minded very much but not because she had returned to his house, or that she wanted to see Tommy. He minded very much that her hand was in another man's hand and of all the possibilities that implied. He minded mostly that it was Jake's.

Kelly could feel his resentment and felt gratified by it. Emotionally retarded he may be, childishly stupid and simplistically cruel, but this Neanderthal being could not disguise the stench of his male animal jealousy as it filled the air so reassuringly. Almost as reassuringly as the absence of Sophie, who apparently had not yet ventured from the rehabilitation home she had been moved to.

Carl watched submissively as the conjoined couple explained the workings of the phone to Tommy, laughing together as they jostled each other lovingly.

Kelly's hair fell sexily around her face in tousled strands of gold against her porcelain complexion as his eyes fell onto her perfect mouth. She was chatting but Carl could hear no sound for he was mesmerised by the soft glossy lips that had found his hundreds of times.

He followed the curve of her throat to the soft skin his hands had caressed so carelessly and unappreciatively. The contour of her breasts under the white tee shirt reminded him of their sweet perfection, and how her deep pink nipples would become erect under his touch. Her manicured hands which had lovingly explored every inch of him, and the feel of her entire body pressed against his. He tried to shake away his memories and forced a smile.

Tommy was delighted with his phone, and to an onlooker, this would have seemed like a happy scene with all conflict laid to rest, and all ill feelings finally resolved.

Carl should have been feeling the relief that Kelly had granted him his freedom. That she had kept her council and managed to stay in Tommy's life without destroying his family, but the tightness in his chest seemed to be stopping him from breathing. All he could see in the happy scene before him was that another man was stealing his woman and it was the worst pain he had ever felt.

After they left, Carl paid little attention to the remainder of the party, something he would later reprimand himself for, knowing he had allowed his jealousy to impede on his son's big day. Lying in his bed, lonely and confused, his hand began to stroke his penis for comfort, for relief and release. As he stroked, he tried to visualise himself with Sophie. The nights of stir fry and tv football on the sofa before they would fall off and make love on the floor. He remembered her scent and her touch, but they raised no more than a reminiscent smile.

The only images capable of exciting him were those of Kelly's body as she sat astride him with her hands raking her hair upwards as she pleasured herself against him. He tried to swot her away again, but she was right in front of his eyes, his hands gripping her thighs as she rode him, taking him further and faster towards the most intense orgasm of his life. He continued to thrust into his hand hating himself with every stoke until the power of those images sped him to the delicious convulsions of climax.

"Damn it!"

Sunday morning brought a little winter sunshine and with it a more positive mood. Carl was determined to get on with his project of rebuilding his family and that would be with Sophie and Tommy, the way it was meant to be. He showered and dressed and took Tommy egg and soldiers in bed as a futile attempt to make up for his lack of enthusiasm for the party.

Tommy was already messing with his phone and Carl was very much aware that he had probably been texting Kelly.

"We will have to put you some more numbers in that phone" he laughed "Like mine and Grandad's and Sophie's."

"If you want." Tommy was nonchalant but un-obstructive.

"I'll do it later then?"

"Ok." Tommy was dipping his bread into his egg but keeping an eye on the phone's screen beside him as though expecting a response to something.

"Are we going to see Sophie today?" Tommy asked miserably.

"Yes, well if you want to?"

Carl was aware that his relationship with his son had changed. There was less affection between them, but he never made the connection with the day he had collected him from school instead of Kelly. The day Carl evicted his mum.

"I don't mind."

It wasn't a direct refusal and Carl took that as positive progress. He pulled out a jumper from Tommy's wardrobe and then resorted to completing the outfit of trousers and tee shirt by dragging dirty ones from the laundry basket. He had to stop doing this he told himself, as he dampened the corner of a towel under the tap and tried to rub off the dirty marks from the knees. He did it far too often, since Kelly left.

He folded them neatly and tried to smooth them with his hands to make them look presentable for his son, but Tommy didn't even notice. He didn't care what he wore today or how he looked for his visit to the rehabilitation hospital. All that mattered was the reward he knew he would get for going. The visit to the ice-cream parlour.

Carl was oblivious to the to the fact that he was bribing his son to visit Sophie. He chose to believe Tommy was warming to Sophie as he walked purposefully back to his own room to smarten himself up for Sophie.

Kelly had got her man and he was going to get his woman back. Sophie would soon be sexy and fun again. Her body would tone, and her hair would regain its glossy waves and very soon she would be the focus of his lust. He would want her more than he ever wanted Kelly, much more, and it was all starting today.

As they left the house chatting normally, it felt like things were finally falling into place. Sophie was back and all his waiting had paid off. Kelly was happy with someone else and it was the best outcome he could have hoped for. Everything was perfect.

He entered the building full of optimism for the smile that would welcome them. The smile that had kept him hoping through the darkest of days through those endless years as he held on, praying for a miracle and now his prayers had been answered. All he needed to do now was to turn back the clock in his heart, to the day he had comforted her as she left that final morning to visit her mum in hospital.

He knew he had to get her home if they were to have a chance of making that happen. He needed to get her out of the rehabilitation home, away from the clinical surroundings and institutionalised routines. As soon as he'd checked in on her he intended to set the wheels in motion to bring her back under the same roof. He knew that if she slept beside him again, everything would come flooding back.

As they approached her room, he could see her still scribbling on her bits of paper, the bits of paper that had multiplied in both size and quantity over the weeks. She had become obsessed with her snippets of random sentences. Her bedroom had taken on the persona of a police incident room with connecting arrows here and there and question marks dotted around like she was trying to solve some giant puzzle.

He was momentarily filled with compassion and sympathy but as she caught sight of them and glanced his way Carl's blood ran cold. Her sunken eyes with their dark sickly circles were full of contempt and anger, as though she was furious that they had disturbed her puzzle, and although she cleverly curtailed her reaction, he could not shake the feeling.

"Hi." She smiled falsely, in Tommy's direction.

"Hi." Carl returned the greeting, trying to dismiss his doubts and re commit to his plan of inviting this woman back into his bed. It was going to be fine; he would make it fine and he would start by determinedly rekindling his affection and attraction for his returned lover.

She was gathering her papers again, and trying to pretend this was not an unwelcome interruption to her day.

"Why does she write all these things down?" Tommy asked in a whisper

"She's just trying to remember stuff. The doctor's idea." Carl lied as he appraised her.

Her eyes were red and her complexion blotchy. Her hair still greasy and lifeless. At the back of her head it had separated, revealing the flat greasy rosette where she had slept. Nothing had changed.

She was clearly making no effort to recapture his desire. He became irritated that she was not playing her part. He was doing all he could to want her again, but she was making no effort at all to help him. She was blatantly sabotaging his plan. How did she expect him to desire her when she looked like that? More importantly, how did she expect him to exorcise the image of Kelly astride him as she gently rocked him to ecstasy? His irritation turned to anger.

"Have you even washed your hair recently Soph!" It was a statement, not a question.

"Nope." She smiled. It was a statement, not an apology.

He looked at her dry flaky lips, her translucent lard-like complexion and her bony shoulders draped with a soiled cotton shirt. He felt enraged and frustrated at her lack of effort, but it was anger born of fear. The same fear he had felt when her hand had fallen from his, as they looked out from the top of a mountain many years ago. The same fear that had prevented him from asking her about the little lists of his strengths and weakness which he'd found in draws and handbags, as though she'd been trying to make a decision based on logic not love. The fear that she didn't really love him. Not then and not now. The fear that so many years had been wasted.

"You could do with a bit of a makeover and a few trips to the gym girl." He was testing the water.

She looked down at his stomach indignantly and gave it a firm slap.

"Looks like you could do with the same old man!"

Tommy laughed as Carl looked down at his own body.

It was true that the shape he had now was far from the profile Sophie would remember. His six pack had melted into a single soft curve causing his pants to sit below it, held by a belt that was barely visible due to the overhang. He blamed fatherhood for the less frequent sessions at the gym and on the football pitch, but he also wondered if he had taken Kelly for granted in more ways than he realised.

Had he worked harder when he was with Sophie, knowing that her heart was always out of reach, while Kelly's heart was a sure thing? or did he just crave Sophie's admiration more?

"Perhaps you should have spent less time moping at my bedside and more time at the gym!" She laughed sarcastically.

He couldn't believe she was ridiculing him as though she had every right to. This was not the woman he remembered, and as she continued to laugh, Tommy moved closer to him for reassurance.

"Can we go now daddy?"

Carl gave him a reprimanding look. "We've only just got here and that was a rude thing to say. Apologise to your mother."

His mother wasn't listening to either of them. She had returned to her investigation, still giggling to herself, and for a moment Carl doubted his conviction. Kelly had hinted that Sophie was no saint and he wished he'd pushed her harder to explain.

"She's not my mother! I don't like her, and I don't want to talk to her."

Carl wanted to reprimand him further, but as he looked at Sophie crawling around on the floor like a mad woman he couldn't argue.

Sophie started to pay attention. She knew she might need Tommy to help her, and causing him to back away like this, was definitely counterproductive. She got up from the floor and walked over to them before Carl had the chance to respond to his son's behaviour.

"It's not his fault Carl, it's mine."

She took both of Tommy's hands in hers and bent down until her face was level with his, ignoring as he flinched.

"You know I've been asleep for a long time Tommy?"

Tommy nodded.

"Well while I was sleeping, a lot of things were going round and round in my head, and so that I can stop thinking about them,

I need to remember them all, and write them down. Do you understand?"

Tommy shook his head.

She took a deep breath and tried again.

"Sometimes when things don't make sense, if you write them all down and then read them, they seem easier to understand, and when you understand them you can stop thinking about them. Does that make sense?"

This time he nodded, and she smiled.

"As soon as I understand it all, I can put all this away and spend all my time trying to be a proper mum to you."

"How long will that take?"

"I'll be as quick as I can. How does that sound?"

Tommy shrugged but Carl felt elated. The trepidation he had been feeling only a few moments ago vanished instantly. He needed it to vanish and she had given him the perfect excuse to push it aside, along with the doubts he'd been having about her love for him.

"You don't know her yet," he whispered to Tommy as she moved back to tidy away her papers. "she's absolutely wonderful. You'll see."

He hoped he was right. He had to be right, because the possibility   that he might have trampled Kelly into the dirt for this woman who had never wanted either of them, was beyond devastating.

As for Kelly, well she had been the author of her own misfortune, by knowingly trying to steal his love from Sophie. Soon that love would be back on track because very soon Sophie would start to make the effort, she'd just said as much, and before long he'd be showing off his sexy fiancée again.

"Has Sophie told you the exciting news then?" Anne's voice interrupted his thoughts.

"No. What news?"

"I was just about to,," Sophie's tone was far from convincing, "he's barely been here a second."

"We've suggested she goes home for a weekend. Either to her father's house or with the two of you"

"That's wonderful. Of course, she must come with us. That's what you want isn't it?" Carl asked without waiting for her reply. "That's what you want too. Isn't it, Tommy?"

Tommy didn't answer either but his eyes pleaded with his father to prevent this woman from entering their home.

"Tommy? "He repeated in the voice that urged his son to mind his manners, although secretly sharing his son's fears.

"Suppose." He finally said sulkily as he played with his phone on which Carl could see a line of kisses on the end of his latest message to Kelly.

Anne smiled. "Good, so everyone is happy."

No-one was happy, including Sophie. She was about to lose the privacy in which she could study her evidence and plan her way back to her real family.

As Carl and Tommy walked away Anne took Sophie's arm firmly and spoke firmly.

"Don't mess this up Sophie. Forget this other phantom family of yours. I had a case very similar to this before and the woman refused to accept that it was all in her head."

Sophie was noticeably stunned.

"What happened to her?" She eventually whispered.

"She's in an institution on suicide watch! Don't let the same thing happen to you. Be careful Sophie."

Sophie nodded in appreciation of the advice but secretly she felt a little excited that this had happened to someone before.

When Carl and Tommy returned home, Carl started to prepare for Sophie's visit but the excitement and enthusiasm he had been anticipating over the years didn't come. As he packed away the few remaining items Kelly had forgotten, into a box and wiped the shelves and wardrobes to make room for Sophie it was with a heavy heart.

He hadn't opened Kelly's side of their wardrobe since the day she left, and now as he wiped her away with a damp cloth, he remembered how excited she'd been when he allowed her to have the ones she wanted. The ivory wood with the pale pink inlay was typically Kelly, and no matter how hard he wiped, he knew that he could never wipe away the pure joy on her face on the day he had them delivered. They would always be Kelly's wardrobes.

Reluctantly, he brought down the boxes of Sophie's old clothes from the loft and despondently hung them in neat rows. None of the familiar items resurrected the emotional nostalgia he had been expecting. He gave them a shake to try to get rid of the creases and quietly closed the doors.

He had decided to give Sophie the master bedroom out of chivalry but there was no denying the feeling of betrayal from moving her into the bed he'd shared with Kelly, nor of allowing her clothes to occupy the space from which the pink satins and cream chiffons had been brutally evicted. Dejectedly he folded his clothes and took them to the spare room.

By Friday night, all three participants had prepared themselves for the ordeal of the weekend ahead with equal ambivalence. The long-awaited occasion. The momentous return of the long-lost partner and mother to her family, was no more than a car journey of silent tolerance and uneasy dread.

As Carl showed her around the house with the respectful courtesy of a hotel proprietor welcoming a guest, the contrast to his long-standing vision of this moment, physically hurt. He had lived it a thousand times in his head. The moment when he would carry her over the threshold of the home he had made for her, laughing and kissing as he spun her around and threw her on the bed causing her soft waves of hair to bounce over her face as she landed.

He turned to check that the frail, pasty, solemn faced woman was still following him as he moved from kitchen to lounge. She was shuffling obediently behind him, and for a moment his heart went out to her. She looked like she was resisting the urge to run.

He reached out his hand and touched hers. It was not desire or love or even affection, it was nothing more than the simple compassion extended from one human being to another.

"Come on." He led her up the staircase keeping her hand in his for support.

As she breathlessly climbed the final step with her hand in his, she resolved to give this a shot. To play the part at least, until she was lucid enough, and informed enough, to be sure of what was real.

Carl led her to a wardrobe door and opened it for her to look inside. There, hanging neatly, were most of her old clothes. She recognised them immediately and the sight took her breath away.

"You… you." She stammered.

"Yes, I kept them all for you. I couldn't bear to part with them even though they may be a little dated now."

Tommy followed them into the room and frowned at the wardrobe full of unfamiliar clothes. Carl shot him a warning glance and he kept his silence.

"Oh, I don't know," Sophie replied, "It doesn't seem like fashion has changed dramatically over the last nine years. Well not as dramatically as the seventies did from the sixties anyway."

"The sixties!" Tommy yelled "How old are you? Were you alive in the sixties?!"

"No" Sophie laughed "I'm a similar age to your dad but I remember the sixties fashion from my mother." It was the first genuine smile Sophie had made, and suddenly things felt a bit less bleak.

"Would everyone like Chinese tonight?" Carl was trying to build on the positivity.

Both nodded, and Sophie put her hand on his in recognition of the effort he was making.

"That would be lovely."

In a few minutes Carl was issuing instructions on the warming of plates and as he drove into town, he felt genuinely happy. Things were heading in the right direction. This was everything he had hoped for, his wife and son back together, a Friday night takeaway and a future to look forward to.

He ramped up the radio and tried to sing along, quickly realising that he hardly knew any of the words. He never knew the words. It was Kelly who knew every word of every song and she would sing along with everything. Even the impossible jabbering of rap. He smiled as he imagined the concentration on her face as she hit every syllable while her hands animated the storyline.

He had to stop the car for a moment to deal with the blow. The impact of those silly, joyful memories of the woman who had given him more support and devotion than any man deserves, had knocked him sideways. The woman he had kicked a thousand times but who, like a faithful dog, had returned again and again but who was now safely in the arms of another man. A man who appreciated and deserved her love.

He banged the steering wheel several times in frustration and anger. There were no winners here. Everyone was holding a consolation prize. He took a very deep breath. It was too late now. Everyone was going to have to make the best of it.

On the return journey, chop suey and chips for all on board, he selected a different playlist. A playlist from 1999 when he and Sophie used to go out clubbing in Scarborough. The carefree days of dancing into the early hours, tipsy taxi rides home and hangover lay-ins. The days before the Millennium bells tolled, and his life changed forever.

He was still singing as he put his key in the door, pushing it open with his shoulder as he hung on to the large box of food.

"Leave me alone, leave me alone!!" Tommy was screaming in the distance.

Dropping the box on the floor he took the stairs three at a time in his haste to get to Tommy.

"Dad!! Dad!!!"

Carl burst through the bedroom door where Tommy was sitting on his bed with his knees tucked tightly to his chest and his head buried into his knees. Sophie had her hands firmly around his wrists.

"What on earth is going on?" He bellowed.

"She's mad, she's mad!! Get her away from me!" Tommy was hysterical.

Sophie instantly let go of his wrists and turned to Carl with an expression in her eyes somewhere between desperate and crazy.

"I heard him." She whispered angrily.

"Heard what?" Carl was making no attempt to hide his rage.

"He was talking to her!" Sophie snarled.

"To who?"

Sophie swung her legs from the bed and walked over to where Carl was standing in the doorway with the confidence of someone who was about to justify her actions with some terrible truth.

"He was talking to Becky."

"Who the hell is Becky?"

Sophie stared at him like he was an idiot and then quickly realised she could not speak to Carl about this. Carl mustn't know she is in love with John. She had backed herself into a corner here. Slowly the desperation melted from her face as she started to mellow.

"Nothing. It doesn't matter. I'm sorry."

"It damn well does matter!" Carl bellowed as he put a comforting arm around his son.

Sophie walked calmly downstairs and started to plate up the food. She needed time to think. She'd made a mistake out of desperation and now she had to calm down.

"It's Ok. She's just confused mate."

Tommy looked up at his father pleadingly.

"She's mad dad. She needs to be in the hospital. I'm scared of her"

Carl pulled him close "She would never hurt you, or me, she loves us."

"No! she doesn't dad. She loves Becky."

"Who is Becky?"

"I don't know. She's cuckoo."

"Don't say that!"

"It's true. She thought this Becky was here in my room. Send her back dad. Please!"

"What did she say?"

"She just ran in and said she'd heard me talking to this Becky. It was horrible."

Carl tried to play the incident down, but his blood ran cold as he listened to Tommy's account of the outburst.

"Come on. The foods getting cold. Everything is gonna be fine. You'll see." He assured as he put an arm around the little boy and guided him downstairs.

He knew everything was going to be fine because he intended to sleep in Tommy's room tonight, and tomorrow he would re-evaluate the safety of having this stranger in his house. She was definitely not the girl he had fallen in love with so many years ago.

Still with his arm around Tommy he gingerly pushed open the dining room door. Sophie was sitting at the table smiling warmly. She knew she needed to do everything she could to redeem the situation, but deep down she still thought that Tommy was lying to her. He might be her son, but he was lying and eventually she believed that if she managed to stay in this house, he would provide the contact she craved with her beloved Becky.

"I am really sorry I frightened you Tommy."

Tommy shrugged and sat down at the table.

"I just thought I heard something in your room. That's all."

Tommy shrugged again.

"Am I forgiven?"

"Guess so."

Sophie put her hand out and for a while Tommy ignored it.

"Tommy?" Carl prompted.

Slowly Tommy took her hand only to retract it as though it had burned him.

Sophie smiled "It will never happen again. I promise."

Carl smiled at her, and as she smiled back, he remembered the curve of her lips. It was the first glimmer of the old Sophie he had seen.

They ate the meal in polite silence and Sophie offered to wash the dishes.

"We have a dishwasher," Carl laughed, "it just needs loading."

"Oh. We could never afford one of those before, could we? They were a bit of a luxury."

"Almost everyone has one now"

Sophie's heart sank. This was another bit of evidence that her life with John wasn't real. They had lived in the Docklands in London and later in an affluent area in Chelmsford, yet she had not had a dishwasher. Maybe she had just never considered buying one but, if they had become commonplace, surely John would have been keen to have one. She dismissed the notion as neither proving nor disproving anything and proceeded to load the machine.

They all went to bed at the same time and it was a relief for everyone. Tommy didn't want to be alone and neither Sophie nor Carl wanted to be left alone together.

Sophie lay in the strange double bed noticing that the duvet cover wasn't particularly masculine. She wondered if he had bought the floral set just for her. She examined it closely and decided that it wasn't new. Perhaps Kelly had done most of his home décor but why did she even care who had bought the sheets? She had more important issues to debate with herself like her stupidity with Tommy.

She knew she hadn't been mistaken and took out her notebook from her case to write down what she'd heard. It wasn't that the words themselves had any significant value, but she needed to write down the exact words in case she ever found herself doubting the inference of it. She tried to recall his exact words. He had definitely whispered the word 'Becky' several times as though asking for confirmation that she was listening. He had also said "Your mum's here in the house," but then she must have burst in and grabbed him by the wrists demanding that he explain what he was doing. She should have waited longer. Next time she would not interrupt, no matter how desperate she felt to shake it out of the boy.

She knew she needed to bond with him and gain his trust and if she was clever about it, he might start to open up to her, giving her vital information, taking her closer to securing her ticket home. She decided to pop her head around the door to wish them both goodnight, so she padded down the hallway and gently knocked before pushing down the handle and leaning into it. The door remained shut and she could feel that something heavy was pushed against it.

"Did you need something?" Carl called casually

"No. I just wanted to say goodnight."

"Ok. Goodnight." He called without offering an explanation for the blocked door.

"Great," she whispered to herself as she trotted back to her room, "now they think I'm a psychopath."

The remainder of the weekend passed without incident because Sophie made sure it did. She cooked breakfast and made some effort to push the vacuum cleaner around a couple of times. She played Lego with Tommy for hours and even had a go at some violent game on his play station. She laughed and cheered and hated every damn minute of it, but she loved that she was manipulating Tommy so easily. This little wretch with his lies and fake tears was no match for her!

On Sunday it was time for her to leave and she asked if Carl would take her to visit her mother's grave on the way. He agreed, but didn't want to expose Tommy to any more emotional outbursts, so he asked Kelly if he could stay with her for a couple of hours.

Naturally Kelly was elated.

As they pulled up outside it was Jake who opened the door, greeting Tommy with an enthusiastic high five. Carl clenched his jaw in resentment whilst simultaneously feeling some gratitude for making his son so welcome. Contradiction seemed to be a constant element in his life in these days.

As he pulled the car door shut, the ambience changed, as though he had trapped it inside with them. That sudden awkwardness that takes you by surprise when you become instantly alone with someone. It was the first time he had been alone with his fiancé since he had offered to drive her to visit her mum on that fateful morning. It felt ironic that he was now driving her to visit the grave. Almost like a natural continuation of where they had left off.

Neither of them spoke but they both felt it, and although the silence was suffocating, neither of them tried to breathe any air into it. Carl's heart was bursting to grasp this moment, to resolve everything and to trigger the full return of his gorgeous girl but Sophie was counting the seconds between Kelly's house and the graveyard hoping that the silence could make it.

As he parked the car and walked Sophie to the white headstone with the tiny cherubs, he instinctively took her hand in his, and although she didn't reciprocate, she allowed her hand to remain loosely in his until they reached the spot.

"Do you want to be alone with her?"

"Yes please. Do you mind?"

Carl shook his head and squeezed her hand before letting go and returning to the car.

Sophie read the headstone "Beloved wife and mother" and noted the date 10th October 2000. Gently she sat down on the faded autumn grass and stroked the ground affectionately.

"Oh mum. How can you have been down there since 2000 when you took Rebecca to the doctor with me only a couple of months ago? I've watched you play with Becky and Tori and I've seen how you love them. I must be totally insane or something because I remember everything we shared in those years and every visit. I hope you can't hear me because I hope none of this is real, and soon I'll be telling you all about it in person. Nothing more than another episode of my condition."

As she started to get up, she rested her hand on where she believed her mother's head would be, and as she did so she remembered every line on her mother's face. Her mum's 55-

year-old face and not the 46-year-old one that was supposed to have been buried here. She wiped away her tears and got up from the wet grass which had to soaked through her coat onto her cold wet thigh. Dejectedly she loitered her way back to Carl who was pacing back and forth beside the car, occasionally blowing into his hands to keep warm.

They greeted each other with some genuine affection and Sophie rested her head on his shoulder for the remainder of the journey.

Chapter 13

Having returned to hospital with a successful visit behind them, it was only a matter of another week before the suggestion was made that Sophie could return permanently to her family, after a couple more weekend visits.

Sophie volunteered to take the box room as she felt awkward occupying the largest room, when the house wasn't even hers. Carl was relieved to keep his room, so it was settled.

He was also secretly pleased to be able to remove her clothes from Kelly's wardrobe, and Sophie was secretly pleased that her new room was right next to Tommy's, enabling her to eavesdrop through the single brick wall. Carl had put locks on all the rooms as a precaution, disguised a gesture of privacy. Everyone smiled their approval, but each harboured their respective private views on the subject.

Tommy was still in fear of this sickly woman with the explosive temper. He didn't want her in his life, mother or not. He wished she would climb back into her hospital bed and go back to sleep forever leaving a space back in their lives for his real mum. For Kelly.

Carl wasn't sure about taking the situation on full time. He wasn't sure if he wanted to take Sophie on at all. There seemed no sign yet that she might metamorphize back into the woman he loved instead of this distracted, miserable, bad tempered, and astonishingly unattractive version of her.

Sophie was the only one who felt some excitement about the idea. She knew that if she moved in full time, Carl could not possibly manage to chaperone Tommy constantly, which meant she would get time alone with him. All she had to do was to convince them that she had made progress, and that meant making some effort to be her old self. She would try to be a real mother to Tommy and better company for Carl. If Tommy was connecting with Becky in that house, then that was the only place she wanted to be.

There are few things more astonishing in life than the human ability to adapt to a situation. To develop a routine to the extent that the abnormal becomes normal and the remarkable becomes very unremarkable.

In this household, during the remaining weekend trials, three people adapted. They developed a routine of normal family life around the abnormal practices of eavesdropping, mistrust, bolted doors, fear and suspicion.

Each night, Sophie listened at the adjoining wall for any hint of her old life in Tommy' bedroom. Carl watched both his housemates with a nervous interest, hoping to see signs of bonding, and tried with all his heart to find some desire for Sophie.

Nothing seemed to be changing as the days counted down to the planned moving in day. The barriers precluding them from real family life were neither eroding nor building, and so when the weekend visits were extended to permanent residency there was very little fuss about it. No-one celebrated it and no-one protested about it. It was just how it was.

Much to Carl's annoyance, Tommy was communicating with Kelly on a regular basis and had even spent the occasional night over at her house. He tried to discourage it but as Sophie was totally in support of ridding herself of the burden of motherhood from time to time, he was fighting a losing battle.

It gave her the opportunity to rummage through his room for evidence, or just to sit on his bed and listen for any sounds of John or her children, any glimmer of hope in escaping this hell she was now living.

She had no interest in pursuing a romantic relationship with Carl, and took every opportunity to lock herself away to research what she begun to refer to as, 'her book' She had told Carl she was writing her memories down in diary form, in the hope of getting it published one day.

In the quiet of her room, while Carl watched tv and wallowed in his own misery and regrets, she continued collating the facts from her previous life, anything she could remember from postcodes and phone numbers to the names of friends and work colleagues of John's. Surely, she could not have made all this up? and the postcodes definitely matched the area she thought she had lived in.

As she searched for logical explanations, she considered the possibility that she may not have jumped back and forth to another world but to another time in the same world. This explained the continuity and the idea gave her more than hope, it excited her each day as her certainty grew. She recalled those duplicated days right at the start and the more she scribbled and arranged her evidence the more convinced she became.

If this was some hiccup of time, then John and her girls had trod this earth and she needed to prove it. There were many bits of paper marked with physical facts but there was one that would not be dismissed. As she tirelessly categorised and recategorized her data, there was one weathered scrap of hospital notepad catching her eye. Written in the faintest of pencil in the smallest letters yet rising from the puzzle like a beacon, haunting her, willing her, and urging her to plot an expedition to find it.

She still had regular sessions with Anne and as they sat opposite one another one morning, while Tommy was in school and Carl at work, Sophie brough out a thick notebook which she knew would intrigue her guest.

"You assessing me now, are you? Or are you writing your memoirs?" Anne laughed as she took out her usual large folder.

"Maybe I am." Sophie smiled without clarifying which question she was responding to.

The two women smiled condescendingly at one another and then each took a sip of the coffee in front of them.

Both women were desperate for information from each other. Both wanted to get their hands on the ramblings of the other, but neither allowed it to show.

Anne was struggling with the paper she was writing on Sophie's case. She needed to draw similarities to her previous case, but apart from the early bursts of fantasy, Sophie seemed to have returned to normality. Either that, or she was cleverly concealing her illness.

Sophie was struggling to fill in the gaps of her disjointed collage, and believed Anne had the answers in the notes on her other case, the institutionalised suicidal woman of mystery. Either that, or she had made it all up to frighten Sophie into behaving.

Is wasn't a battle of wills here, it was a battle of strategic manipulation and in this, Anne should have had the edge.

"So, what do you present as the secret to your recovery in this publication of your memoirs?" Anne asked finally.

"Well, then it wouldn't be a secret would it?" Sophie smiled

Anne smiled back but she noted Sophie's demeanour. This woman was playing with her and if she was going to get her to open-up, she had to change her approach.

"I'll be honest with you Sophie. I'm trying to find similarities with you and my other case."

"Yes, I know you are," Sophie was still in the driving seat as she continued, "you are hoping to see some matching chaos inside my head."

"Is there any?"

"Why don't you tell me what you're expecting, and I'll tell you if anything matches?"

Both women toyed protectively but teasingly with their respective notes. Both wanted to trade but one was bound my patient confidentiality and the other by the desire to hold onto her liberty.

Anne was the first to speak.

"Have you ever had suicidal thoughts?"

"No."

Anne looked disappointed, as Sophie predicted. She knew the other woman was on suicide watch, so it was an obvious question.

"I did at one point," Sophie continued, "I thought it might have been a way back but now I know it isn't."

"How do you know?"

Sophie had the worm almost on the hook.

"I was only in a coma but if you're dead, you're dead right? No matter where your head is?"

Anne seemed disappointed and irritated.

"My other patient believes that dying in one life means only that."

"It's an idea I suppose, bit of a risk though, what makes her so sure?"

Anne couldn't stop herself. She needed the similarities and Sophie hadn't provided them adequately.

"Her mother killed herself because she believed there was a better life waiting, and just after she, did the dual existence started. The exact same experience her mother had written about in her diaries and when it happened, she found her mother again."

Sophie was scribbling in the back of the otherwise empty book.

"She said her mother only existed now in this other place, the better place."

Sophie was the one finding the similarities here. Her life with John had always been the better life. She stopped writing and stared at the page for a moment as she imagined the poor girl's desperation. She had felt it and she knew how powerful and urgent it felt. Anne was still talking.

"I suppose we all hope we are going to a better life eventually, don't we?" she mused, "we say it all the time."

"I'll write up a copy of my notes for you if you want?" Sophie offered, "perhaps you'll find the similarities earlier in them. I'm maybe just happy to be alive no matter where I ended up?"

Anne checked her watch and gulped the remainder of her coffee.

"That would be great. Will you have them done for next week?"

"I'll try."

Anne left the house feeling apprehensive. She'd said far too much and hadn't got anything out of it.

Sophie put the cups in the dishwasher feeling elated. She'd kept everything to herself and got exactly what she needed.

It felt like she was getting closer, unlike the poor girl Anne knew. Sophie wasn't on suicide watch, she had no-one shackling her to this world.

As the days passed by Tommy was also filling her with renewed hope.

Sometimes, late at night, she would listen with a glass to his wall and hear the whispering that had become so familiar to her. The whispering that Carl dismissed as sleep talk, but which she knew to be his secret contact with her family.

The jokes and secrets this little boy denied, filtered through the glass into her straining ears, always quiet enough to prevent her making sense of it, but loud enough to taunt her with the names of the people she loved. He was hiding his secrets and enjoying her misery. Bit by bit her resentment for her own son was growing inside her like a tumour and with it grew her determination to make him pay.

Chapter 14

Tommy was always full of life and fun, when he returned from one of his regular visits to Kelly's house, spilling out lots of amusing stories about her and Jake. The contrast to the home he was living in, was blatantly obvious and both Carl and Sophie had come to dread the first hour of his return.

Sophie knew the game he was playing. Trying to show his dad what a huge failure she was as a partner and mother, in comparison to what other people had. It would cause the lioness in her to awaken as she resolved to rise to the challenge, but her efforts were usually short lived.

Carl tried to be happy for Kelly. He knew he had treated her badly and she deserved some happiness, but from every one of Tommy's stories jealousy burned. He consoled himself with the hope that they were all a clever act Kelly was putting on to get this exact response. To make him throw Sophie out on her ear and ride on his white stallion to get her. It had to be, because in all the years he had lived with her she had never once hosted a family Karaoke or face-painting contest. But when he lay alone at night, and the image of Jake now prevented him from using Kelly as his fantasy relief, he considered the awful possibility that she may be genuinely happy. This latter thought was more than he could bear.

Sophie noticed the effect Tommy's accounts of his visits were having on Carl, and she knew he had to be making comparisons to the dull existence he was now living. If she wasn't careful, she could lose Carl as well as John and, as she watched him sip from his bottle of beer, she was reminded of a time long ago, when they would cuddle up contentedly on the couch together.

Those blissful years after his proposal, and before she stupidly started to question their love with her ridiculous doubts and lists of pros and cons. He seemed to feel her gaze and turned to smile straight at her. It was more than his recent smiles of polite acknowledgement. It was a plea for her to fix this and it closed her throat with dread and pain. The pain from realising that she'd thrown away the life they'd been heading for, of missing her mum's final moths, but mostly the pain of missing the years they should have shared nurturing the baby they had made together. The child she knew she would have loved, the child she now despised.

As she loaded the dishwasher, she knew that current situation was not sustainable, and the dull routine of three people tolerating each other whilst all preoccupied with their own agendas had to change.

She looked over at Tommy sitting at his dad's feet and wondered what he really thought of her, and of his life now that she had returned. She knew she'd been a huge disappointment to him, and her maternal instincts had failed them both. He'd expected her to wake up and sweep him into her arms, desperate to make amends for the missing years and instead, she had rejected him. She had done worse than reject him, she had resented his existence which had replaced that of her daughters.

It wasn't his fault and she knew she had to try to force her heart to accept him as her own. She was a firm believer that behaviour breeds behaviour and maybe if she started to act more warmly to her son, he would start to return some of that warmth.

She closed the door of the dishwasher with a lighter heart. Nothing but good could come of her efforts to transform this fiasco into a real family.

It would be a slap in the face for Kelly who was still gloating in the glory of being Tommy's only functional mother. It would also stop Carl from worrying about leaving Tommy alone with her, and from regretting the fact that she ever woke up in the first place. As the machine sprang into action with its gush of water, she walked cheerily for the first time, to join her two boys in the lounge.

Winning their affection became her new priority because it was the only direction that offered any chance of change. She needed things to change. She needed her relationship with Tommy to change because if he learned to love her, he might stop taunting her and lying to her. He might invite her into his world of whispers and open the door she was so desperately seeking.

Tommy however, seemed content enough with his lot. He still had his dad's full attention and regular visits to Kelly where he was spoiled rotten. He had even found some positivity in the freaky woman who had returned from the grave to wreak havoc over the household, because her behaviour provided him with endless funny stories to relay to Kelly and Jake. They would reel with laughter when he did his impressions of her in her 'incident room' with its ever-changing arrangements of the same bits of paper. There were times when he wanted to blurt out the secret of his dad's love affair with Kelly just to hurt this pathetic intruder, but Kelly had given him reason to keep his silence.

"If Sophie knew about your dad and me, she would never allow you to come here and visit." She whispered to him one night when he was having a tantrum and threatening to tell her.

It was a good reason to keep the secret, the best reason, and he was not going to risk his visits to Kelly's for anything. Kelly felt secure in Tommy's life. She had held onto her position as his mother, and she loved that Carl and Sophie were still in separate rooms. She loved to recall all the reassuring stories of disharmony Tommy passed on as she slept soundly in Jake's arms. She loved that Carl's dream, the dream that had tortured her for all those years, had finally been delivered to him in a pile of ashes and there was no chance at all that anything would transform it into the fairy-tale he'd imagined.

The next night Sophie showered before Tommy got home from school. She pulled the straggles that had become her hair into a top knot and secured it with a pin. She brightened her face with a shimmery moisturiser and curled her dark lashes with black mascara. Her reflection was still a long way from the radiant young woman who had last peered back at her from a mirror, but it was still a big improvement on the listless bedraggled being who had been mooching around unwashed for the last few weeks.

By the time Tommy arrived home she had stew and dumplings on the stove, and the sweet aroma of spiced apple crumble wafted warmly in the air. Tommy commented immediately as he threw down his gym bag and pushed back his rebellious blonde fringe.

"Mmmmmmmm!"

Sophie smiled to herself as she stirred the stew. This was going to be much easier than she'd imagined.

"Go and get a bath to warm you up love. I've filled it with bubbles, dinner will be ready soon."

Tommy didn't need telling twice and within seconds Sophie could hear the water splashing around.

As the door opened for the second time, she was ready with a glass of red wine for the man of the house. He took it from her, too shocked to speak. She could see the suspicion in his eyes as he wondered if this was another manifestation of the same madness, but she ignored his scepticism and proceeded to dish out dinner.

Tommy retuned from his bath and started a conversation about bonfire night plans. Sophie knew this was an opportunity to unite her new family and to steal the reins from Kelly, who had been the unchallenged organiser of all family celebrations since Tommy's birth.

"Can we go to the one in Scarborough again dad?"

"We could have our own bonfire in the garden." Sophie suggested.

Tommy's face lit up.

"Can we dad? Can we have one of our own and build it ourselves?"

Carl gave a few seconds of consideration for his lawn before re-aligning his priorities.

"I suppose we could. It would mean I could have a beer for once"

Sophie and Tommy were finally united in a simultaneous triumphant smile.

"Can Kelly come?" Tommy gushed.

"Of course." Sophie made sure she was the first to reassure him as she hid her annoyance.

"Great. What can we make to eat?"

Sophie collected his empty plate and playfully ruffled his hair in exactly the way Carl did so often.

"I'm sure we could make a few toffee apples and jacket potatoes!"

Tommy smiled at his dad, but Carl's smile was more restrained, as he tried to fathom what was behind this sudden personality change, and how long it was likely to last.

After dinner, Tommy showed her his iPad and she became instantly interested in how it might help her to find evidence of her life in London. Tommy showed her some maps and she knew it could help her to at least verify or disprove some of her memories of places and street names. Tommy's air of superiority was humiliating but welcome, as he showed her some of the things it could do. She smiled at the possibility of getting some time on it in private, she also smiled at how easy it was to gain the trust of a stupid child.

After tucking him in bed, she sneaked the gadget to her room and attempted to use it, but she couldn't even get into it. She'd forgotten the part about the password! Angrily she returned it to the dining room, knowing that it might arouse suspicion if she woke Tommy to ask for it. Deflated and annoyed with herself, she curled up on the sofa in her pyjamas and stared blankly at the tv screen as she retreated into her world of memories and hope.

Although Carl and Sophie were living together, there had been no resurrection of any physical affection between them. It was a difficult topic to raise after all this time living as house mates, and there was no naturally progressive courtship going on.

It seemed hard to imagine how such a thing might start up again, especially as they had fallen into the routine of sitting in separate chairs and engaging only in conversations of a practical nature. The platonic status quo, however, suited Sophie perfectly as her devotion and loyalty to John failed to diminish, and the love she remembered failed to fade.

Carl had his own reasons for making no attempt to resume their sexual relationship, but it had nothing to do with loyalty or love. He simply didn't fancy her. Nothing about her attracted or aroused him. He could clearly remember how passionately he used to feel, but he found it impossible to accept that his vibrant sexy fiancée and this dull mousy woman in fluffy pyjamas could be the same person. The chemistry simply wasn't there in the way it had been when she had been a curvy, healthy, glowing young woman with thick shiny dark hair and a tanned, toned body. Shamefully it was that simple.

So habitually sprawled across his King-sized bed, Carl stared at the ceiling and fantasized about the nights Kelly had filled the empty space beside him, while Sophie wrapped her own arms around her boy-like chest in her single bed and tried to sleep.

In the early hours one day, a remarkable thing happened, she woke from a dream in which she had been with John. It was an actual dream in the way that she remembered dreams were meant to be. A series of random events without detail. Snippets and flashes of people and faces and short conversations with no logical progression. She sat up in bed feeling the dampness of her pyjama top, as it clung to her back with perspiration. She peeled her wet hair from her neck with a sweep of her hand and expelled the air from her lungs as though she were blowing out a candle.

This was the kind of dream she remembered. The kind of dream everyone thought she had been having. It was nothing like. There was no comparison. Today's dream had been normal, and she knew that the John in it had been no more real than fairies in the garden. She knew the difference. In that single moment she knew without doubt, that her other life with John and the girls had not been this sort of dream, it had been real. She didn't know how it was possible or how she could explain this wasted body, but she did know that she had been somewhere all these years, and that it had definitely been no dream.

She lay awake for the rest of the night trying to find a logical explanation. The possibility that her spirit or soul or whatever you may choose to call it, had found an alternative place to reside. A place where she had another body and another world of souls to share her time with. That maybe there are several worlds coexisting at the same time but very few people have the ability to move from one to the other.

Her inner ramblings became more and more absurd as she became mentally and emotionally exhausted until she finally drifted off to sleep only moments before the rest of the house woke up.

As she sat at the kitchen table filtering through the possible scenarios that had infiltrated her mind during that long restless night, there was one recurring idea. If the key was time, then perhaps one world might cross over the other eventually. If she could find a single piece of physical undisputable evidence here that belonged to her other life.

The tea she thought she had poured only a few seconds ago was barely warm as she had been lost in her thoughts. How easily time loses perspective. As she took another sip, her attention flew once again to that small scrap of paper written in faint pencil.

The one piece of her giant jigsaw that never failed to draw her eyes to it, taunting her and compelling her to act on it. She left the table and returned to her room where she slid the collage out from under her bed. She didn't need to search for the note she wanted, as she knew exactly where it was. Sat between the notes of 'red sports car' and 'six strides north' was the word 'pepper pot.'

As she prepared Tommy's cereal she was already plotting. As soon as the house was empty, she was on her way to the small garage to buy herself a road map.

"You're lucky we even have any of those," the man laughed, "everyone uses Google nowadays."

"I like something real." She smiled with bitter irony

As she opened the pages of the map, she felt new optimism. If she could get back to the mountain, she was sure she could find the place it was buried and if it was there, it would at least prove if her two lives were sharing a physical world. Optimism grew to excitement as she found a hotel close to the foot of the mountain on the map. She hadn't noticed the name of the hotel they stayed in, but it was there, and the fact that a hotel existed in the place she remembered was enough to fuel her excitement.

She knew she was on the right track and finding the little pot would give her the certainty she needed. The courage to find John and be reunited with her little daughters who will be wondering what happened to their mummy. She had to go, and the urgency of it grew as she cleared the breakfast dishes. She was going to return to them…whatever it took.

She sat back down with the map and tried to work out how long the journey would take and if it was possible to do it in a day. Carl had arranged to take Tommy out for the day on Saturday. They were going for fireworks for the bonfire party with Carl's parents, having lunch in town and then to the afternoon football game. If she got everything ready the night before, she could be out of the door the moment they left and be back before they noticed.

She scurried to her room and bundled together some warm clothes, stacking them ready for her escape. She found an old rucksack in Tommy's room and a trowel and torch in the shed. She was ready.

On Friday night, curled up in her usual chair she tried to establish the exact timing for her escape.

"What time do you want Tommy to be ready for tomorrow?"

"Tomorrow?"

"Yes, you're taking him to pick the fireworks with your mum and dad and then to the match remember?"

"Oh shit! I totally forgot. Do you mind taking him Soph? I have to work tomorrow."

Sophie couldn't believe this was happening to her.

"Work? You never work on Saturdays!"

"I know but I've got so many MOT s to do, I said I'd go in and get them done. We've got a real backlog and if I don't work Saturday you won't see me until midnight every day next week."

"I don't believe this!" She snapped wishing she didn't have to see him at all, on any night.

"What's the big deal? I'm sure you're capable of driving him for fireworks and having a bit of lunch with mum and dad. I don't know why you avoid them so much. They were thrilled to have you back and you hardly speak to them now.

Sophie couldn't explain the real reason she felt uncomfortable around his parents because it was just a memory from what he would describe as her 'mad dreams' She could hardly say that the last time she saw them was at his inquest when they had spat their hatred at her for killing their son.

She thought for a moment, knowing she had to back off a bit "I don't mind seeing them I just feel embarrassed at how I look and I'm just not ready for them gushing all over me."

"Yes, I get that, but we really need the money now I'm the only one bringing a wage into that house Sophie. You might even enjoy the match. You used to love footy."

"Yes of course. Don't worry I'll sort it." She smiled, already trying to come up with plan B, while totally missing his slip up on revealing that there used to be more than one wage coming into the house.

She was too pre-occupied with her dilemma to listen to his excuses and now there didn't seem to be a way of making this happen. Carl had ruined everything.

If she postponed it, she might not get another chance for weeks. She was going and that was that. It was his own fault if the fireworks were not collected and his parents didn't get lunch with Tommy. All she had to do was to get away. Once she was on the road, he couldn't stop her, and she didn't care what he'd have to say about it when he found out. She could deal with that later. Her only issue was what she could do with Tommy.

Before she allowed herself to drift off to sleep, she came up with a plan. Desperate it might be, but a plan, nevertheless.

On Saturday morning she stayed in bed until she heard Carl's car leave and then rushed to wake Tommy.

"Morning sleepy head. How would you like to go on an adventure?"

Tommy was still extremely nervous around Sophie and sat up a little defensively.

"What kind of adventure?"

"The kind that takes you up a mountain looking for treasure?"

"But we are supposed to be getting fireworks this morning? Does dad know about it?"

"No but we can call him later and tell him about the change of plan."

Tommy's frown deepened and Sophie knew she was frightening him.

"Look. Let's get ready and then we can ring dad and ask him what he thinks."

"Ok." Tommy took the clothes Sophie had picked out and headed for the bathroom.

While he was getting washed, she rang Carl.

"I have been thinking about using today to spend some time on my own with Tommy instead, if that's ok with you?"

"You already have the day planned Sophie. Fireworks and lunch with mum and dad then footy remember?"

"We can get fireworks in the week and football doesn't do much for conversation does it? I'm trying to bond with our son here."

"Fine by me. But you'll have to cancel mum and dad. Good luck with that."

"Might be better coming from you?"

"Fine, fine. Put Tommy on."

As Tommy returned, Sophie handed him the phone.

"It's dad," she smiled, "he said it's fine to have our adventure"

Tommy took the phone from her and went out onto the landing. Sophie could hear him whispering as she paced nervously. Eventually he returned.

"So, are we going?" She asked trying to sound enthusiastic, fun and friendly. Resentfully masking the annoyance she was feeling, for having to cajole the stupid boy.

Tommy shrugged "Guess so."

"Come on then, let's have our adventure." She grinned as she moved the trowel from her bag to his school bag and replaced it with a cake slice in hers.

"Tools for the mission." she grinned, wishing she could drop him off at his grandparents on the way and get on with this alone. The little boy smiled back, he was temporarily back in favour for not causing a fuss, and within ten minutes they were in the car with sandwiches and tools on board.

As she started the engine she looked over at the little boy. His innocent, trusting blue eyes illuminated his cherub like face and she felt an unexpected warmth for him. He noticed her gaze and frowned at her. She smiled back with genuine affection. The kind of affection between a mother and child. If this really was her living son, then maybe it was time to allow some maternal feeling through. If today turned out to be a fool's errand, if her other life was nothing more than a coma induced fantasy, then she could do much worse than to embrace this new life. Maybe Carl and Tommy could give her more satisfaction than she dared to believe.

Tommy switched on the radio and they both sang along to "Single Ladies" They had sung the chorus a couple of times when the relevance of it registered with Sophie.

"What year did this come out?"

Tommy shrugged.

"Tommy, we both know the words!"

Tommy frowned. He wasn't getting the point.

Sophie, on the other hand, was consumed by the point. She had danced around the room to it with Becky and Tori not that long ago.

"Did anyone play music to me? Did they play pop music? Did I ever speak any of the words? Did this song get played a lot?

Tommy didn't respond to the bombardment. He looked frightened by her sudden outburst. She needed to calm down.

"Tommy?"

"What?"

"Did anyone play this to me?"

"I don't know."

"Well think."

Silence.

"Tommy!"

"I don't know!" His face was starting to crumple but Sophie was desperate for him to concentrate on what she was asking.

"Please think about it." She tried to be more gentle.

"I am thinking."

"You're not. You're messing with your phone!" She snatched his phone and held in the air as ransom.

"Maybe. I think so. Yes. I don't know."

"Is it yes or you don't know?"

Tommy resorted to a shrug and she knew she had to stop bullying him. She handed back the phone and smiled through her anger.

"I'm sorry Tommy. It's just that some things feel really important to me. You understand, don't you?"

"Suppose." He shrugged again and she fought the temptation to shake him hard.

After a long silence he spoke.

"Dad used to play lots of music to you, and he told grandad that he knew you were listening to it more and more, as the years went on."

"Do you know when?"

"When what?" He frowned.

"When did he start to feel that I could hear it?"

"Dunno. He said you were different when I was a baby, so he stopped doing it for a while, but as I got older something changed."

"What changed?"

Silence.

"Tommy. What changed?"

"I heard him telling grandad that you were on your way back but when I asked about it, he said not to tell anyone. Not about that and not about the extra visits to wake you up, because they were a secret surprise."

"Not to say anything to who?"

"To Kelly of course." He had spoken without realising what he'd done.

Sophie's eyes became fixed on the road ahead, as she fought to rationalise Tommy's words. She missed her junction. She pulled up and turned the car around still without speaking. Her mind was incapable of processing anything at all.

"Have we gone the wrong way?" Tommy was looking frightened again.

The atmosphere had changed dramatically, and she knew it. She had to follow her plan and deal with this later. Perhaps it wouldn't matter later anyway. She tried to get them back on track by talking about the adventure they were about to have.

"So, are you ready to look for buried treasure?"

Tommy looked even more uncomfortable and didn't answer.

"Tommy?"

"What treasure?"

"It'll be fun. You'll see. I buried something a long time ago and we are going to see if we can find it."

Tommy became more interested. He remembered the stories Kelly had read to him about pirates and treasure chests buried in secret coves.

"Is it gold?"

"No exactly, but if you help me find it, I'll buy you something nice as a reward."

Tommy was back on side as they made their way westward, along the roads Sophie had travelled with John, when she had filled his car with crumbs so many years ago. After a couple of miles, they pulled into a layby to eat their sandwiches and share stories about pirates and secret maps.

It was well after 2 pm when the formidable outline of the Mam Torr rose before them, just as she had remembered it. Hostile and barren it stood against the winter skyline. The sleeping Giant with the power to deliver or shatter her dreams with the secret it held in its soil.

She parked the car at the foot of the mountain and looked toward the footpath she knew so well. The familiar wooden gate she had last opened with her other hand resting in John's. She looked around to try to get her bearings and establish the direction of the hotel they had stayed in, somewhere between the mountain and Loose Hill. Perhaps she may recognise it from higher up the mountain. She took Tommy's hand and gently tugged him towards the path leading to the foot of the mountain.

"Are you ready to climb?" She smiled. It wasn't a question.

"Yup" Tommy was looking much happier and almost excited, as he strained his neck to try to get a peek at the summit.

Hand in hand the little boy and his biological, estranged, unstable mother stepped through the small wooden gate, onto the cobble path and started the accent.

She tried to keep his spirits high by singing songs she hoped Tommy would know, but the gusts of wind stole most of the lyrics, blowing them back down the mountain before they could be heard. The mountain felt intimidating and threatening with its desolate trail now only visible for a few yards in front. The fog had descended quickly, and as they pushed forward against the gusting wind, those few yards of visibility seemed to be shortening with each twist of the slippery path, and the already failing daylight.

She marched on, with Tommy obediently holding her hand but the atmosphere between them had changed. She could feel his fear, and she knew it wasn't fear of the mountain, but fear of her sanity. His previous chatter about the treasure and his reward of new trainers had quietened.

"It's not far now," she said cheerily, "another few turns in this path and we can dig for the treasure and then go home."

She heard him mutter something, but it was inaudible, and it didn't matter anyway. She tugged him along as he battled against the wind, which repeatedly thrust him backwards in ever increasing gusts. He had taken his trowel out of his rucksack in readiness at the foot of the mountain, holding it akimbo like a sword into battle, but now it hung limply in his small frozen hand. She wished she had remembered the gloves a mother would have remembered.

Suddenly the ground flattened. Sophie let go of Tommy's hand to protect her eyes from the wind, as she tried to peer through the patches of fog that were being swirled around them, offering small windows of visibility that were snatched away again as quickly as they appeared.

"We made it!" She cheered as the small summit monument flashed momentarily before her.

She made an attempt to celebrate with a high five, but she heard the clink of his trowel as he slumped down onto a small boulder with exhaustion. She suspected he had started to cry, but she didn't have time to pander to him right now. She needed to get her bearings, but nothing looked familiar through the pockets of visibility.

She started to wonder if she had made the accent with John from a different direction, but there were no other man-made tracks to the summit that she could see. Fear started to creep over her as she began to doubt that any memory of this mountain was real. Any chance of finding her bearings from the view, or the hotel nestled between the hills, had been swallowed by the damn fog and now every direction looked the same.

She stood at the monument, trying to turn her back on the place she thought the track had ended, and took six large strides. It took her to a plateau. A flat stretch of earth with no outcrops. It wasn't the place.

As she walked along the top of the mountain, the daylight deserted them, stealing the colours away with it, and as the green grass turned to iron grey tufts, and shadows played their tricks on her memory, she recognised nothing at all. She took out her torch with freezing hands and flashed it desperately in each direction. An outcrop of rocks a few yards away struck a chord.

"This is the place Tommy. I'm certain of it."

Her burst of enthusiasm and triumph, stirred something in the frozen little boy, who had been looking forward to the digging part, and now that he had suffered to get here, he didn't want to miss the good part. He picked up his bag and walked towards her voice.

"What does it look like?" he shouted, "this treasure?"

"You'll see!" She called back as she started to stride out six large paces from the monument in this new direction. It took her to the exact spot she recognised.

She took out her cake slice as Tommy started to dig in the spot with his trowel.

"We can start here and then widen the search." She was already digging.

The icy wind burned her cheeks, and her hands were numb, as she tried to stab the cake slice into the hardened ground. She looked over at Tommy who was rubbing his frozen dirty hands together for warmth and looking over to her defeatedly, as though anticipating the declaration of an end to this madness.

Sophie looked at his forlorn figure, silhouetted against the dusky sky, battling to keep balance in the vicious wind, stamping his feet for warmth, and appealing to his mother to save him from this hostile place. But her heart wasn't melted by the pleading eyes of her gentle son, because this might be her only chance to find the pepper pot, and she wasn't going to give up until she was absolutely sure, one way or the other. This was no time for molly coddling, so she merely punched him playfully and went back to her own spot.

The ground was frozen solid, and the cake slice curled on impact. She looked over at Tommy who had the steel trowel, which was barely disturbing the soil at all, as he nudged the tufts of course grass back and forth in a token gesture to appease her. It had only ever been a game to him and now it was a game he didn't want to play anymore, and as she tried again to thrust the fragile slice into the unyielding ground, her frustration was building. She dug and watched, dug and watched. Could this arrogant boy really believe this was all about him? That she'd gone to all this trouble to give him an adventure? She tried to use the slice as a spoon to make use of the curl at its point, frantically scooping at the stubborn roots while pulling at the grass with her frozen hands, but after half an hour of digging there had been almost no progress at all.

She slumped back to rest for a second and peered over at Tommy again. He was wafting the trowel back and forth over the tips of a patch of long grass humming to himself.

She jumped to her feet and ran at the boy, lurching for the trowel so aggressively that she knocked him from his squatting position face down on the ground, seizing her prize as she screamed at him.

"What the hell are you doing! Do you think this is game you stupid spoiled brat?!"

Tommy made no attempt to get up. He turned his head to look at her, but remained face down in the grass, as though terrified that any movement might trigger another outburst.

Sophie took her precious trowel and started to dig with renewed vigour. She was going to find the pot with or without him and now she had a fighting chance at it. As she ripped out clumps of mountain grass, she threw them over her shoulder to give herself a clear view of the patch of soil she needed to dig. Tommy didn't move.

She stood up to appraise the patch of open soil which now resembled a tiny allotment. A rectangle of brown earth cut neatly into the overgrown grassland. She rechecked the paces back to the monument and nodded her satisfaction. It was somewhere in this patch, and as renewed hope lifted her mood, it also lifted away the anger towards Tommy who had raised himself to a sitting position.

"Come on soldier, show me what you're made of. I can feel how close we are to finding it now. Only losers give up. You are not a loser, are you?"

Tommy shook his head slowly from side to side and as she took his hand to relocate him to another digging spot, he obediently complied with the flimsy bent cake slice held forlornly in his small red hand.

"Dig down to about four inches. No deeper than that."

"Ok." Tommy replied with neither enthusiasm nor reluctance, as they started their task from opposite ends of the allotment patch.

It was completely dark and the torch, which she had tried to prop up against tufts of grass, provided meagre visibility.

"Use your hands to feel for it," she bellowed into the wind, "you won't be able to see it now."

Tommy didn't answer, but she knew he was still there from the sound of the cake slice stabbing the ground with more gusto than his previous effort. Perhaps he had learned his lesson.

She had made progress to about halfway when his crouching figure came back into view, and she heard his phone beep.

"What's that?"

Tommy paused before replying.

"Nothing."

"Is someone texting you?"

Tommy shrugged, but his body language told her he was hiding something.

"Have you been texting someone?"

"No" He said, immediately protecting his pocket with his hand.

"Who have you been texting?" Sophie became worried that he had told someone exactly what they were doing.

All maternal feeling evaporated once again, taking with it any previous pledge to try to love him as her son.

This wretched child was going to ruin everything, and when it came down to choosing between John and her pathetic son, there was no contest.

She had chosen John over everything, time and again. Over Carl, over Niki, over Tori's treatment and over life itself. Nothing was more important, even though she knew it was wrong. She knew her desire to please him was poisonous, and this dreadful fear of losing him was malignant, but it was still her only goal. Here on this mountain, behaving like a mad woman, with her own son half frozen and scared to death, it was still the only thing that mattered to her. The only thing she was living for… or would die for.

Tommy returned immediately to his digging with renewed enthusiasm, as though trying to distract her from the conversation about his phone. It worked, because even if he had been texting there was nothing more important to her right now than the last few feet of untouched earth, and she was content that he had returned to help.

Another half hour passed, and the freezing fog numbed her bleeding fingers, as she clawed at the earth with one hand using the trowel in the other. Her nails on one hand were broken and clogged with soil, the wrist of her other hand ached from the persistent jamming against the handle of the trowel and her knees were numb from the pressure of kneeling on her fleshless bones. Tommy was now no more than a small crouched shadow a few yards away. He didn't seem to be digging any more, but trying to protect himself from the icy wind, as he held his legs close to his body with his arms.

Somewhere deep inside her heart there was an ache for the plight of this fragile motherless, frightened child, she could sense the emotion that would have compelled her to embrace him, to forgo this madness and take him home to warmth, comfort and sanity. The protective instinct had, at last, been roused but still it was no match for her obsession with proving John's existence. In an instant, it was snuffed out as easily as a damp match. The only remnant of the moment was translated into a few words of kindness for the boy.

"Won't be long now" She comforted, but Tommy didn't reply. He remained steadfast in his position as though no longer hearing her.

Sophie realised she was going to have to cover the remainder of the patch on her own, but it didn't matter. In a few minutes she would know the truth and she was not going to give up now. In the distance, some way down the track she caught sight of a flickering light which seemed of little importance until Tommy also spotted it and jumped to his feet.

"It's just a light from the village!" She shouted over to him, through the gusting wind, which was now infused with fine icy rain, cutting through the fog.

Tommy didn't reply but seemed to be anxious about the light as he paced up and down, peering along the track below, tracking it as though it were an approaching demon.

Sophie was making good progress, but the pepper pot had not yet been found. She thrust both hands into the soil and rummaged frantically like a child destroying a sandcastle. Briefly her hand hit something solid. Solid and round, but she had already rummaged past it before the information had travelled to her brain and back to her hands. Slowly she retraced the trail her hands had made, and after a few slow deliberate swirls she felt it again.

She could hear her own heart beating, feel it pounding against her chest, pumping blood so strongly against her lungs that she could barely breathe. Slowly and gently she drew the item out of the dampness as she reached for her torch with a hand that shook so rapidly, she dropped it several times before finally capturing it in a determined grip.

As she held it up into the light, soil fell from it and as the soil continued to fall, the small solid cylinder emptied. Its weight lightened until she could barely feel any weight at all. She held the torch on it for the longest time, hoping that it's illumination would transform the small section of plastic pipe back into the pepper pot she had imagined. The plastic pipe remained a plastic pipe as the last few grains of the impacted soil that had tricked her, fell mockingly onto her lap leaving the shell in her hand. Her hope drained with it, leaving the empty shell of her heart now barely beating at all.

She moved the torch to the meagre patch of untouched ground yet to be searched, but the huge disappointment had taken its toll, and she needed a moment to recover.

In the distance she thought she heard a voice.

Quickly she resumed her search as though time was running out.

"Toooo-mmy!" It was the kind of singsong voice one uses when calling a missing dog

She listened for a moment, and then turned to speak to Tommy. The skyline around her was empty. Tommy's pacing figure had disappeared, and the disappointment was quickly replaced with anger at his disobedience, when she already had so much to deal with. There was not even a single second in which she worried as a mother, for his safety.

Just a few more minutes and her questions would be answered. She picked up the trowel again and stabbed fiercely at the remaining patch

"What the fuck?" Carl bellowed.

Sophie looked up into his horrified eyes, as Kelly's silhouette emerged at his side. Wrapped firmly around her waist were Tommy's arms, clinging to her like a baby chimp to its mother, with his terrified face half buried in her breast.

For several seconds no-one moved or spoke. As the wind blew around them, over them and through them, they remained steadfast as each assessed the others. Each waiting for another to speak.

Kelly was the one to break the deadlock as she tugged Carl aside to whisper to him in private, but the wind swept up her whisper and delivered it efficiently to Sophie.

"She's insane, how could you leave her alone with Tommy?!"

Carl's expression softened from rage to sympathetic acceptance, as he extended his hand to Sophie's. He took her soil encrusted bloodied hand in his, and helped her up from her neat, rectangular patch of madness.

"Come on Sophie. It's ok." He said softly, as though trying to coax an animal from a cage.

Her dirty blood-smudged face turned upwards as her wild eyes searched his expression for any signs of trickery. There were none. Gently he peeled the straggles of windblown hair from her damp face and eased her to her feet.

She leaned against him defeatedly, as he guided her in the direction of the footpath to start the descent. Kelly and Tommy were also still coupled as they led the way. She felt grateful for Carl's gallantry and support, but she knew everything had changed.

Defeatedly, she started the journey down the mountain, consumed by the taste of regret she knew she had yet to feast on in the wretched days to come. The futile mission, the acceptance that there was no pepper pot on this earth, the knowledge that she had sabotaged her only family. But there was another bitter taste starting to seep in. It came from the inadvertent revelations of a careless little boy's chatter. It was the taste of betrayal, and as she walked behind Kelly, who was still comforting the clinging chimp, she was haunted by it.

Had this woman, who saved her from certain death, then proceeded to steal her life? She didn't want to believe it. She didn't want it to destroy the gratitude and love she'd been feeling towards Kelly, and replace it with hatred, resentment and jealousy.

She flashed her torch directly at Kelly and watched those perfectly rounded buttocks sway back and forth in crimson, size ten ski pants and black puffa jacket, embellished with perfectly matching crimson trim, and marvelled at how, in the heat of an emergency, Kelly had still managed to turn herself out so impeccably. This was, without a doubt, a woman who was hell bent on impressing a man.

Chapter 15

Earlier that day, Kelly had been sipping a cup of coffee whilst waiting for Mrs Adams hair colour to take, when her phone announced the arrival of a text. She had picked it up, expecting a saucy remark from Jake in response to the one she had sent ten minutes before, but was surprised to see it was from Tommy.

Her heart skipped a beat, as it always did whenever there was an unexpected opportunity to make contact with Carl. She was really trying with Jake, but any sign of being wanted or needed by either of them still awakened something in her. It breathed life back into the hope, she had tried to lay to rest a thousand times.

"I'm scared. Don't call." Was all the message said.

Quickly she sent a message back.

"Why? Where are you?"

"Sophie has taken me to a mountain, but she is acting crazy. It's getting dark and I'm scared."

"It's ok Tommy. Do you know where you are?"

"No but it took hours to get here."

"Do you know the name of a town or the mountain?"

"I think it was Mam something."

"Mam Torr?"

"Yes! Yes, that's it."

"I'll get dad. Keep your phone close – we're on our way."

Without checking on Mrs Adams, Kelly fled from the shop to the car outside, calling Carl on the way.

"What on earth were you thinking, letting her take Tommy anywhere?" She screamed down the phone, but Carl was too distraught to defend himself.

Within ten minutes they were heading west towards the M1 and silently praying for Tommy's safe return to them. Kelly was barking directions at Carl, like he had never driven the familiar road before, whilst she continued to send messages to Tommy with shaking hands. Stress and urgency had manifested itself in mis-spelt muddled words, that she had to keep erasing and re writing as the car veered left and right on the country lanes.

Gently Carl's hand touched hers and she looked over to him despairingly. Instantly the bond between them was repaired. They were parents in fear for the safety of their child. This was a feeling neither Jake nor Sophie would ever understand because the reality was, that she and Carl were his only real parents, and both would lay down their life for him.

She stoked his trembling hand.

"I know. I know." Nothing more needed to be said.

"What are you doing?" Kelly messaged.

"Climbing the path but she might catch me texting."

"Don't text any more then darling. Dad and I will find you... I promise" It was a promise Kelly had no intension of breaking.

Hours later they finally arrived at the foot of the mountain and saw Sophie's car

"Should we have called the Police?" Kelly panicked suddenly.

"Text him again and check he's ok." Was Carl's response.

Kelly tapped at her phone and waited. It pinged reassuringly and she smiled "He's ok."

Leigh Oakley

"Come on then." Carl pulled her by the hand as they raced toward the wooden gate. The blustery rugged path, which had proved such a difficult climb for a little boy and a frail, wasted woman, was a piece of cake to two comparatively fit parents desperate to rescue their child. Striding swiftly and methodically they cut through the wind like it was a nothing more than a mild summer breeze, and as they arrived together at the summit sweating and breathless, Kelly took a few deep breaths and then called Tommy's name.

There was no reply. Hand in hand they marched along the path as Kelly continued to call.

"Mum! Dad!"

"Oh, thank God," Carl sobbed, "thank God." As he scooped Tommy into his arms.

The three of them clung together for a few moments, as they allowed the relief to dissolve the fear and anxiety of the past few hours. Kelly cuddled Tommy tightly in gratitude. It was gratitude to fate for his safety, gratitude to God for allowing her to be the person to save him, and gratitude most of all to Tommy for screaming the word mum the moment he saw her. He had healed a part of her she hadn't known to be damaged, and once again she was re-evaluating her life.

They gently released one another from the embrace and continued along the path in search of the mad woman who had caused this. After a short distance of walking along the path a spectacle came into view. Sophie hadn't heard them approaching as they moved closer to view the mumbling, crouching figure frantically tearing at the dark damp earth of the mountain summit.

As they returned to the two parked cars, Carl ushered Sophie towards the passenger seat of her own car and nodded to Kelly to take Tommy in his. It seemed sensible to keep Tommy away from her, and Kelly was relieved to be able to comfort Tommy alone. She also wanted to make sure Carl would be taking Sophie directly back to the hospital, but they had no privacy to have that conversation.

Tommy slept soundly in the back seat all the way home, and Kelly was content to have him in her care. She was looking forward to tucking him into his bed and intended to insist on spending the night with him. She had a warm gush of nostalgia as she drove towards the house that had been her home, with the child that had been her son, safely sleeping behind her. The undeniable feeling that she was going home.

As she took the final turn onto the street, she felt the blood drain from her face when she saw Carl's car already parked. He hadn't had time to drop her at the hospital or anywhere else.

Gingerly she peeled Tommy from the back seat and guided him sleepily up the path to the front door.

Inside Sophie was sitting at the kitchen table and Carl was making tea.

"I'll take Tommy to our house" She announced without negotiation.

"It's ok," Sophie said softly, "I don't blame you, but I am no threat to Tommy I promise."

"Well it's a chance I would rather not take if you don't mind." She spat hugging Tommy closer.

Kelly was feeling angry at the entire situation. She felt angry that Carl had put Tommy in such danger in the first place and even more angry that he hadn't dumped her off at the nearest loony bin on the way back. She was angry that she'd had to leave work to sort their stupid mess, but most of all she was angry at herself for being the mug. Again.

The reckless drama had catapulted her back into Carl's life so completely, and all progress she had made in emotionally dissecting herself from it, had been undone in a matter of hours.

She had been summoned back into her role as mother and wife and had fulfilled those roles admirably and without hesitation. She also knew that she had left devastation in her wake. Devastation in the form of her relationship with Jake, not to mention Mrs Adam's hair!

She looked over at Carl as he sat down beside Sophie on the couch with his favourite 'Best Dad' mug. The mug she and Tommy had bought him for fathers' day last year. If only she knew how Carl was feeling right now.

How could he possibly fancy Sophie with her sunken beady eyes and bad breath? And how could he bear to be stroking those bony fingers with the lovely hands that had explored her own body so many times. It had to be an act he was putting on to try to pacify her until he could get her removed.

If he would just give her a sign or take her aside to explain. If he would look her way, and let her know that he wanted her back, she would change her life in a heartbeat, but his attention remained on Sophie and she was not going to give him yet another opportunity to humiliate her.

"Come on Tommy. Get some clothes and let's go. I'll send Jake for pizza and we'll watch a late film."

Carl finally looked up at her as Tommy left to gather his overnight things, and she hoped that slipping Jake's name in, might have caused the reaction.

"You don't have to take him Kel. He can stay here with us. You've done enough today."

Kelly hesitated for a moment, trying to decide if leaving Tommy would prevent intimacy between him and Sophie, or if taking him might whip up some jealousy.

"I think he needs to feel safe tonight."

Carl didn't argue, but he did take his hand from Sophie's and Kelly felt easier about leaving them alone together.

She arrived home with Tommy, who went straight upstairs to dump his bag in the room he regarded as his own. Allocating and decorating a room for Tommy had been part of the bargain when Kelly agreed to move in, and Jake considered it a small price to pay to have Kelly full time.

Jake was sitting on the couch, still playing with his phone and made no attempt to open the conversation. A part of her wished he would throw a tantrum about her ties to Carl and her obsession with his family. It would give her the opportunity to retaliate and hand her the justification to cut him out of her life and focus on getting back into Carl's, but that was not his way.

She went into the kitchen to wash the soil form her hands and as she returned, he met her in the doorway a huge glass of red wine and an enormous hug. She laid her head on his shoulder and she felt safe, so safe that she could feel the emotion bubbling to the surface. No words were needed as they held each other in silence and his entire body moulded to hers.

If only her heart could learn to live in this warm safe place with her, she knew her life would be perfect. To truly love a man like Jake and to be loved in return was the utopia she had dreamed of and here it was, right in front of her, all there for the taking, so why was her heart struggling to wriggle free from this embrace and why was her imagination wandering back across town to the house she had just left and burning with jealousy at the mere fact that someone else was in the same house as Carl?

In reality, Carl and Sophie were not just in the same house, but also in the same room. Carl was not yearning for Kelly nor burning with jealousy at the images of her with her lover and his own child. He was trying to coax something from the skeletal being who was sitting dejectedly on his couch. He was searching her face for any hint of recognition.

For some small glimmer of hope that his sexy, witty, curvy, ambitious fiancée would be resurrected and take her place back in his life, as the woman he desired and craved. The woman who teased and challenged him, who made him strive for her attention, who held his heart with an air of mystery and by being always that little bit out of reach.

"What on earth were you hoping to dig-up?"

Sophie didn't answer. She hadn't had the time or motivation to try to justify her actions, without landing herself in some institution.

Carl crouched in front of her and took her dirty hands in his.

"Look. I have no idea what this is like for you. What you are thinking or feeling but if you don't start to share some of it nothing is going to change."

She sighed. She knew she couldn't tell him anything of what she was feeling because all her feelings were based on betrayal and repulsion.

"I'm finding it hard to accept that I've slept through a huge chunk of my life," she stammered, "do you have any idea how frightening it is?"

Carl nodded empathetically giving Sophie the confidence to continue.

"I dreamt a lot, and those dreams feel so real that I just needed to prove to myself that they weren't. I wanted to let go of them and just got the urge to prove to myself that something I buried in a dream wasn't there"

"What was it?"

"It doesn't matter. Just something I buried with a friend up there."

"Did it work?"

Sophie smiled the false smile that always fooled Carl.

"Now it has," she said softly, "Carl, I'm back."

Carl kissed each of her filthy hands in turn.

"I'm still your guy. Are you my girl?"

"Absolutely." She lied, and they kissed for the first time in a decade.

That night Carl slept beside her, but they didn't make love. Sophie was grateful for the company, which helped to distract her from her incessant plotting and analysing, and Carl was grateful that at last she was making some sense and communicating with him again. Both were grateful that the other didn't want to make love either. Just Carl and Sophie, together at last.

He turned over to face Sophie's pyjamaed back, wondered if he could dare to believe that they were back on the path that would bring them together again. He thought it would be a nice gesture to extend his arm around her. He thought about it for the longest time, about how it might feel to hold her again. He wanted to, or at least his head wanted to. It was the right thing to do. The moment was begging for it. This was the love of his life returned from the grave and the mother of his son.

Instead he turned onto his back and starred into the winter darkness. The mother of his son was not here, nor was the love of his life for she was lying in the arms of another man, his big black arms around her silky white body, beads of sweat chaffing their chests as he thrust into her, owning her, possessing her and making her his. Carl could feel it. He knew it as he tried to breathe through the pain, and the spectacle played out in the darkness before his eyes.

Sophie woke to the gentle breathing of Carl beside her. There was no arm around her nor was his body within touching distance. This would, until yesterday, have been a relief, but there was something about the events of the previous day that had awakened in her a primitive desire. The desire was not for Carl but purely to reclaim her man.

 The man that she suspected had been stolen from her while she slept. Tommy's indiscretion about Carl hiding his visits from Kelly, had struck a chord that was ricocheting around in her head. Had Kelly muscled in on her relationship? Seduced Carl while she lay in a coma? It was unthinkable but she'd witnessed them together when they joined forces to rescue their beloved Tommy. They acted like a couple.

Quietly she got out of bed and went downstairs to make tea, stopping on the way to wash her face, put on some moisturiser, tidy her hair into another updo, brush her teeth and put on a bit of make-up. She was going to knock Kelly out of their lives onto her scheming ass even if she didn't want him for herself. This was a matter of pride and self-esteem. Carl was hers and always had been and she needed to prove it.

On the way back with hot tea, she glanced at her reflection as she passed the bathroom again and was as satisfied as she could be, considering what she was working with. She pushed open the bedroom door with her elbow and gave a cheery greeting.

"Morning sleepy head. Tea?"

Carl looked around anxiously as though trying to get his bearings before lying back down and stretching.

"Thanks." He yawned.

"Shall we go pick Tommy up and do something as a family today, since it's Sunday?" She smiled.

"Perhaps he should stay with Kelly today."

"With Kelly?!" Sophie snapped, "why should he stay with her?"

"You gave Kelly quite a scare yesterday Soph, I think she may want to be with him today."

"You're leaving him there for Kelly's sake?!"

"No. Not just for Kelly's sake. For both their sakes. Tommy had a scare too you know."

Sophie huffed like a defeated child and Carl raised his eyebrows disapprovingly.

"I'm sorry," she sighed, "I guess I'm just anxious to put things right."

"It's fine." He replied harshly, noticing his own grumpy mood this morning.

He had woken up with the vivid images of Kelly and Jake still in his head and, leaving Tommy with them, might at least prevent Kelly from hosting one of her all-day sex sessions with their running bed buffets and massage intervals.

The ones she used to host for him on wet Sundays when Tommy was at his Grandad's.

"Carl he's your son not hers. He is our son not hers. She has no rights over him, but she acts like his mother." Sophie whined, jolting him from his daydream of memories.

"I'll speak to her," he relented, "but not today."

Sophie was far from satisfied, but she smiled and thanked him for the small victory.

As she took a shower, she could hear him speaking on the phone but couldn't make out many of the words. She could hear that the tone was somewhat confrontational though, which pleased her as she shampooed her hair and mentally selected an outfit from her wardrobe. One that would make the best of her recovering body.

She purposely made no reference to the call as she continued to dry her hair and re-apply her makeup. Eventually it was Carl who reopened the conversation.

"I spoke to Kelly this morning to check on Tommy, and I mentioned the situation we are all in. She suggested that we all go somewhere together. Maybe for a meal or something?"

"All?" Sophie tried to hide her displeasure, "you mean the four of us?"

"No. Five" It was Carl's turn to try to hide his displeasure.

"Fine," she smiled, "I just thought it might be easier to discuss things without Tommy. As two couples."

"We are one family in this Sophie," he retorted, "who is coupled to who is irrelevant." His grumpy mood had returned the moment she tried to couple his Kelly with Jake.

"I said we could meet them for lunch today."

"Yes, that's fine." Sophie spoke the words while already planning how she would make sure Kelly would be left in no doubt that this was a family she was no longer a part of.

Jake, Kelly and Tommy were already seated, when they arrived at the country pub which served traditional Sunday lunch, and which had been highly recommended by Jake.

Sophie quickly took the seat beside Tommy who was then sandwiched between her and Kelly. It was almost symbolic. A small child nestled between the two woman who were making their jealous claims on him. It was Sophie's way of reminding Kelly that her place was beside her son, but it backfired instantly when Tommy quickly jostled his chair closer to Kelly's.

When the menu's arrived both women jumped in to try to help Tommy decide, but the confrontation became blatantly obvious and Carl stepped in.

"I think Tommy can make up his own mind."

The elephant in the room had been banished to the corner, for the time being.

Sophie was struggling to find any topic of conversation that might be of interest to Tommy. She was losing ground fast and decided to go to the ladies' room to kill some time until the food arrived.

In the mirror of the powder room she gave herself a talking to. She needed to decide if this real-life family before her was really what she wanted and if so then she had to be less aggressive in her approach to secure it. Her failed mission to find the makeshift time capsule had seriously damaged her resolve on the existence of John or her cute little Tori or her frail frightened Becky. She was trying to accept that they didn't exist. That they never did, and they never will.

She gave her updo a few tugs to try to create the illusion of volume. Her updo's always looked so spectacular when she had longer thicker hair but now it sat there like a pathetic tiny knot.

She needed to work on her nutrition and allow it to grow back into the wavy mane it used to be. Full of determination, she squared her shoulders, and rustled up a smile. It was time to embrace reality. It was time to rebuild a relationship with Carl and to start another one in earnest, with the little boy to whom she had been an unforgiveable disappointment.

It was time to evict John and her children from her heart because the torment of their presence there, was standing in the way of her happiness. It was time to knock Kelly into the middle of next week!

On returning to the table, she could see that the food had arrived but as she approached her seat nothing could have prepared her for what lie before her eyes.

On her plate was a selection of vegetables beside which lay a perfectly halved chicken breast and a perfectly halved gammon steak, both of which had been pushed together as though joined. She froze in the moment as she scanned the plates of everyone else, Tommy had the identical plate, and as she tried to control her shaking hands, he looked straight at her.

Carl was the first to speak, "Are you ok? Tommy said you couldn't decide so he thought he would share with you. Isn't that cute?"

Of all the adjectives Sophie was thinking of, cute was not one of them. She sat down carefully, without saying a word, whilst giving herself some time to process the situation, to quieten her pounding heart and gather some composure while she considered what it meant.

Tommy was tucking into his meal with a cold wry smile on his lips. A smile that filled Sophie with terror and excitement in equal measure. Her son was playing with her, and it was unsettling that a child of his age possessed the steel to take her on, but beyond that it meant something else.

This boy really was in touch with her other life, he really was the imaginary friend of Rebecca.

She sliced calmly into the chicken of this 'the cut and shut' before her and as she lifted a forkful to her mouth, she returned his cold wry smile perfectly.

He looked back at her with arrogant confidence. She held his stare and he hers. Neither was afraid of the other.

She couldn't wait to get him alone.

Chapter 16

The next evening, after Tommy returned from school, Sophie paid attention to his outwardly innocent behaviour. His submissive angelic expressions, and his manufactured nervous disposition were acts worthy of rapturous applause. She had underestimated the boy and she needed to plan her approach with caution.

There was nothing to be gained in trying to befriend him because it seemed he had already picked a side. He was playing for team Kelly. She also knew she couldn't bully him. One word to his father was likely to result in his removal from the house again, or more likely hers. Either way she wouldn't get her explanation for the half and half meal.

As she cupped her lukewarm coffee whilst contemplating her next move, there was a knock on the door.

"Anne! What are you doing here?" Carl blurted on opening the door.

There was no audible reply, and Sophie assumed his question had been responded to by some silent expression.

"Look who's here." He smiled as he showed her into the kitchen where Sophie was now scowling into the congealed remnants of her cold coffee.

"How nice," she smiled sarcastically, "I suppose Kelly summoned you to restrain the mad woman?"

Anne huffed humorously then turned to Carl

"Could you give us a moment Carl?"

Carl left the room gratefully. He didn't want any involvement in this discussion, and he had neither the energy or desire to try to understand any of it.

Anne shot a reprimanding look in Sophie's direction which took her somewhat by surprise. She had been expecting Anne's 'tea and sympathy' approach and had prepared herself to be the stubborn arrogant patient, but Anne's coldness put her on the back foot.

"Now listen here Sophie. I don't know what you are trying to do by going off up mountains like a demonically possessed lunatic, but if you aren't careful you could lose your liberty completely. Do you understand?"

"I suppose Kelly raised the alarm then?" Sophie replied sulkily.

"Kelly is worried about you. Everyone around you is worried and you put your son in danger and scared him half to death."

"He's fine. You don't know him at all. I could tell you a thing or two."

"You don't know him either Sophie. Are you listening to me? You could lose everything!"

Sophie slammed down her cup like a defiant child.

Anne scowled again "I've seen this happen before Sophie. You know that!"

Sophie suddenly became interested, more so about the detail of the patient's delusions than her fate.

"When was it though? Who is she? You didn't tell me the whole story."

"That doesn't matter and it's confidential, but I can tell you that it was a girl who was also claiming to move between existences."

Sophie's full attention had been captured.

"Where exactly is she now?"

Anne sighed "She's in an institution like I said, on twenty-four-hour suicide watch. I can't tell you where, but she's been there for three years."

"Is she trying to get back to her other life?" Sophie asked hopefully.

"I don't know what she's trying to do. I spent months on her. She was convinced that she had the ability to step into the afterlife"

"The afterlife?" Sophie frowned having never considered this.

"Yes, but that's irrelevant. Her mother killed herself when she was fifteen and this condition grew as the result of being abandoned, I think."

Sophie thought for a moment, "Or it could be that the condition is hereditary?"

"It's possible I suppose, but that's not my point. My point is that you have to acknowledge that it's a condition. It's an illness, and unless you start to accept that and stop this obsession of getting back to your coma world of dreams, attractive though they may seem, you could well end up in an institution."

Sophie nodded and smiled but her smile was not one of gratitude or acceptance but of hearing that she was not the only person who had the ability to move between existences. Everything seemed to be making sense.

Anne left her some pills which she agreed to take and thanked the woman for potentially saving her from the nut house. They parted on a positive note, but Sophie had learned the value of deceitful acting very well and smiled her satisfaction as she placed the tablets in the drawer, one of which would be flushed away daily.

Her attention then turned back to Tommy. She had to be patient.

Sometimes there was, what seemed to be, a knowing glance between them, but it was never enough for her to directly challenge him. Not that was, until bonfire night.

The family bonfire in the yard had originally been Sophie's idea, but that was before her hatred for Tommy had embedded itself in the pit of her stomach.

Resentfully she prepared for the celebration, adverse to doing anything that might bring him the slightest joy. Trying to salvage this family life was no longer on her agenda, and as she watched from the bedroom she now shared with Carl, she poured herself a large glass of mulled wine.

Jake and Kelly had arrived early to help, and as Jake threw large tree branches onto the pile, Kelly stood beside Carl, watching awkwardly. This was going to be another occasion tainted by all the issues associated with the secrets and jealousy of tangled romances.

She gulped down the contents of the glass and poured herself another one. Carl's parents pulled up, and as they got out of the car and collected trays of food from their boot she gulped again and smiled. Perhaps today she could manage to have a conversation with them without feeling the compulsion to apologise for causing their son's death.

"Anybody want a potato?" Tommy asked, looking proud that he had been given the responsibility for something.

"I will." Sophie smiled. She was playing the game. Hoping that he would become bored of her disinterest and try to provoke her.

He cut up the potato and placed it on a plate with a sausage from the barbecue. Then he removed one of the halves onto his own plate along with half the sausage and marched over to Sophie cockily handing her the plate of the other halves.

"There you go."

Sophie took the plate and thanked him loudly through the noise of the music. She knew he was waiting for her reaction, so she deliberately pretended not to see any relevance in the plate he had handed her. He watched her face for a moment and then leant forward and said something she could hardly hear, but she definitely made out the word 'secret.'

As he walked away, she caught him by the arm, but he snatched it away shrieking with the nip she had given him.

"What did you say?" she hissed, "who told you about the cut and shut meals? Was it Becky?"

"I didn't say anything. Let go! You're hurting me."

His face started to crumple as he searched around for the attention of someone he could fool. His act was convincing, forcing her to let him go before he had the chance to turn his false fear into something audible.

For a moment he did nothing other than to turn away from her. He stood with his back to her for several seconds before slowly turning back around to face her. The crumpled face had been replaced by a smooth solemn stare. His unyielding eyes met hers as he savoured the moment before speaking.

"I found it."

"Found what?"

"The fucking pepper pot."

She rocked backwards as though his words had punched her in the face. She was physically reeling. Reeling from the wine, from the revelation, from the foul language erupting from the rosebud mouth of this blonde, blue eyed child.

She tried to get her balance as the wine continued to impair her senses. She could see him heading towards the house and set off in pursuit.

"Where is it?" She hissed as she caught up, stumbling drunkenly against a bush.

"I don't know," he snapped, "I threw it away."

Sophie lunged at the boy, spinning him around to face her as she caught his wrist and pulled him into the bushes. "No you didn't! Where is it Tommy!"

"Let go! You're hurting me!"

She tightened her grip on the boy's frail wrist "I said where is it?!"

"I hate you! Daddy! Kelly!"

Carl's father pulled her away sharply.

"What on earth are you doing?"

"You don't know the half of it!" She slurred as she let go of his wrist.

"You're drunk!" he barked, "you're not fit to be around a child."

As Tommy ran into the house, Sophie called after him.

"Go on! Run away. I know what you're up to!"

"You'd better calm down lady." The man she had once bonded with as her future father in law was staring at her with repulsion in his eyes. She and Jack used to be closer than she was with her own father, during her years with Carl.

"Now go and sober up before I tell Carl what you did."

It seemed that their closeness had not been forgotten, and he was prepared to give her a second chance.

She nodded gratefully and returned to the garden where the group of meaningless people were smiling and chatting, munching happily on hot potatoes and drinking mulled wine. They were irrelevant to her. They no longer mattered because now she knew without doubt, that John was not a figment of her imagination and her only goal had been restored. Her goal to find him and her little girls.

As she sipped her wine and stared into the flames she was trying to decide on the best way to handle Tommy, the best way to spy on his secret meetings with Becky or if she should try to win him over and get all the information she needed. As she looked into the flames she was taken back to another bonfire, a bonfire when she'd been happy.

The woody smoke wafted into her nostrils and the familiar combination of burning face and freezing back, transported her to her old house, her real house. She remembered how Tori had been terrified of the bangers and John had been the only one who could console her, as he swept her up into his arms like a new-born baby causing her anger and annoyance to replace the fear. She had been crying and laughing at the same time as he refused to stop rocking her like a baby. How she missed John's smile, Tori's giggle and Becky's skinny arms around her.

She was so distracted that she hardly noticed anything else around her. She definitely didn't notice the amount of time Kelly spent with Carl nor the obvious displeasure this gave to Jake who continually tried to bring her back to his side.

She didn't notice her fiancé s longing glances at every part of Kelly's body, nor his over enthusiastic laughter at her jokes. She certainly didn't notice that for a time Carl and Kelly were missing at the same time, and Jake was asking incessantly about their whereabouts.

None of this was relevant to Sophie. Nothing about the evening was relevant except the chance to talk to Tommy again when the wretched bonfire finally ended.

In her seesaw existence the scales had tipped dramatically back towards the possibility of her happy married life with John and consequently, any potential romance with Carl had become unthinkable. She was thankful that the platonic status had not been breached so she could run back into John's arms with a clear conscience, and a faithful heart, the moment she found the conduit that would enable her to return to him.

Kelly and Carl had certainly been missing for a while. Kelly had gone into the house to use the toilet and on her way back Carl had been waiting at the kitchen door. He pulled her onto the path down the side of the house, full of jealousy, lust and frustration.

"I hate it Kelly. I can't stand it."

Kelly snatched her elbow back from his brutal hand.

"Hate what? Seeing me with someone else? Well, welcome to my world."

"What do you mean? You know I haven't slept with Sophie."

"Carl, you've been sleeping with Sophie in your head for years. I've always played second fiddle and now you're just annoyed you can't have it all."

"I don't want it all. I want you."

"Well that's a little bit unfortunate isn't it? You have a fiancée in your bed remember? The mother of your child? The love of your life?"

"She's not the love of my life. You are. I wish I'd married you years ago."

"Well that's a co-incidence because I wish you'd asked me years ago."

"Is it too late for us Kelly?"

"I don't know. Is it Carl?" She snapped, "what you gonna do about Sophie? Put her back in her coma?"

Carl made a grab for her as she started to walk away.

"I can't just throw her out Kelly. She used to be everything to both of us."

"Oh, here we go again! Back peddling already. Poor Sophie, poor Sophie. I've heard it all before Carl. Tell you what, you call me when you've got rid of her. I won't hold my breath waiting for that call."

As Kelly marched off, he tried to catch her by the arm again, but she wrenched herself free, glared at him and strode away.

"You can hold your breath Kell, she'll be gone sooner than you think."

Carl watched until she was gone then took a deep breath to regain his composure and set off to return to his guests. As he left the path Sophie's dad stepped out from behind the bush beside the kitchen, where he had rushed to urinate after finding the toilet occupied.

The next day the atmosphere between Sophie and Tommy was obvious, but Carl seemed content to leave it alone for now. She assumed he was letting them find their own way, but the reality was that he hadn't noticed any difference. He's spent the entire night at Sophie's side thinking about Kelly.

Sophie had no intention of letting this drag on and on. She'd wasted enough time already and was not prepared to spend the next few months trying to befriend Tommy again. He was too smart for that and she was too annoyed for it. She needed to confront him without raising the 'lunatic alert.' She had to find a common goal.

When Carl was around, they both played their parts, talking of plans for Christmas and of shopping for gifts but one evening when Carl went out on a breakdown call, she seized her opportunity.

"I'm sorry I nipped your arm at the bonfire Tommy."

He shrugged and continued watching TV.

"I was just surprised you hadn't told me about finding the pot after we had dug together for hours. Didn't you want me to have it?"

He shrugged again.

"Perhaps we could help each other here?"

He continued watching the screen for a while but when Sophie left the suggestion hanging, he finally looked up.

"You'd like to spend more time with Kelly I know that, and I don't blame you. I could help you with that."

"How?"

"If we work together. If you help me work everything out. Any bits of information you have? Then I could get your dad to let you go over there. Maybe even for Christmas?"

"You think he'd listen to you?"

"Oh yes," she smiled, "your dad always listens to me."

She saw his body language change. The tenseness became relaxed as he slowly started to realise that maybe they both wanted the same thing. She took her chance.

"So, when did you last see Becky? She asked gently.

Tommy looked startled at her forthright approach.

"It's ok Tommy," she encouraged, "I've heard you talking to her."

"Not for a long time. See you in the morning." He got up from the floor and started to walk away.

Sophie had got an admission and was not about to let it go.

"What happened to the pepper pot?"

"I put it in the dustbin."

"Why? You knew how important it was to me."

"I know it was. That's why I did it. I was pissed off"

"Did you open it?"

Tommy smiled "Of course I did"

Tommy then went on to accurately describe the contents of the pot as Sophie sat open mouthed. Shock gave way to excitement and excitement gave way to hope.

She so wanted to push him harder, but was afraid he might clam up altogether, so she just asked one more question.

"Did Becky say where her mum was?" Sophie was desperate to find out if anything had happened to her on the last night she remembered, the unremarkable night when she'd slid into bed beside John.

"She said her mum was in bed as it was the middle of the night. It was just after you woke up, I think."

Sophie kissed him out of sheer gratitude that she had finally got him on side. She wasn't sure if he'd grasped the full implication of helping her. Of getting her out of his life so he could be Kelly's son again, but it seemed enough for him to realise they had some common ground.

He wanted more time with Kelly and quite frankly, she wanted to disappear and leave them all to it.

That night she slid into bed beside Carl with a lighter heart and sleepily started to go over the facts. At least Becky was not aware that she was missing the last time Tommy spoke to her. Of course she would still be sleeping, because of all the times she jumped worlds and returned to John, never once did he ask her where she'd been. Time hadn't move on in his world and the days continued in sequence.

Did this mean that no matter how long she spent here, she could return on the same day she left without ever being missed? Yet in this life, time had definitely moved on without her. Suddenly she was wide awake again and trying to establish the logic behind the facts she was gathering.

As she lay there beside Carl he moved suddenly. She kept perfectly still to avoid any conversation. He continued to move. His arm was rocking rhythmically, and it soon became startlingly obvious that he was masturbating on the assumption she was asleep. She felt disgusted and guilty at the same time. The man had needs, he also had virtually no privacy, and she had now driven him to finding relief on his own, right beside her in their bed.

She wanted to interrupt him but also to spare his embarrassment, so she lay there quietly. Quietly listening to his breathing as it quickened. Quietly being rocked gently back and forth, on her side of the bed, by the movement which was gaining momentum. As she listened in the semi darkness, she imagined how she would feel if this were John. John would have been doing it purposely to tease her and she would have leaned over to kiss him and join in the pleasure. If this had been John, she would not be lying there pretending to be asleep and feeling nothing but guilt and disgust.

After a few moments she felt his body jerking against hers, but she couldn't move. His stifled grunts were almost directly in her ear he was so close. As his body convulsed and jerked forward in the throes of orgasm, she felt the hot wetness through her nightdress at the base of her spine. She closed her eyes tightly and gritted her teeth as she whispered to herself "Dirty bastard!"

Carl was snoring within minutes and as she tried to peel her damp night dress away from her body, she turned her thoughts back to her alliance with Tommy and how she could speed herself back to the family she loved.

Consequently, she was the one to tuck Tommy up every night from that day, adorning him in the 'cupboard love' that opened the door to information about his night visitor.

Her confidence grew as he described Becky's big garden and her little sister. Tommy seemed to enjoy watching the reaction on Sophie's face as she recognised the life he was describing. He was telling her about a life she already knew, a place she had already lived in, and of a little girl she had held a million times.

Carl seemed warmed by the new connection she had made to their son and this new reinforcement of his family made him more determined to expel the love he had for Kelly, but Kelly was a force to be reckoned with.

He tried desperately to rekindle the deep love he used to have for Sophie, but the feeling just refused to return. Something was broken. Something had changed and no matter how much he wanted it to change back, it just wasn't happening and for that, he cursed Kelly several times a day. A curse for every time she popped into his thoughts, squeezed his heart or caused his hand to grasp himself whenever he found himself alone picturing her soft naked curves.

He took to sifting through old photographs of the days he and Sophie first moved in together. He could see the love and passion in his former self as he smiled at her adoringly. He could see it, he could remember it and he could imagine it, but he couldn't feel it.

Meantime, Sophie had got to the point where she decided she had enough evidence to confide in someone and since she no longer trusted Kelly, she arranged another lunch with Niki.

She led into the conversation carefully, assessing Niki's reaction after every small revelation, but as Niki seemed receptive, she soon found herself excitedly gushing out every bit of information she had been given by Tommy.

"He knows every detail of my other life, don't you see Nik, this means it's not been all in my head?"

Niki smiled weakly, and for an awful moment Sophie feared she may have been humouring her.

"You do believe me?"

"Of course, I do, but I am really having trouble believing that any of what he says is true."

"Well how else could he know all this stuff?"

"I don't know." Niki shook her head gently.

"He knew everything Niki. I'm telling you that he has that pepper pot. He knew what was in it and he took great delight in describing every detail of it, the words in our note and even the cotton bud, red with our blood."

"Stop it. You're giving me the creeps Soph. I just find it all too spooky."

"I know. I know you do and so would I but try to understand that I've lived another life. I'd almost convinced myself it wasn't true but deep down I knew it. I knew it was, and this proves it. Oh God, I know how this sounds."

Niki put a sympathetic hand on Sophie's and then rubbed it playfully, to lighten the moment.

"Give yourself some time to consider all this Sophie. There's probably a plausible explanation. Don't let it consume you."

"I won't." Sophie lied whilst already planning her next conversation with Tommy.

"What do you think Tommy is going to be able to help you with anyway?"

"I don't know but I think he probably has the answer to how I can get back there, but he just doesn't know it."

"Sophie just promise me you won't do anything stupid again."

Sophie cocked her head to one side as if to say, "of course not," but she didn't actually say the words.

Later that evening she tucked Tommy up in bed and the conversation was all about the approaching countdown to Christmas. She couldn't bring herself to spoil the jovial atmosphere, so she kissed him gently but reluctantly, and returned to the living room to exchange meaningless pleasantries with Carl.

As she sat beside him, he extended an arm around her, a gesture of warmth that felt colder than the air outside on this December night. In response she reached for his hand and pulled it gently around her neck as though welcoming his attempt at affection, but it was equally cool, empty and devoid of feeling.

They sat in this position for almost an hour watching TV as though neither of them wanted to move the situation in either direction, to back away or to develop it to greater intimacy, each had gone as far as they could bear.

Eventually a programme ended, giving them both the excuse to legitimately disentangle themselves from the embrace and seek solace in the private space that their turned backs afforded them in their barren bed.

After a few minutes she heard Carl's breathing change to that of gentle slumber, leaving her to wrestle with her own passage to much needed sleep, a door which was firmly blocked by the incessant ramblings of her overactive preoccupied mind.

Notions passed through her head with the familiar regularity of novelties on a merry-go-round, each passing her again and again, thoughts and ideas without beginning or end and always in the same order. She knew that the compulsive replaying of these scenarios achieved nothing, but the cycle was impossible to break.

As she fought to slow down her brain, she heard a voice in the distance. A whispering coming from Tommy's room. Hushed, excited whispering that made the hairs on the back of her neck stand up. Slowly she lifted the duvet and quietly swung her legs out of the bed, placing her feet carefully onto the carpet. Her heart raced as she crept nearer and nearer to the sound.

Step by step she stole over the landing towards Tommy's door where she waited for a moment trying to silence the faint sound of her own breathing. She was terrified of breaking the spell, of sending whatever this visitation was, catapulting back across the vastness of the unknown into the place she couldn't reach. She was going to do nothing to trigger its recoil and stood silently frozen to the spot trying to make sense from the muffled mumblings wafting through the half open door.

She couldn't quite make out the words of the generic bland whispering. It could have been anyone saying anything, but still she strained for any hint of recognition, holding her breath in pursuit of absolute silence. Gently she put her hand on the handle and turned it slowly, gently and quietly she leaned her weight against the door until it crept open inch by inch to allow her to enter the room where the whispering continued as she did so.

Tommy was chatting to someone, but she couldn't see who. He wasn't sleeping, he was sitting on the edge of his bed in full conversation with an invisible being. Sophie waited in the hope that the person would respond, she needed to hear Becky, she needed to know for sure that this was real but before Tommy finished speaking, he spun around in her direction.

"What are you doing here?" He snapped from behind the part open door.

"I heard voices. Who are you talking to?"

"No-one." He said guiltily as he jumped up onto his feet.

"Was it Becky?"

He looked up at her and nodded. Sophie's heart missed a beat as she scanned the room as though expecting to catch a glimpse of her daughter.

"Where is she?"

"She's gone."

"What did she say?"

Tommy's expression softened.

"She said she misses you."

"Did you tell her I'm here?"

Tommy looked startled as though he hadn't even considered it.

"You interrupted." He said defensively.

Sophie frowned. She shouldn't have barged in like that and she knew it. If she had waited a few more minutes she might have heard Becky's voice.

She couldn't interrogate him further for fear of waking Carl, so she quietly left, leaving the door ajar as before, but instead of returning to her room she stood in the hallway and waited.

Almost immediately the whispering started again. She could hear the rhythm of it, it was a conversation between two people, but the whispers were too similar to tell them apart. It felt hopeless and she was freezing in the hallway, but her feet refused to move and the hairs on her neck were reminding her that this boy was in contact with the family she thought she had lost.

Then the moment came. The moment her whole body shook. As clear as day, Tommy's words emerged from the incessant inaudible whispers. Loud and perfectly audible.

"She won't do it. Not even for you. She doesn't have the balls Becky," he laughed, "you may as well tell your dad she's staying with us."

Chapter 17

At 11 pm On Tuesday 7th December 2010.Sophie Taylor walked northward from the town along the sea front heading for the top of Filey Brigg. Her head bent against the driving sleet and arms folding her open jacket around her body. The sea front was deserted, but even if there had been some solitary dog walker along this path they would probably have failed to notice the heavy ruck sack dragging at her right shoulder or the rope dangling from the partly open zip which wormed down the back of her legs, to the loop attaching it to her right ankle.

They would probably have failed to notice her thin plimsoles which were totally unsuitable for the deep slush they were splashing through, or the blank expression on her face, as she failed to flinch from the sting of the hail as it dashed against her cheeks.

She couldn't feel any of it. It was of no concern, for soon she would be far away from the misery of this bitter wind, this cruel December night and this vile existence.

Tommy's laughter rang again in her ears as he told her beloved little girl that her mother wasn't coming back. She would wipe the smile off his arrogant face the next time he spoke to Becky and discovered she was back where she belonged.

She'd had the key to this prison all along but had been too afraid to use it, but the doubts which had held her back had gone, and this time there would be no mistake. No coma caused by an interfering bitch, or from an inadequate car crash, from a lucky fall or from a misfired gun. This time she was returning home for good and the heavy load on her back was her one-way ticket.

From the top of the Brigg she could see the swirling dark water below, hear the deafening roar of the waves as they crashed against the jagged rocks. There was something threatening about the night sea in winter, dramatic and frightening but the power and size of the waves rising from the water in turn, looming upward to full height then crashing down like closing jaws held no fear for her. It was on their force and strength she was relying for they must, for her, force open the gates to her heaven or hell. It was in their relentless brutality, their ability to overpower any desperate attempts she might make to survive, that would open the front door back into the warmth and love of home.

She had to make sure this would be swift, clean and absolute. She looked down and her stomach turned a somersault. It was too risky from this point. There were too many protruding rocks that might bounce her right or left, possibly leaving her mutilated but alive on a ledge or dangling from an overhanging rock.

She needed a clear drop into the water where she would be consumed instantly. She was sure her heart would fail within seconds after she hit the icy water in her flimsy nightdress, but she was taking no chances on being washed back onto the rocks and being discovered in the nick of time by some passing Samaritan. She needed a point at which the water was deep and uninterrupted.

She walked along until she saw a patch of water without surface ripples as the waves retracted. A deep pool without rocks was directly below an overhanging ledge only two feet from the top. This was the place. She climbed carefully down and stepped onto the ledge. Her stomach turned again causing her to inhale deeply and then blow out again. Below her was a clear drop into the water below. Water of sufficient depth to carry her back to John. The jagged rocks chafed the soles of her feet through the thin shoes in which her toes were now freezing and soaking wet. Her bare hands, numb against the slippery surface as she grappled for makeshift handles in the sharp crevices, struggled to hold her firm as she commenced her preparation for the passage home.

Somewhere beyond this watery grave her mother smiled with open arms for her return, her children's laughter beckoned, and her soul mate waited patiently for the reunion of two hearts that were withering in the despair of this cruel separation.

She put down the heavy ruck sack and took out the bolder which she had wrapped in fishing net and secured with the other end of the rope. Scooping it up like a baby in her arms she held it close to her chest as though hugging it for comfort before kissing it gently in recognition of the part it would play as her executioner and her beloved passport.

Earlier that evening Niki had finally got round to emptying her over-full kitchen bin into the dustbin outside, when a small bandage dropped to the floor. There was nothing remarkable about the white piece of tangled linen that had covered the cut of Pete's finger a week before, but as she held it up against the light she gasped. The blood on the bandage was no longer red, it was brown. How could she not have realised that when she last spoke to Sophie. Blood left for only a short time doesn't stay red. Tommy was lying! Tommy was probably making the whole thing up to torment her. She looked at the clock as she went back into the kitchen. It was 10.30. They would be in bed by now. She would tell her in the morning.

Sophie closed her eyes for a moment in silent prayer. This was no time to lose her nerve. She had made this passage back to John many times and she knew how it worked. She prayed again, her last plea for some divine force to take pity on her and convey her speedily and painlessly from this torment into the safety of John's arms.

Still muttering gently with eyes closed she stepped off the top of the rock and sped through the icy air. She felt the impact of the of the water as it engulfed her, still speeding her downwards through the noise of the gushing water as all sounds from the world above were extinguished.

Shocked by the speed at which she was still descending, at the pain of the cold as it crippled and knotted every muscle in her body and the frightening realisation that her heart hadn't stopped on impact, terror replaced hope. She was hurtling through the thick darkness hearing only the dulled echo of the rushing water through muffled ears. Onwards and onwards she sped on the power of the tide, not knowing if she were travelling downwards or sideways out to sea.

She could feel the rope dislocating her ankle as it dragged her away from the light, and the chunks of seaweed and ocean debris, pounding her face and body. Suddenly the instinct to fight for air overpowered all else. She could hear her heart pounding in her ears. Grasped by blind panic, she held her breath, hoping to feel her face break back through the water into the air above.

She started to swim, arms fruitlessly pushing back the water as she remained anchored. She reached down for the knot in the rope at her mutilated ankle. The rope she had tied tightly with all her strength to deliberately prevent such an escape. Inwardly she was sobbing, as she tried to hold onto that last breath.

Another surge threw her away from her anchor, ripping at her hip and causing her mouth to open in pain. She lurched for the rope again with both hands causing her to roll forward as her nails ripped on the unforgiving fibres. What followed was a pain so severe that she froze in the grip of it. She hadn't felt the intake of water involuntarily sucked in, as her body gasped for air, but she felt the pain of it hit her chest. The water that trapped the air in her lungs delivering excruciating pain as it flowed down her throat expelling air out of her body into the darkness around her. Pain and panic consumed her in the terror of these moments, as she fought for life and instinct thwarted hope. There was no afterlife, no family waiting, and the magnitude of her sheer stupidity dawned.

Then something changed. The battle between air and water was over. The battle, won by the sea, allowed water to flow in and out of her lungs painlessly as she continued to inhale and exhale instinctively.

She could feel the seas debris pass through her nose and mouth, but there was no choking or discomfort as the cold water passed peacefully back and forth. Her eyes were open, and she could see faint shadows through the darkness as the gentle movement of the deep water rocked her back and forth as far as her tether would allow. There was a beauty in this moment, a peace born of acceptance, as she drifted alone with her inner self, with her soul and with her God once again.

She had felt this moment before. Hope returned and she knew that at any second, she would feel John's arms and hear his voice. She waited in the darkness but there came a force she hadn't felt before. A gentle diminishing, a fading of her conscious thoughts, stealing her will, like huge hands laying her to rest.

Chapter 18

Wednesday morning started like any other for Carl as he stretched and yawned, before mooching in the direction of the shower, with a bathrobe in hand to cover his nakedness As ever, it never got past the grip of his hand, and was casually hooked onto the back of the bathroom door, from which it would later make its return journey with equal uselessness.

He called to Tommy to get up, and then down to Sophie to establish if she was making the breakfast or if she had gone for a run and therefore, he would need to do it himself. There was no reply, so he continued his shower, singing Christmas carols as he lathered his hair.

Christmas decorations were stacked in the hallway, which triggered a kind of childish excitement in him. He squeezed past them smiling, as he anticipated opening the boxes later with Tommy and Sophie. Of decorating the house, with Christmas music playing while they drank the traditional glass of sherry. This was their first Christmas as a family, and he intended to do everything he could to make it a memorable one.

He shook some the cereal into Tommy's bowl but left the milk beside it, as Tommy hated it soggy He poured the juice and popped a slice of toast in the toaster.

Tommy arrived in the kitchen and started his breakfast without speaking, which was exactly as it had always been. Neither of them were morning people. The silent ritual continued, until Carl picked up his jacket and car keys and shouted his goodbye.

"Mum's out on a run. Be getting ready for school."

Tommy didn't acknowledge his father.

Carl's car was frosted up and he cursed as he searched for a CD case to use as a scraper. Rubbing his hands together for warmth he started the engine, turned the blower on full blast before dragging the plastic case back and forth over the driver's side of the windscreen. He got back in and crouched down to peer through the slit he had made in the layer of frost.

He was already later than he wanted to be and driving whilst looking through this tiny slit, had definitely been a ridiculous attempt at speeding up the journey. Further hindered by a queue of traffic along the tiny seafront road was adding to his frustration, as he cursed the clutter of emergency service vehicles which were taking up most of the other lane. Sirens and flashing lights were everywhere, as the trickle of northbound cars took their turn to seep through the single lane.

Eventually he arrived at work and as he laboriously arranged the job tickets for that day, he flicked on the kettle. Now, as part owner of the same garage he had worked at since his apprenticeship, he felt adequately satisfied with his achievements.

The winter months were lucrative for mechanics, as an endless flow of easy jobs came their way. Flat batteries, frozen locks and starter motors and the towing away of cars from the many accidents caused by icy roads and poor visibility. It was going to be an easy but busy day, and it would pass quickly. As customers came and went, each had their own take on the number of emergency vehicles from the morning traffic jam, but each shared the same fact that an unidentified woman had been discovered by a jogger, her body left on the rocks by the receding tide.

The stories varied from a drug related murder to a dramatic suicide, and Carl nodded agreeably to each as he ploughed through the tickets, in the hope of an early finish to start the decorations. He was fed up of hearing about it, but it was very big news in the sleepy winter seaside town and as the day went on it became the only topic of conversation.

A phone call from Tommy at around 4 pm annoyed him more than worried him, when he heard that Sophie wasn't home, and Tommy was therefore alone in the house. He called her number, but it was Tommy who answered with the greeting…..

"I already tried that."

Carl became more irritated that she had left her phone behind and his first idea was to ring Kelly but, before he dialled, he checked himself. It wasn't fair on her, and anyway he didn't want her to know the kind of mother Sophie had turned out to be, so instead he decided to wrap up early and go home.

He made a quick call to Niki to check if she had gone for one of her chats, but Niki was still at work, so he threw the phone onto the passenger seat in temper and pulled out onto the road.

The slow-moving traffic added to his frustration as the seafront activity was still causing mayhem. The rock face had been cordoned off and incident vehicles still littered the pavement, from what was now rumoured to be a murder enquiry over the death of the unfortunate woman found early that morning.

When Carl entered the house, Tommy was watching TV completely unconcerned that he had been left alone. Carl reiterated to himself that this was hardly the point, and that

Sophie had some explaining to do. Still carrying the anger and disappointment, he started to make an omelette for himself and Tommy, deliberately excluding Sophie from the meal.

Father and son ate together, watched some TV and as they watched, Carl's anger quietly started to transgress to that of concern. Tommy went to bed around 7.30 without asking after Sophie, and Carl grabbed a beer from the fridge and sat back down in front of the TV.

Another hour passed in which he had called Niki again and then Kelly. He then called her father who was the one to turn Carl's concern to panic. His daughter was missing, and no-one had raised the alarm. He was furious.

It wasn't until Carl dialled 999 and he started to speak to the operator that he suddenly started to shake. His voice dried up as he suddenly connected the absence of his fiancé to the incident that had consumed the entire town all day. The lady on the other end of the call had already made the connection, and the tone of her voice told him that this was the call they had all been waiting for.

The events that followed this phone call took on a life of their own as the incident team launched into action, and a series of events tore through his home at a phenomenal pace.

By the time the Police arrived, Sophie's worried father had made the short journey and sat silently in the kitchen with Tommy who was now up again. The old man was trying hard to make normal conversation with the child, but fear and trepidation were stealing his words and contorting them into sterile syllables of little meaning.

Kelly, Jake and Niki all arrived at once to find Police and a family liaison officer already established in the living room. Carl was staring out of the window with an absent-minded ambivalence to the many voices around him. He wasn't answering any of their questions, as he fixed his eyes on the garden path as though expecting Sophie to return at any moment and save him from the ordeal. Anxiety had left him, and grief, guilt and horror had not yet filled the empty space.

It was now 10 pm and he was in no doubt that Sophie was dead. Everyone knew it. He knew it. The confirmation was a formality, but for the time being it was too early for condolences and too late for hope. This was the void of nothing. The lonely bridge between speculation and devastation. The empty hours filled with weak smiles, soft hugs and tea.

He was asked questions about her clothing and what might be missing from her wardrobe, but he was of little help. He had known every item in the years he had lovingly guarded them but today he couldn't remember them. He didn't want to.

He continued his stare until they stopped asking him and contented themselves with recent photographs of Sophie and statements from Kelly and Niki about her mental state. No-one approached Tommy who sat beside the chubby liaison woman with her motherly dark curls and sympathetic patting.

Carl watched suspiciously as she continued to make notes, speak quietly to Sophie's father and whisper on her phone. He suspected she had been planted to spy on them. Perhaps they thought he had murdered his fiancé after she had returned from the dead as a huge disappointment and thrown her into the sea.

It would make quite a headline, and vultures like these loved a good headline. He wished everyone would leave but he didn't want to be alone. He wished someone would speak but he had no ability to listen if they did. He just wanted the inevitable confirmation to end this timeless pocket of nothing, as everyone sat with bated breath for the news that would change their lives forever.

Finally, the knock came at 11.30 pm and the fateful blow was delivered quietly by two detectives of similar appearance. Overly tall, overly young and overly sombre. Sophie's father was asked to identify the body, as Carl slumped beside Tommy to offer him the comfort he didn't need. Kelly and Jake were getting up to speak to Carl before leaving when one of the detectives interrupted.

"We would like you to come with us Carl. To answer a few questions."

"I can't right now. Maybe tomorrow if it's all the same to you?"

"I'm afraid I have to insist. I'm sure it won't take long."

Carl's demeanour changed "Am I a suspect or something?"

"Just a few questions that's all." He tried to pacify Carl who had drawn himself up to his full height in protest.

"Surely you don't think I did something to Sophie? She's the love of my life! The only woman on the entire planet I've ever loved!" his words fell like missiles as Kelly rocked from the blows. Carl was oblivious as he continued his careless assault, "I've waited a decade to have her back. My life on hold for almost ten torturous years of praying and hoping. It's all I've been living for and it's been years of tedious monotony and now she's finally here you think I would kill her? You're insane!"

"We're going to need you to come with us Carl and also we need Kelly?" He looked around waiting for someone to answer.

"That's me," Kelly's voice was barely audible, "why do you need me to come?"

"We'll explain at the station." The detective said reassuringly as they ushered Carl to the car outside.

Kelly started to follow, but one of the officers stepped in.

"You will need to wait for a separate car I'm afraid."

"What? Why? Are we under arrest?" Her heartache was turning to resentment as she processed every syllable of betrayal and degradation that had fallen from Carl's lips.

"No. Of course not. We just need you to answer some questions to help the investigation."

"Well in that case I'll take my own car if you don't mind."

The officer nodded but continued to escort Carl to the Police car.

"Daddy, Mummy!" Tommy screamed as they stepped through the front door. Sill in his pyjamas, he tried to push his way through the door, but the fat arms of the chubby woman fell around him and guided him back into the house.

"Can you stay for a while?" She asked Niki.

"Of course." Niki nodded without telling the woman that she hardly knew Tommy at all.

Jake and Niki looked at one another for an instant. They both knew what this meant. Surely, they were not suspecting Carl or Kelly of causing Sophie's death. It was preposterous! Jake shook his head reassuringly and whispered to her.

"They'll be fine."

At Scarborough Police station, Carl was settled into an interview room and given more tea, but the hospitality didn't hide the fact that the two look-alike detectives were treating him differently, and there could be only one reason for that. He was a suspect. He wanted to ask if her was under arrest but was afraid that asking might heighten their suspicions. Better to pretend he hadn't even considered it.

They waited in silence while, a few miles away in the morgue, an old man was shown the bloated, battered body of his daughter. The little girl who had ridden on his shoulders along the cliff path above the Brigg a thousand times. She had patted his head in rhythm to the song she was singing and squealed as he pretended to wander too close to the edge. The edge she had calmly stepped off of, without a single squeal as she plummeted to her death.

He could tell it was her, but her face had taken on a monstrous expression, as though she was possessed. The cover fell loosely around her shape, and although he was only shown her face, he could see that one of her feet was grotesquely twisted back up her leg as though only partially attached, and her body seemed to be leaning to one side. He assumed the damage had been caused by the fall and no explanation was given by the officer.

It would be much later, after the post-mortem, that the poor man would be exposed to the heart-wrenching facts. How her ankle had been torn away and her hip pulled from its socket by the force of the tide pulling against her anchored foot. He just nodded numbly and left the morgue for the Police station.

Carl answered the questions put to him as best he could. Her mental state, her movements on the previous day, their relationship in general and his own movements in the previous twenty-four hours. He had nothing to hide and answered as honestly as he could, except for the questions about their relationship. He decided to embellish the truth in the hope of avoiding any red flags.

"So, your relationship with Sophie was as strong as ever?"

"I loved her before this happened and when she came back to me is was a miracle. Yes. I loved her just as much."

"It must have been difficult to break up your new family when she came out of the coma?" The detective said smugly, as he put on a pair of glasses making it easier for Carl to tell them apart.

"My family?"

"Yes. We know you had moved Kelly into your home. She'd lived with you as your common law wife for some time I believe?"

"She helped to look after my son." Carl said forcefully.

"If you say so."

He looked from one to the other. He wondered if Kelly would say the same thing, or if she would tell them everything.

"Ok. Yes, we were in a relationship, but as soon as Sophie came out of the coma, we ended it."

"Like I said. It must have been hard?"

"Yes of course it was hard, but it was the right thing to do. She's Tommy's mother."

"She *was* Tommy's mother you mean?"

"Yes" he sighed.

"Ok. That's all for now."

"I can go?"

"I'll get someone to drop you off."

As he walked through the waiting area, he saw Jake who rose quickly to his feet.

"What's going on Carl?" He boomed accusingly.

"I have no idea" Carl said defeatedly. "Why are you here? Is Kelly still in there?"

"Yep. I followed just after you left but she'd gone in before I could talk to her."

Jake sat back down and put his head in his hands causing Carl to instinctively pat him on the shoulder.

"It'll be fine. You'll see."

Jake didn't react. He sat with his head in his hands wondering how anything could be fine. The coma woman was dead, and Kelly was being questioned about it. Even if Carl was right, it meant that there was now an empty space in his bed again. He hoped Kelly was incriminating him. He hoped Carl got convicted.

Carl was taken back home in a Police car and as soon as he got back into the house, he started trying to ring Kelly. He left Niki to deal with the departure of the annoying spy woman and to deal with Tommy's questions, while he remained in the hallway.

Niki watched him pacing the hall as he tried desperately to reach Kelly. Dialling, cursing, pacing and then dialling again. She didn't like how it looked.

At the police station Jake had Kelly's phone in his hand. He watched it light up again and again as Carl's name repeatedly appeared. Eventually he snapped and answered it.

"Kelly? Thank God."

"Don't thank God, it's me. What do you want?"

"Is Kelly there?"

"No. She's still being questioned about the death of your woman. What do you want?"

"I just need to talk to her."

"Need to get your stories straight do you? You know what? I don't care anymore. You deserve each other."

"Jake? Jake?"

Niki watched Carl put his phone back in his pocket as he covered his mouth and nose with his hand. She thought he might be crying but her attention was back on Tommy, who was still watching TV as though nothing was happening.

He saw her watching and smiled politely. She didn't know Tommy. Anything she knew about him had come directly from Sophie, but she was hardly a reliable source of information. He looked like any other boy of his age but there was something chilling in that polite smile. His biological mother had just been dragged from her watery grave and the woman who'd raised him had been arrested, yet he sat calmly in front of the tv screen smiling politely. Something wasn't right.

She recalled Sophie's account of his behaviour, his whisperings and teasing of her. Was it possible that he had somehow managed to convince Sophie that her fantasy world was real? Had he managed it so convincingly that she'd actually thrown herself off the Brigg to get back to them. She shuddered. It was a massive accusation to make to a small child.

She turned back to watch Carl again. His panic at being unable to speak to Kelly. He was acting strangely for someone who's fiancée had just died. She couldn't shake the look of desperation she'd seen on his face. He wasn't consumed with grief he was consumed with guilt and fear.

She didn't know what to believe. She tugged her jeans up over her spare tyre, pulled her sweatshirt back down, raked her fingers through her tired hair and sighed. Competing for a man's attention, consumed by jealousy and heartache were the rules of the game she had never played. Today she was thankful for her choice. For the quieter dependable love of boring old Pete.

Carl left the hallway at last and started to walk towards her, when there was another knock on the door.

"Sorry to disturb you again but I need you to come back to the station for a few more questions."

Carl was ushered into the police car again and Niki was left alone with Tommy.

As the police car pulled up back outside the station, Carl saw another car in the carpark. A car he recognised. It belonged to Sophie's dad. He couldn't believe they were hounded her father instead of leaving him alone to grieve, what possible information could he provide that couldn't wait a few days?

Carl was taken back into the same interview room as before. The one at the end of the corridor that passed by the one David was in. David, who was re-telling the eager officers, the word for word conversation he'd overheard on bonfire night.

"So, you are sure those were his exact words?" The lady officer asked him again.

"Yes. I heard him clearly. He shouted after her, "you can hold your breath. She'll be gone sooner than you think.'

"And this was to Kelly?"

"To Kelly, yes."

"About your daughter?"

"About Sophie, yes."

After the Police car pulled away Niki made herself a strong cup of coffee and went to sit beside Tommy on the sofa.

"So? "she said calmly.

"So what?" He said without taking his eyes from one of the many scenes of Starwars he knew by heart.

"How did you do it?"

"Do what?" she still didn't have his full attention.

She snatched the remote from his hand and switched off the tv. He was startled by the abrupt removal of the background noise. He was alone with this woman and he didn't like it.

"How did you find out about all that stuff?"

Tommy frowned. He genuinely had no idea what this strange woman was talking about.

"What stuff?"

"About Sophie's other life. Her daughters, her husband and that bloody pepper pot?"

The blood drained from Tommy's face. For a few seconds he was ghostly white but as Niki held her stare, his heart started to pump wildly, and the blood rose again creeping upwards until his face became crimson red.

"I didn't do anything" It was a childish defence. The kind Niki had heard a hundred times from her own children when they weren't entirely sure which crime had come to light.

"Don't mess with me Tommy!" she had his wrist firmly in her grip, fuelled with anger at the possibility that this evil child could be behind it all, "she told me everything and I don't believe you'd throw away something you'd found, so where is it?"

"I don't have it!"

"Come on!" She wrenched him from the Sofa by his wrist causing him to fall to his knees, but she didn't wait for him to get up as she dragged him bodily towards the door.

"What are you doing? I don't have it!"

She continued to drag him into the hallway and up the stairs to his room while he screamed and cried for her to let him go.

"You're hurting me! Please let go! Please let go!" He was terrified.

"Not until you show me the damn pot!" She threw him through onto the landing.

"Which is your room?"

He pointed to his bedroom door without trying to get back on his feet. He looked up at her, as he tried to force the words through sobs, his eyes wide with terror and columns of snot connecting his nose and mouth.

"I don't have it! I really don't!" He sobbed.

"No, you don't do you?"

He searched her face for some hint of where this was going.

"You don't have it because it never existed! You made it up, didn't you? There was no cotton bud of red blood was there? Blood doesn't stay red stupid, it turns brown. A blackish brown that you would never have known was blood."

"I'm sorry," he pleaded, "please don't tell my dad."

"Tell your dad?" she laughed sarcastically, "what did you do? Where did you get all that information you spewed out at her?"

Tommy gave up on trying to speak as he curled into a ball on the floor and wailed.

"How Tommy! How did you know? because I don't buy all this bullshit about whispers in the night!"

Tommy fell silent. His heaving body relaxed and slowly he rose to his feet and headed for the door. Niki followed quietly as he went into the room Sophie had occupied before she moved into his dad's room and pointed under the bed. Niki crouched down and pulled out a folder from which bits of paper were protruding in all directions.

The room fell silent. All sobbing, protesting and accusing had ceased, as Niki sat quietly on the bed and opened the scribbled testimony to Sophie's madness.

"You used this?" she whispered, "you used this to torment her? Why?"

Tommy shrugged. "It was just a joke."

Niki's anger rose again.

"A joke?! A fucking joke?! It wasn't a joke though, was it Tommy? You wanted her to think her other family were wating for her, didn't you?"

It was Tommy's turn to snap.

"Yes! Yes, I did! I wanted her to go back to them and leave us alone."

"So you whispered in the night, when you knew she was listening? You told her you had seen some pot that belonged in her fantasy? Well how did you expect she would go back to them Tommy? Tell me that."

"Dunno" He shrugged again.

"Yes, you do know!"

"I don't!" He started to cry again.

"Well I know that you do, and you've murdered your own mother you evil brat!" She put the slips of paper back in the folder and stood up.

"What are you going to do?"

"I'm taking this lot to the Police station and I'm going to tell them some things your mum told me about her plan to get back to this fictitious family. I'm going to get your dad and Kelly released, that's what I'm going to do."

"Will I go to prison?" He asked quietly.

Niki pulled him towards her and looked him straight in the eye.

"I'm not going to put your father through any more heartbreak than he already has," she hissed "you're lucky that I care more about your dad and Kelly than I do about watching you pay for this. Come on, you're going to your grandad's while I take this to the station."

Back in the same interview room Carl sipped the sweet tea, in an attempt to lubricate his throat, which was so dry with nerves it was almost closed.

"Are you aware of Sophie's weekly meetings with Anne her therapist."

"Yes of course."

"Do you know the content of those sessions?"

"No, not really."

"Did she never speak of them and you never asked?"

"No."

"Why not? Not interested in her progress?"

"It's private and she had a lot of stuff she didn't want to talk to me about."

"Would it surprise you to hear that in those sessions she had stated that your relationship with her was not particularly good? That you had not had a physical relationship with her since she moved in, or that you displayed no desire for her?"

"I guess not."

"So why did you infer you were a devoted and loving couple?"

"Because I thought it sounded bad."

"You mean it might have led us to believe that you would want her out of the way?"

"I guess so."

"Would it also surprise you to know that, in those sessions, she often spoke of her suspicions that you were in love with her friend Kelly, the woman who had been in your life for quite some time?"

"That's rubbish."

"What would you say if I told you her father heard you talking privately with Kelly on bonfire night and that you told her that Sophie would soon be gone?"

"I want a solicitor."

"Interview terminated 11.45 pm pending acquisition of a legal representative"

Niki pulled up outside Sophie's father's house, but his car wasn't on the drive.

"Damn it! Do you know where your grandad might be?"

"No" Tommy shook his head, still trembling from his ordeal.

"It's midnight for God's sake. Where the hell would he go at this hour?"

She sat for a moment to think. She needed to do this now, but she wasn't going to take the devil boy along.

"Ok. Show me where your Grandma and other Grandad live."

Fifteen minutes later she pulled up outside Carl's parents' house.

"Can Tommy stay with you for an hour or so?" She said, already pushing the boy through the open door.

"What's going on now? Where's our Carl? Do you know what time it is?"

Niki didn't have time for this, and she knew if she told them he'd gone back to the police station they'd be there in a shot leaving her with no babysitter.

"Carl's fine" She assured him, as he glanced back and forth between Niki and Tommy, frowning beneath his bushy eyebrows.

"Why isn't he taking care of Tommy then?"

He didn't believe anything she was saying but she didn't care.

"Can he stay with you or not?" She snapped hoping to bully him into submission.

"Yes ok. Of course he can stay. Tell Carl to call us."

"I will." She lied as she hurried to the car and jumped back into the driving seat through the open door she had left swinging in the road.

She arrived at the station and parked without noticing any of the cars that might have been familiar to her.

As she entered the front desk area, Jake looked up.

"Jake! Surely, they don't still have Kelly in there?"

"Yup. Makes you wonder doesn't it?" He said blandly as he frowned at the folder she had tucked under her arm.

She sat down for a moment beside him.

"I can assure you; Kelly has nothing to do with any of this."

"You don't know that."

"Yes, I do. I promise you, they'll both be back home tonight."

She squeezed his hand and he tried to smile. He didn't know what or who to believe or what revelation might be coming his way, so he accepted her compassion and remained silent.

Niki placed her folder on the desk and asked to speak to someone who was dealing with Sophie's investigation. After only a few moments, a woman Police officer emerged to escort her through the back to the interview rooms. She walked past several rooms displaying illuminated occupied signs, one of which contained Kelly who was calmly answering every question they asked.

She sat calmly on the plastic chair, as Niki and the lady officer walked past the door. She answered every question with complete honestly. She admitted to being Carl's common law wife because it was true, and she had nothing to hide. She liked the sound of it, and she had a solid alibi. She had been with Jake the night before, and admitting her relationship with Carl, and even her resentment of Sophie's return, was not a crime. She was innocent and nothing she said was a danger to her so she spilled out the details of her relationship with Carl and the officers devoured it as quickly as she could toss it before them.

"Do you think Carl wanted you back?"

"Yes, I do."

"You think he was disappointed with Sophie?"

"Of course he was," she smiled, "did you ever meet the woman?"

She sat back in her chair and assessed the situation. She wondered if she had gone too far. Perhaps Carl didn't have an alibi? She assumed that he did, but what if he didn't.? She started to sweat as another possibility ran through her mind. Perhaps he really was involved in Sophie's death and she was helping to put him away.

She stared blankly at the wall behind the officers' heads. Perhaps Carl had removed Sophie from their lives so they could get back to how it was before. Had he killed Sophie for her and now she was betraying him? Had he at last realised that he loved her and not Sophie? It was unlikely. He didn't have the balls. Even if he had, he would never hurt his beloved Sophie, and especially not for her. She had just heard him say so. Sophie had always been the symphony while she was nothing more than monotonous white noise.

Yes, she had given her evidence carelessly. She had done it because she knew he would now be wracked with guilt, blaming himself and maybe blaming her too for Sophie's tragic death. He would probably continue to worship her grave the way he'd worshipped her hospital bed. She'd wasted too many years competing with Sophie and didn't intend to spend the rest of her days competing with a ghost.

She had given her evidence carelessly because it didn't matter anymore. Carl was on his own now, and he would have to deal with it. He would have to watch her with someone else for a change.

"Would you like a break?" The round-faced officer asked her politely.

She stared at him, suddenly noticing how fat he was. She hadn't noticed that before. She wondered why people let themselves go like that, as she picked at her manicured nails. Perhaps he didn't have anyone to impress. She looked at his fat fingers and his gold wedding ring. Or perhaps he was just loved for who he was, the way Niki was loved. She sighed. Perhaps all the flabby, straggly haired women she used to pity, with their plain, bare, ugly faces were the ones she should envy. The ones who didn't have to toil every minute of every day to claw their way back up the slippery slope, after cruel words cast them down and weak careless hands fail to save them, hands that always let go. Those plain happy women who don't need to strive for beauty out of fear as they try to substitute love with lust.

"Yes please, a break would be nice."

The officers left and she sat alone for a while wondering how Tommy was and who he was with. She heard voices in the corridor and wondered if Carl was still being held. She imagined him being accused of murder and how terrified he would be. She imagined how he would feel when he learned that her own evidence had compounded his situation, but he deserved nothing from her.

She could feel the changes happening again. Changes in her heart that she knew too well. Her pathetic heart that was already justifying his outburst to the police. Lies he had to tell them to defend himself. He hadn't had the chance to explain to her. She hadn't given him the chance, and now she had made everything so much worse when fate had just handed her the perfect situation. He was totally free now and already her heart was trying to reach into the space Sophie had vacated.

The door opened.

"We don't need any more from you right now. You are free to go but we may call you back at a later date."

Kelly stood up dejectedly. They had probably got all they needed from her to hold him. She walked back down the corridor and Jake jumped to his feet.

"What's going on?"

"I really don't know Jake. Let's go home."

"Do you know Niki's here?"

"Why would she be here?"

"She seemed to think she could prove Carl had nothing to do with this. She had a folder in her hand. She seemed convinced she had enough to clear you both."

Kelly perked up immediately. Perhaps Carl need never know of her betrayal after all. She had no idea what possible help Niki could be but that didn't matter.

"Maybe he'll be out soon then? Let's wait for a bit."

Kelly sat down but Jake remained standing.

"You've gotta be kidding? It's after three in the morning. Come on, we're going!"

"You go," she said as though doing him a favour, "I'll wait on my own for a while."

She clearly hadn't grasped Jake's point.

"Kelly. Now listen and listen carefully. You can either come with me and come now, or you can wait here for Carl. You are free to make that choice but think before you choose because if you stay here for him, then I'm done!"

She stared up at him in genuine surprise.

"What are you talking about?"

"You heard me."

"Jake, you're being ridiculous. I need to wait and see how he is."

"You don't need to wait Kelly; you *want* to wait and that's the big difference."

Jake marched through the door. Kelly remained seated.

She heard his car door slam shut, the engine fire up and the screech of his wheels leave the carpark.

A few yards away, Niki was showing the investigating officers the bits of paper detailing Sophie's fantasy life. The life she wanted to return to. The life she had told Niki she would never let go of, and the conversation that had made Niki so worried she had forced Sophie to promise she wouldn't do anything stupid.

"So, you suspected she would try to take her life?"

"I did for a moment, but she promised she wouldn't, and I believed her."

Niki failed to mention the reason Sophie was so convinced her other life was still there for the taking. She didn't mention the scheming child who had methodically and coldly manipulated his mother into taking her own life. Removing her, so he could reinstate Kelly back into that role. He was just a child.

The officer with the glasses lifted them, to peer at the scribblings in Sophie's handwriting.

"She confided in me years ago before her first suicide attempt," she said resignedly, "she was trying to get back to this John person then, and she was doing the same now."

"You didn't tell the Police at the time?"

"No, I didn't because for a while I thought she was going to pull through any day, and as time went on it didn't seem important anymore."

The officers looked at one another then one of them nodded.

"There's similar evidence in her early therapy sessions, but they're recorded as a temporary and a normal stage of recovery. Seems she had everyone fooled or her doctors missed something. Either way, clearly her delusions were still alive."

"Very much so. I just wish I'd raised the alert."

"You can't blame yourself." He said dropping his glasses back down to look at her.

She didn't blame herself and she resented taking any of the blame. The blame rested firmly with Tommy who was probably sleeping soundly while she carried the can for him.

Hours passed and Kelly felt obliged to check in with Jake. She knew he wouldn't have slept after their tiff, and she begrudgingly decided to make peace, so there would be one less irritation to endure. She dialled his number several times, becoming increasingly annoyed and agitated each time she stepped outside for privacy and returned again as his voicemail kicked in.

He was sulking, and she knew he had a point to make but still she was angry. She was angry that he dared to ignore her because she was the one who calls all the shots and he was the one who backs down. That's just how it was, and this was no time to make a stand. It was pathetic and she would make him pay for it when she got home.

She searched for her mother's number. She just needed to hear a friendly voice but before she made the call the door opened, and Carl appeared.

"Kelly!" He rushed over as she flung her arms around him and held him tight.

"They let you go. Thank God."

As she kissed his neck with gratitude, all memory of his declaration of love for Sophie was erased. His outburst to the police had been necessary self- preservation and was instantly forgiven. The idea of Sophie being the only woman on the planet he had ever loved was duly dismissed and laid to rest.

"I think Niki came through for you."

Carl ran his fingers through his hair and closed his eyes for a moment.

"Yes. Thank God for Niki and for the witness who saw Sophie marching along the seafront on her own," he screwed up his eyes as though trying to block out the image of her, "she jumped off the Brigg with a fucking bolder round her leg Kell."

"Oh God. Why?"

"I don't know but I need to find out. I need to know what was so bad about her life with me that she'd do something so horrific."

"So you can blame yourself again you mean, just like last time?"

"If she was that unhappy and desperate then of course I'm to blame!"

"Leave it Carl. She's gone now. She wasn't well."

"I can't leave it. I need to talk to Niki"

A Love to Die For – Tortured Hearts

He peered out of the window; dawn was breaking. It must be almost time for Tommy to be getting ready for school.

"Where's Tommy?"

"I left him at your parents." Niki's voice interrupted from behind.

Carl turned around to face her "I need to talk to you Nik."

"I know."

They were all exhausted, nauseous from sleep deprivation, shivering from shock and barely functioning, but no-one suggested delaying the talk until later. They knew no-one would get any sleep until they'd shared what they knew.

"'I'll pick Tommy up. He's not going to school today." Kelly was already searching for her keys without a thought for what Carl wanted. She needed to see her son and neither Carl's whining nor Jake's tantrum was going to stop her.

"I'll give Pete a call and meet you at yours." Niki whispered, giving Carl a quick hug as he rubbed his arms to generate some heat. He had left home in his vest and sweatpants the night before, but it felt like a month ago.

They left the station to head out to Carl's.

"I've got your key Carl," Niki called, "so you can jump in with me if you like, while Kelly gets Tommy?"

Carl didn't get the chance to answer before Kelly jumped in

"I think he wants to pick Tommy up too. You go ahead Nik. He can come with me. I'm sure he wants to see Tommy first," she glanced at Carl "Don't you?"

"Yes. You put the kettle on Nik. I'll go with Kelly. I need to see him."

"Of course you do." Niki muttered under her breath sarcastically, as the two of them cosied up in the small car.

Chapter 19

Niki boiled the kettle, put out the cups and waited. Still annoyed at how Kelly had manipulated the ride back, and unless they arrived in the next ten minutes she would leave and stick the key under a plant pot. She was not going to sit around while they cuddled up together down some deserted lane, taking her for a fool.

She checked her watch as she tried to calculate the journey time. She could feel the anger rising as she added together the timings. Even if it had taken a full ten minutes to get Tommy out of bed and into the car they should be here by now. She was just about to slam the cups of tea into the sink when she heard the car pull up outside, causing her to take a deep breath and calm down a little.

"I'll speak to Tommy and let him go back to bed for a few hours." Carl whispered through the kitchen door as he tried to guide the sleepy boy towards the stairs, but Tommy stopped and turned around.

"Is Sophie really dead?"

"Yes love. I'm afraid she is." Kelly said softly

"Can you come back now then mum?"

The three adults were stunned into silence as they stared, first at Tommy and then at one another. Niki felt a chill run up her spine.

"Come on Tommy," Carl tugged him away, "you need some more sleep."

No sooner had they disappeared, when Kelly pulled Niki back into the kitchen and closed the door.

"What did you tell them?"

"Who?"

"The police of course."

Niki was still distracted by Tommy's question. She knew he'd caused Sophie's death with his tricks and taunting but had he really anticipated what she would so? Surely, he hadn't intentionally planned it. It was ridiculous. There's no way he could have known she would think death was a way back. He was just hoping his mum was coming home that's all. She turned back to Kelly's question.

"Everything, I told them everything."

"You told them about her imaginary family and how long she'd been obsessed by it?"

"Yep. I told them the lot."

Kelly looked nervously at the door.

"Look Niki. I know it's a big ask but don't let on I knew anything about it will you?"

"He needs the whole truth Kelly. We both owe him that."

Kelly became desperate.

"Look. If he knew I'd kept all this from him he'd never forgive me, and it was the damn promise I made to you that stopped me telling him all these years anyway."

Niki scowled. She didn't see why all this should be on her shoulders, but she knew Kelly was right. There must have been several times when Kelly wanted to blurt out Sophie's obsession with a secret lover, but she'd kept Niki's secret, and it was time for Niki to do the same.

"Suit yourself." She said more loudly than Kelly was comfortable with.

"Shhhh" Kelly pleaded.

"I'll keep you out of it." She whispered as Carl returned.

"I think I need to thank you for whatever you said to the police Nik," Carl hugged her gratefully, "what did you tell them?"

"I think you'd better sit down, Carl"

Niki kept her hand on his as she told him about Sophie's fantasy husband. How she believed she'd lived with him throughout her coma years and the children she was desperate to get back to.

He listened patiently, as Niki described the desperation Sophie had been feeling at being separated from the children she had loved and nurtured in her mind every day of those years, but she didn't mention that all this started long before. That it had also been the reason for her overdose or her plans to cancel her marriage to Carl all those years ago.

All Carl heard was the torture Sophie had been living with, and how she had felt unable to share the burden of it. As Niki's voice fell silent, he was sobbing like a small child.

Kelly's eyes were wide and angry. This was not the outcome she wanted. She tried to catch Niki's attention to urge her to tell the whole truth, but Niki wasn't engaging with her frantic attempts. She knew what Kelly wanted but she wasn't prepared to deliver it.

"I need to go now." She said mildly as she took her hand from Carl's and kept her eyes intentionally away from Kelly's.

The door closed leaving Kelly and Carl alone.

Upstairs Tommy had been trying to listen to the conversation, but they were talking so quietly he could barely make out any of the words. He didn't like the accusing way Niki had looked at him when he asked if Kelly could come back.

Quietly he crept to the corner of his room and lifted up the edge of the carpet to reveal the four pieces of paper he had carefully hidden. The ones he had kept for himself because they made him smile. The ones Niki hadn't taken to the Police station. He took them back over to his bed, picking up each one in turn and tearing it into small pieces of pen streaked confetti. The words no-one else would see. Way home? Sleep? Coma? Death?

Downstairs Kelly heard Tommy flushing the chain, so she waited a moment or two before walking over to Carl and sitting down beside him. Immediately he threw his arms around her and continued to sob. She slid her arms under his and held him tight. It felt good to give him comfort and it felt good to be alone with him, but mostly it felt good to feel him back in her arms.

Eventually he disentangled himself from her and pressed away the tears with the palms of his hands.

"What have we done Kelly?"

"What?" She didn't understand.

"We betrayed her. We both did."

"No, we didn't." Kelly soothed as she put her hand in his open palm.

Quickly he snatched it away.

"Carl. Sophie has gone. It's not our fault. We need each other now."

Carl stopped sniffing and looked her in the eye.

"We weren't there when she needed us because we were too wrapped up in the aftermath of our sordid little affair Kelly."

"Sordid little affair? How dare you!" Kelly stood up to face him.

"You don't know everything Carl!" Her irritation with him was quickly turning to frustrated rage.

"I think I know Sophie better than you, and I think she knew about us. I could feel it, but she didn't ever accuse us. She just tried to deal with it on her own."

"You're incredible! You think she did this out of longing for you? You have no fucking idea what this was about do you?"

"So perhaps you should enlighten me if you have all the answers." His tone was almost venomous.

Kelly's eyes were wide with pure anger, she wasn't going to hold back any longer.

" Her infatuation with her fantasy lover started long before she woke from her coma. I'm talking long ago. Do you want to know when exactly? When she first fell in love with him? It was back in 2000. He was the reason she took the overdose."

Kelly was laughing sarcastically.

"What are you talking about? You're making it up!"

"Ask Niki if you don't believe me. She was trying to get away from you then, just as she did now. She wanted to call off the wedding Carl. She didn't love you, she never loved you. She loved John! Do you hear me? She wanted John, she lusted for John. Wonderful, sexy non-existent John."

"You're lying!"

"Am I? Look me in the face and tell me if I'm lying. This whole fucking tragedy of your pathetic life was about another man. Does that make you hate her Carl? Do you finally fucking hate her, or do you just feel jealous?"

Carl felt the anger and hatred she spoke of, but he aimed it back at her.

"You knew this? You knew she didn't want me, and you let me sit by her bed for years? Wasting my life?"

Kelly laughed out loud.

"You think I didn't want you to know. Oh, I wanted you to know about the cheating bitch you were worshipping, but I promised to keep her wretched secret and I had no proof without Niki anyway."

Carl slid from the sofa onto his knees and banged his fists into the carpet several times before looking back up at her with angry eyes.

"You could have told me! Look what a bloody mess you've made of my life, of Tommy's life and your own. If I'd known this, do you think I would have spent every day of my miserable life wating for someone who didn't even want me? Are you insane? We could have been married by now! We could have had more children by now! We could have had a bloody shot at being happy."

He grabbed her by the wrists harshly and looked her directly in the eyes.

"You stupid cow. You've made a bloody fool out of me for years. Ten years of watching me feel guilty when you knew she didn't deserve it."

Kelly waited until he had finished screaming at her and then spoke softly.

"You wouldn't have believed me."

Carl seemed stunned as she continued with calm defeat in her voice.

"You would have called me a scheming liar who was trying to steal you away from your precious Sophie."

Carl heaved several deep breaths. She was right. He would have done exactly that. He sat back down and looked up at her face. Her brows were perfectly shaped, her lashes beautifully curled and her lips shining. Even now, after a night of questioning and no sleep, she looked lovely.

"I'm sorry Kelly. It must have been hard to watch me obsess over her, knowing what you knew. Wait 'til I see Niki. She let me waste half my life on a lunatic who didn't even want me?"

"Don't blame Niki Carl. She thought Sophie would wake up after a few days but then it turned to weeks and there was the baby. She didn't know what to do, but there was always a chance Sophie would wake up and be part of the family you wanted. Niki was rooting for you and Sophie. That's why she kept away from me. I was the home wrecker."

"You're no home wrecker" He rose back to his feet and put his hand gently on her face.

"What are you doing?" She pulled away.

"I thought…"

"You thought what? That I would come running back because Sophie fell from grace?"

"I just…"

"Yes, you just thought you could pick me up again to plug up the hole in your life just as you always do."

"It's different now. Sophie didn't want me and if I'd known I would have married you in a heartbeat."

"Oh! You mean I was your second choice? Well guess what? I already knew that, and I also know that you expect me to be content with second place! Well not this time Carl. I have a man at home who loves me, yes, he actually does, and he doesn't just love me because I cook and clean and take care of his kid. He doesn't just love me because his other woman fell out of favour or because she's dead. He just loves me and, you know what? I'm going back to him right now"

She flounced out of his house without looking back and for the first time she strode away without feeling her heart pulling her back, the way it always had, slowing her every step. No, this time she strode freely and swiftly back to her car and drove home without a hint of uncertainty and it felt so good. She had a good man and from this day on she would show him what he means to her.

As she drove, she imagined how her new life would be laying in the arms of Jake. Just feeling his huge black arms draped softly around her, made her feel safe and warm in a way Carl never had. The warmth of certainty, of knowing that his love was absolute.

She would keep Tommy in her life of course. She smiled. It would also give her the opportunity to tease and torment Carl. To sabotage any new romance he may find. To punish him and show him every day what he is missing. He had been only man she had ever wanted but now she didn't want him either. He was too dangerous, he hurt her too easily. She would spend the rest of her life making his life a misery. Flaunting her relationship with Jake and the unconditional love she received from him. Her love for Carl had been an unhealthy love, a jealous love, a love tainted by his cruelty and she would make him pay for the damage he had caused.

She put her key in the lock quietly and as it clicked, she gently pushed to open the door. The door didn't move. She tried again and again. It was bolted from the inside. Her time with Jake was over.

Niki had driven home along the seafront where the light of newsagent was the only hint of life in the cold early morning desolation of this sleeping town. She passed the bar and in her mind's eye she saw Sophie running up the street, to meet her and Kelly in the lively bar. She wiped away a tear. The cold January night when three friends had talked of love. When Sophie wanted a love to die for. She wiped another tear.

At the exact spot where Sophie had left this world, she pulled up and got out of the car. She walked along the cliff top and knelt down close to the edge, looking down onto the rocks far below.

"Oh Sophie," she whispered, "I hope you are at peace at last. Perhaps in heaven or maybe even back home in your own little heaven. We love you and I'm so sorry I didn't call."

She knelt in silence for a while, still staring into the water, listening for something, anything. Some sign that Sophie forgave her and that she was alright. Anything to give her the slightest comfort that Sophie's spirit could hear her. The waves flowed in and out, the breeze blew her hair over her eyes, the gulls were starting to take to the morning air above, but not a single sign from the spirit world. Sophie was gone and she would never hear the apology Niki so desperately wanted her to hear.

As she returned to her car, her thoughts turned to poor Kelly, who had spent years of unrequited love on Carl. Then she assessed her own life. She was surer than ever that she had made the right choice. Pete loved her and she liked him a lot. Her life was not hindered by the drama associated with a passionate love. It was neither enhanced nor dampened by it. She was happy with Pete, but if he was swept from her life tomorrow, she wouldn't fall apart, because he didn't have her heart in his keeping.

A Love to Die For – Tortured Hearts

Her heart had been taken years ago by the father of her first child. Amy was not Pete's daughter, but he didn't know it and he never would. Yes, she had made the right choice. Her life had no ups or downs and that suited her fine. She was free to enjoy the little things. Like the angel costume she had left half done on her kitchen table, and the new recipe for steak pie she was going to try tomorrow. She wiped another tear but this time the tear was for herself. It was for the fact that she had gone through this justification to herself over the years as religiously as Sophie's list of pros and cons.

Carl didn't know he was Amy's father. He had been too stupid to match the dates of Amy's birth to the night they had made love a few months after Sophie went into her coma. They had both brushed it off as a stupid surge of emotion and too much wine, but it had been enough to cause Niki to alienate herself from both Carl and Kelly.

She was aware that people thought she had broken contact out of disapproval for Kelly's pursuit of Carl, but it was really no more than an act of self-preservation. She couldn't be around Carl because she didn't trust herself, and she couldn't be around Kelly out of pure jealousy at the closeness she was nurturing with Carl.

Many times, she had almost blurted the truth about Amy to Carl, usually after too much to drink or when Amy had done something cute or amazing as a toddler. She had picked up her phone and dialled his number, only to make an excuse of misdialling the moment he answered, but she knew Carl didn't believe her. He always believed she was trying to make peace with him and Kelly but had then lost her nerve. Never once did he hint that he thought she might be calling about her and Carl.

To him there was no 'her and Carl' and sometimes she wondered if he had totally forgotten the incident between them. The night he had bared his soul to her, made love to her, completed her in the way no-one else ever had and then left, never to return.

He hadn't acknowledged the events of that night in all the weeks that followed and, as soon as she discovered she was pregnant she withdrew from him and Kelly completely. She didn't tell Pete about her condition until enough time had passed for him to be unable to remember the details of their own liaisons, but still, she didn't give up on Carl.

It wasn't until she became pregnant with her second child that she finally accepted that Carl had no interest in her. The night she would remember forever was the one he had forgotten instantly. She wiped away another tear and drove home to her family.

Quarter of a mile away, Carl lay alone in his bed trying to get an hour's sleep before Tommy woke up again. He was an empty shell. Sophie had done it to him again and now she had caused him to lose Kelly, the only woman who had ever loved him. He knew that now, he also had to acknowledge that, deep down, he had always suspected Sophie wasn't in love with him. Yet, even when she returned as a skinny stinking wreck, he still couldn't let go of the memory of how it used to be when he shared a flat with the woman he loved.

He also knew, even in these hours of realisation and momentous regret, that Kelly could never have measured up to the burning, desperate love he had once felt for Sophie.

Chapter 20

On a sunny August morning a young man swung his small rust bucket of a car into the carpark of the exclusive Spa and Beauty centre and parked it directly behind a red Ferrari. He smiled. He loved to block her in. He got out and slammed the door shut without locking it and entered the fragrant, polished reception area.

He loved coming here. He loved to barge through reception without booking-in as the pretty girls smiled at him. Some of them believed he was the owner's son and others just fancied the pants off him, but he loved it either way.

Playfully he flung open her office door, causing her to jump and drop her phone.

"For Christ's sake Tommy. You nearly gave me a heart attack!"

He made a grab for the phone on the floor and looked at it.

"Still stalking Jake are we?" He laughed as he looked at the Facebook posts of Jake's newest baby.

"I'm not stalking him! Give it back."

Tommy visited Kelly's Spa often. In his mind she had never stopped being his mum and she spoiled him frequently. Sometimes behind Carl's back, but mostly to blatantly infuriate him.

"So, when are you going to buy me something nice to replace the rust bucket my dad cobbled together?"

"When you stop driving like an idiot and get rid of your points I guess."

"You're such a meany." He teased.

"You have three bloody points already and you've only been driving six months college boy! Don't forget who's paying the fees for this fancy place you're starting at."

Tommy pulled a sulky face and then smiled. Kelly laughed out loud. He loved to make Kelly laugh and to watch the little lines burst from the corners of her eyes like tiny fireworks. She was still stunning in a sophisticated way. Not as perfectly pretty as the many girls outside her door but when it came down to sassy, sexy sophistication she beat them all hands down.

 He admired the woman she'd become. A strong determined woman who power dressed and delivered direction in her own special way. A polite but ruthless tone of 'don't mess with me" He loved his mother regardless of the lack of biology or legality to support his claim.

Kelly had showed him exactly what a woman could achieve when she put her mind to it. A mind focussed on success. A mind protected from the disruption of romantic love. Kelly was no longer interested being torn apart, on a daily basis, by some self-centred buffoon who had fooled her into believing he cared.

 The truth was that Carl had been the only man she had ever wanted, but not anymore. Now Jake, she would have taken, she would most likely have been happy with Jake, and the cute children she had been looking at on Facebook might well have been hers. It was an enviable scenario but sometimes she looked at the expression on his wife's face and knew it would have been wrong. This woman genuinely adored Jake as she allowed herself to be photographed with messy hair, and ice-cream dribbling down her chin.

She looked over at Tommy who had made himself at home in her office and plonked his legs unceremoniously on her desk. She was happy with her lot. She had Tommy in her life, and Jake didn't deserve a wife who would be spending every day staging those Facebook posts with the single aim of making another man jealous. It would have been a waste of Jake's love, unhealthy and totally exhausting.

"So, how's your dad?"

"Same."

She smiled and shook her head affectionately.

"And how's your step-mum?"

He rolled his eyes sarcastically "Oh the house mouse is still around somewhere. Scurrying along the floors with a mop and hyper-ventilating over my muddy footmarks."

"Really Tommy. She seems really nice. You shouldn't give her such a hard time."

"Yeah, I guess. She's nice enough."

Kelly nodded her approval.

"In her own boring, pathetic, irritating mousy way."

Kelly threw a ruler at him as he ducked.

"Kelly you've no idea," he laughed, "they totter up to the seafront and sit drinking coffee together. When you were around dad used to run in the sea with his trousers on and eat ice cream down there. We all used to dance in the living room flashing torches and pretending it was a disco! You used to do that funny dance that dad loved, the one where you spun on your back. Do you remember?"

Kelly remembered. How could she forget? It was the best time of her life. Just the three of them, as a family. The reminiscent smile gently melted away as she turned her attention back to Tommy.

"We're all a bit older now."

"Well he definitely is! I've even caught them at a garden centre for God's sake! Their idea of a wild night out is half a lager in a beer garden and chips on the way home. Anyway, talking of wild nights out, have you booked our New Year cruise yet?"

The New Year Cruise had become a tradition for Kelly and Tommy. They used to book a family cruise and spend some quality time together doing the crafts and games as mother and son, but for the last three years they'd booked a party cruise around the Med. Tommy loved the fact that he was able to drink cocktails and break the hearts of a dozen young girls, while his mum tried to fight off unhappily married men who sneaked away from their wives, or of persistent 'would be' toy boys not much older than him. They would laugh together every morning when they shared their stories over breakfast. He loved spending time with Kelly.

"Is that why you're here? Making sure I've booked us in?" She couldn't believe he'd turned up on his university registration day. He'd got less than an hour before he had to be there, and he was more interested in making sure his holiday was sorted.

"No, I just wanted to ask if you would like to meet my new girl" He raised his eyebrows several times suggestively as she rolled her eyes.

"I seem to do nothing other than to meet your girls. Perhaps you should wait until you can introduce them without forgetting their names before you rack up my credit card on fancy meals."

Tommy leaned forward as though about to whisper a secret.

"This one is a keeper," he whispered, "I can feel it in my bones."

He shoved a pile of invoices aside and plonked himself down on her desk.

"It could be love." He smiled, giving his eyebrows a few more bounces.

"Yes, and it could be lust, and you're hoping a few glasses of champagne on my card will do the trick."

"Not this time," he said boastfully, "This girl is something else. I spent all afternoon and evening with her yesterday, and guess what?"

Kelly checked her watch again impatiently. He needed to be leaving soon if he was going to make his enrolment on time.

"Go on then. What?"

He smiled that smile that never failed to crack her up. The smile that totally disarmed her no matter what he'd done or said. She was already fighting to keep a straight face when he put his face directly in front of hers and widened his eyes.

"I'm hooked."

She laughed out loud. She loved this boy beyond reason even though he took advantage of her good nature far too frequently. The truth was that she loved being able to give him all the things Carl couldn't, which mainly boiled down to money, an open house for his friends to crash, and a non- judgemental ear to bend.

"Is that a way of telling me you've maxed out my credit card trying to impress her?"

"Nope! I don't need money to impress this one. You wouldn't' understand. This one is happy to sit on the beach with a homemade butty. I think she's the one."

Kelly tugged the invoices from under his buttock and straightened them into a tidy pile.

"The real thing eh? After one date?"

"She could be. She makes my stomach feel like a washing machine. You wouldn't get it."

Kelly smiled. Oh, she got it. She remembered it well, but she hadn't felt it for many years.

"So, what's her name, this girl who's stolen your heart in a single day?"

He grinned "Her name is Vicky and she's studying psychology. We're on the same course."

"So where did you meet?"

Tommy frowned as though it was a stupid question. "At the registration. Where else?"

It was Kelly's turn to frown. "I thought the registration was today?"

"You need to get a grip," he laughed, "registration day was yesterday."

Kelly opened the calendar on her laptop where she had marked the registration in for Monday at 12pm and that was today. She turned her screen towards him.

"Look. I've got it down for today. That's what you told me, and I've never known a college to register on a Sunday!"

"Today's Tuesday!" he said irritably as he took out his phone to check, "have you finally lost the plot?"

As he looked at his phone, his mouth dropped open and then he looked bewilderedly at Kelly.

Her expression was one he hadn't seen before. She tried to smile, her hands were shaking, and beads of sweat were starting to form on her upper lip.

"What's going on?" Tommy stuttered, "Mum what is it?"

Tommy always reverted to calling her 'mum' whenever he felt vulnerable. Today he was beyond vulnerable, she could feel his fear as he searched her face for reassurance.

She rubbed his leg comfortingly as she tried to think of something to say.

"Mum?" His eyes were fixed firmly on hers. He had his mother's eyes, Sophie's eyes, everyone said that. Beautiful, blue, almond shaped eyes, and now they were full of the same terror. The same confusion, the same desperation, as he tried to make sense of it.

"What's happened? Where the hell did Monday go and where was I?"

"It's ok darling. I just need to make a call. You wait here for a minute."

She hurried out of the room and dialled as she stood trembling in the foyer.

"Carl?"

"Yes?"

"Come to my office right away. We need to talk."